Shirley,

THEODORA

Happy reading!

Christina McKnight

La Loma Elite Publishing

Christina McKnight

Dedication
To Amanda~

Who could have imagined a chance post would bring us
to where we are today?
Thank you for embarking on this journey with me!

Prologue

Canterbury, England
April 1819

Lady Theodora Montgomery sat stock-still before the massive table that served as the headmistress's desk and waited for the woman to put down her pencil and greet her. She'd been shown into the inner sanctuary of the headmistress over ten minutes prior by a young woman—Miss Dires—who'd explained that she'd taught history at Miss Emmeline's School of Education and Decorum for Ladies of Outstanding Quality for going on ten years. The woman didn't appear more than a handful of summers older than Theo.

When she'd taken her seat, and Miss Emmeline hadn't so much as looked up to greet her, Theodora decided it was in her best interests to wait patiently until the woman acknowledged her presence. To keep

1

occupied, Theo took in the room around her—it was far more masculine than the office should be since the school proudly boasted an all-female staff with only one male groundskeeper who took no active role in the daily life of Miss Emmeline's pupils.

The problem Theo currently wrestled with was keeping her eyes open and her posture straight. She'd spent nearly two days in a carriage to reach her new boarding school from her brother's London townhouse. She was dirty, exhausted, and wanted nothing more than to be shown to her bed, where she'd gladly obtain a full night's rest. If she had the opportunity to wipe the dirt and grime from her skin, that would be wholly welcome, as well.

"Your application states that you prefer to be addressed as 'Theo' or 'Lady Theo,' is that correct, Lady Theodora?" Miss Emmeline looked up for the first time, setting her pencil aside, and Theo was delighted to see a bit of mischief in the lady's eyes, even though her tone was severe. When Theo nodded, the older woman continued. "Here at Miss Emmeline's School of Education and Decorum for Ladies of Outstanding Quality, we pride ourselves on allowing our young ladies to discover who they are, and providing the time and resources to help them become the women they want to be."

It was in the printed brochure Cart had presented to her nearly three months prior. The name for the school was outlandishly pompous. She and her sibling had had quite the chuckle at it, but they'd quickly settled on Miss Emmeline's school because the mission statement matched Cart's hope for his only sister's future endeavors and education. Their mother, Dowager

Countess Cartwright—Anastasia Montgomery—had reluctantly agreed to part with her younger child at the insistence Theo write her immediately if the school did not suit her needs.

What her mother actually meant was that she felt it improper for her daughter to be well-studied, her belief that educated women had no place in polite society was the foundation she used to justify her own lack of learning.

She was thankful that her brother, Simon—the current Lord Cartwright, and Theo's legal guardian—better known to his friends as Cart, was not of the same dated mindset.

"Lodging," the headmistress said. "My school houses four girls to each room. This allows a sense of camaraderie between students and enables each girl to seek help in a subject they are not well-versed in. Do you take issue with sharing a room?"

Theo didn't know how to answer the question. She'd spent most of her life with only her mother and servants for company until her brother had returned from Eton. However, he was much older than she. She'd always possessed her own room, her own space— even though she'd secretly longed for a sibling closer to her in years; a sister to share her dream with, to accompany her on adventures about her family gardens, or just to act as a companion to laugh with during the long, dark nights.

"A shared room is preferred, Headmistress," Theo answered.

"Do call me Emmeline or Miss Emmeline, dear." The woman's tone was still stark, but Theo suspected she tried to put her new pupil at ease. "Now, to decide on whom you shall room with it is necessary to discover your talents."

A sense of dread washed over Theo as the woman smiled for the first time, her lips pulling back to reveal tea-stained, crooked teeth.

"And how shall we find my talents?" Theo gulped after asking, a clammy moisture overtaking her clasped palms.

"Oh, I have devised a fine method for ascertaining the strengths and weaknesses of each of my girls," the headmistress said in a whisper as if they were plotting a grand scheme together. "I dare say, I would have made an excellent teacher in the applied sciences."

Theo felt encouraged that Miss Emmeline knew what the applied sciences were. It hinted that her days would not be filled with learning social etiquette and needlepoint and utterly neglecting all other subjects: arithmetic, geography, science, and history.

Theo's exhaustion receded as the woman continued. "Each girl is asked to present in three different departments of learning: academics, art and music, and a physical sport. Based on their choices for each—and how well they do at their chosen talent—I select which room each pupil is assigned to." Theo had to admit, it was an interesting method to determine sleeping arrangements. "It is also necessary for each student to learn something from her roommates during their stay at my school."

It was sound methodology, and Theo could not deduce a flaw in the headmistress's plan, though she was extremely tired and her mind had been sluggish since her arrival at the school.

Theodora

"Are you ready?" Miss Emmeline asked as she stood.

"I am to present now?" Theo squeaked. She thought to have a day—or at least a night—to ponder her known talents before being presented to the other students. Even a decent meal would be appreciated. "Is it not nearly time for the evening repast?"

"You will need a bed in a few short hours, correct?"

"Yes, but..." Theo quickly stood, running her hands down the front of her wrinkled traveling gown. It would be the height of embarrassment to be seen by the entire school in such a filthy dress. They would think her nothing more than a country miss. Not that Theo had ever labored over long regarding the opinions of others, but her time at Miss Emmeline's was important to her.

"You are correct, all of the girls will be gathering shortly for our evening meal." The headmistress touched her coal-stained hands to her upswept, mousey brown hair before running them down the front of her dark grey dress—leaving behind a trail of black streaks. "Wait here while I ready the girls in the music room for your first talent. I will send Miss Dires to collect you when all are seated." The fear must have shown clearly on Theo's face for the headmistress hurriedly added, "Do not fret. Every girl is called upon on her first day here."

Nothing about her reassurance made Theo feel...reassured, but at least it completely dispelled her fatigue as anxiousness set in. Her heart beat at an erratic rate.

The moments passed, feeling like hours as Theo awaited Miss Dires. She progressed from exhaustion to anxiousness to outright dread. She scanned the headmistress's desk for a blank piece of paper. How long would a note, begging her mother to rescue her, take to arrive in London? Certainly longer than Theo had before she was called to the music room.

Dashing her final hope of avoiding the coming discomfiture, Miss Dires returned and motioned for Theo to follow, her smile kind. Upon closer inspection, Theo noted the woman's slight limp as she walked— maybe she was older than she appeared.

The music room was off the main hallway—the only hallway Theo had seen since her arrival—and boasted high ceilings with several chandeliers for light. Large, long cracks in the walls could be seen from the doorway. The door she entered was at the front of the room, and belatedly Theo realized that while she'd been taking in the architecture and disrepair of the space, the other girls had been given the opportunity to inspect her.

Theo thought it best to keep focused on the task at hand and not the many eyes assessing her.

On the raised dais was a piano, a harpsichord, harp-lute, ditalharp, a flute, table of bells, and a guitar— all positioned far enough apart to enable the entire audience an unobscured view of Theo.

Theo hadn't applied herself to any musical instruments, outside of the occasional lesson at the piano. She'd studied many varieties of harps at the museum where Cart was an assistant curator, but she'd never touched one. Wind instruments were not in her repertoire, as her brother had never allowed her to even so much as hold the Greek panpipe—purportedly crafted by Hermes himself—that resided in his collection. As soon as Theo had a moment to herself, she planned to write a strongly worded letter to Cart, denouncing his actions at not allowing her a turn with the panpipe. Certainly, it was a severe detriment to her learning career. Since wind instruments were out, she took in the bells and guitar—both beyond her realm of knowledge, as well. There was no hope—not a single instrument did Theo feel competent in performing with.

"Students of Miss Emmeline's School of Education and Decorum for Ladies of Outstanding Quality, please welcome Lady Theodora Montgomery— though she prefers Lady Theo or just plain Theo." The words rolled off the headmistress's tongue as if she said them daily, and no tongue twisting was necessary to say the name five times. "Lady Theo will first apply her hand to a musical talent—either the piano, harp, guitar, bells, or vocals."

Theo's singing voice was dreadful—far too high to be anything but a screech.

"Next, she will present her academic talent," the headmistress continued. "Lastly, her physical sport, which we will all adjourn to the outdoors for. When everything is complete, we will return to the dining hall for our nightly meal."

A loud cheer with reserved clapping filled the room; however, Theo wasn't sure if they applauded her or their promised meal. The only thing she was willing to celebrate at the moment was a warm bed—it did not even need to be comfortable, only cozy…and quiet.

Though she doubted with all these students Miss Emmeline's was ever a quiet place.

Theo surveyed the many instruments before her. There was truly no choice to be made—it was the piano, or flee the room in disgrace.

With a weak smile to the gathered crowd, Theo sat behind the piano and set her fingers to the ivory keys as she'd been taught. The keys were smooth under her touch from years of use. Her nails were chipped from toting her luggage from the carriage, and her hands were pale and clammy. It was odd these were her thoughts as she sat before roughly forty girls her age while they awaited her piano solo.

Theo was most comfortable reading about adventure and tense situations from the comfort of a soft chair, snuggled under a warm blanket with a fire roaring nearby—or in the garden under a large shade tree with the sun beaming. To actually be an active participate in such a situation was entirely different than reading about it in a book. The sensation of her blood humming through her veins in anticipation, her labored breathing caused by her nerves, and the sheen of perspiration was something no writer could accurately describe with the written word. She tucked the theory into the back of her mind, planning to write her brother about it as soon as she'd had some rest. It made for an interesting observation, certainly, something they could discuss during her Christmastide holiday.

The thought of home and her family brought Theo a bit of comfort. She was here, in Canterbury, and they were in London. Her brother was sacrificing much to afford the tuition at Miss Emmeline's School, and Theo knew she could not disappoint him or her mother by begging off and crying to return home.

Theodora

With a calming breath, her fingers began to move across the keys in a melody she'd only played a half-dozen times, though the memory of the music sheet with the notes was clear in her mind. All she need do is concentrate on visualizing the sheet music and block out the rustling of clothes, the various whispered comments between girls, the echo of a book being dropped onto the hard floor, and the congested cough coming from the back of the room.

The tones floated about, bouncing off the bare, cracked walls and high ceiling, slower than the composer had intended, but in line with Theo's musical ability. She'd rather play at her leisure with accuracy than speed through the intended music and risk missing a key change. It was a soft melody, increasing in tempo as the song progressed. She pictured the final line of notes as her fingers found their rhythm and sped up, pushing gently on the smooth keys.

Only a few strokes left, and it would be over; she'd be able to move on to something a bit more familiar to her.

A door slammed somewhere in the room, and Theo's hands slipped across the keys in fright at the sudden noise, the song ending on a sharp note and not the quieter culmination intended for the piece.

Laughter broke out, and several instructors could be heard shushing the girls.

Theo kept her eyes on the piano, and her head lowered, afraid to face the merriment currently taking over the room at her less than stellar performance.

"Wonderful rendition, Lady Theodora," the headmistress said, returning to the stage. "And now, it is time for presentation of your academic talent."

Theo hadn't thought past her time in the musical round. Certainly, she had many talents revolving around academia, and selecting one should not be overly difficult, but any knowledge she possessed had fled with the other student's laughter in the face of her last failure.

Standing from the piano, Theo made a show of returning the bench to rest slightly under the keys. It gave her a moment to think.

"Many of our girls focus on history for their talent—Lady Josephine is skilled at reciting every British monarch going back five hundred years. Miss Alexandria has memorized every great battle in recorded history. Others find great interest in the sciences or literature, expounding on formulas or reciting lengthy poems." The room became still and silent as Miss Emmeline spoke, even Theo found herself holding her breath. "I will give you a moment to prepare. Remember to speak loudly and clearly so all can hear."

There was no mention of her missed final key— nor words of encouragement for success in the next round, and Theo sensed the headmistress was not one to coddle her students.

Theo raised her gaze to the crowd, noting the various clusters of girls. Many whispered behind their hands or paid her no mind at all. She spotted one pupil drawing in a notebook. Theo brought her hand to her long braids. Most of the girls favored a more mature look with their hair loose around their shoulders or upswept in elegant fashion rivaling many of the women Theo had seen shopping on Bond Street or promenading in Hyde Park.

The headmistress cleared her throat.

"May I return to your office and retrieve something?" Theo asked.

"Of course, Lady Theodora."

Theo cringed at the use of her full name; even her mother had acquiesced to calling her Theo when in private. More giggling could be heard circling the room as she fled the same way she'd entered. She found her way back to the office and snatched her book of maps, holding it close to her chest as she returned to the main room.

Theo knew the talent she planned to show was highly obscure, but with such a short time to decide and no time to prepare—and the haze that had settled over her due to her exhaustion—this was the best she could do.

The headmistress clapped, calling everyone back to their seats, and Theo returned to her place at the head of the room.

"What have you chosen as your academic talent, Lady Theo?" Miss Dires asked from her seat between two groups of girls close to the front of the room.

The woman's encouraging smile pushed Theo to speak. "I have a great passion for maps." Again, the other students moved about restlessly, losing interest in Theo's presentation, but she continued. "One of my talents is spotting mistakes within books—namely, volumes filled with maps."

A few *Oohs* and *Ahhs* could be heard around the room, though they were said with a certain mocking intent.

For the second time since her arrival, Theo deliberated writing to her mother and begging Lady Cartwright to come collect her; stating she'd been horribly wrong in her decision to seek an education outside the tutors available for hire in London.

Even now, Theo could be ensconced in her family's library, debating the merits of the scientific principles with Cart and his wife, Judith. Or playing with Olivia and Samuel, her niece and nephew. Instead, she was far from home, surrounded by a roomful of strangers who had no interest in her or her talents.

Theo opened her book to a marked page and held it high for all to see. "For example, here, on page seventeen, the illustrator mislabeled two cities in France, and utterly forgot to add the Sicilian Island off the coast of Italy."

Miss Dires, bless her kind soul, motioned for Theo to approach her so she could have a closer look at the text. Next, Theo moved down the front row of girls, showing them the erroneous errors.

"In this book alone, I've found forty-two such inaccuracies."

"And what exactly do you do with this knowledge?" Miss Emmeline asked from the stage.

Theo smiled at a blonde girl in the front row as she inspected the page before she returned to the headmistress's side. "Nothing at this time, but my future plan is to work with mapmakers to increase their accuracy in not only their labeling, but also land proportion versus oceans. I would also like to consult on a new method of tracking elevations on printed maps."

"Very commendable of you." Miss Emmeline nodded, her first sign of approval since Theo's arrival. "We all wish you the best in your endeavors."

Theo allowed a small grin to settle on her lips, then closed her book and tucked it under her arm. Her presentation had gone far quicker than she'd expected—and had not been as embarrassing as her piano performance—though she suspected her talent in academics was no more fascinating to the gathered girls than her song choice.

"Next, we shall all venture outside." Everyone stood as if they'd been waiting for the chance to escape the indoors. "Lady Theo, please inform me if you'll need to change into a riding habit."

Dread infused Theo. She'd never in all her days ridden a horse, nor did she own a riding habit. Her mother had spoken of the need to acquire the skill, but the large beasts frightened Theo. Even when she journeyed to the stables, she steered clear of their stalls, preferring to sit in the straw and cuddle the ever present kittens. "No, Miss Emmeline."

"Very well." The headmistress waved her arm in the direction of the double doors—pushed wide to reveal a grassy area with several stations, each housing equipment for various outdoor activities, most Theo didn't recognize. She followed the rest of the girls outside, the sun beginning to set on the far horizon. The headmistress stopped beside her and spoke once more. "We also have a lake not far away if your talent lies in rowing."

"Rowing?" Theo gulped. No amount of studying books had prepared her for all of this. "No, certainly not."

The other teachers, along with the students, hurried to an area set up for spectators and watched with anticipation as Theo walked between the five stations. Two held gear she could not identify or align with a known sporting activity. Another was set up with shuttlecock, a game she'd seen played at several garden parties she'd accompanied her mother to, but Theo had never bothered to learn the rules. Moving along, the next station held a row of guns—she didn't even bother with pausing to inspect them. The final area had a row of pegs with archery bows hanging in perfect order from a half-wall obviously erected for the sporting area. Several yards away, a line of hay-stuffed targets with red and white circles painted on them stood, each dotted with holes from use.

Theo and Cart had studied force and trajectory just months before as *Silliman's Journal* had dedicated an entire volume to the principles behind the study. They'd spent days dropping different items from the roof of their London home—much to their mother's dismay— and skimming rocks across the ponds in many of London's parks. They'd calculated the force and angle necessary to accurately throw a pebble across the water as opposed to the power needed to do the same with a much larger rock.

Surely their discoveries could be applied to the use of an archery bow and arrow.

Theo eyed the various sizes of bows hanging from the pegs as she calculated in her head the distance to the target and the length of the weapons. Though her thoughts were muddled, she should fair far better at archery than at the piano—and if not, an unpredictable flying arrow would captivate her audience more than her skills at error detection.

"You can use my bow," a dark-haired girl stepped up beside her and retrieved one from its peg.

"Thank you," Theo said with a tentative smile.

"I am Josie—err, Lady Josephine." The girl returned Theo's smile. She was one of the students who preferred to allow her hair freedom from its pins; her long, brown tresses—almost the exact color of Theo's—hanging loosely about her shoulders.

"I am Theo." She immediately regretted her words as the headmistress had introduced her before the entire gathering in the music room. "Thank you, again."

"Good luck," Josie called before hurrying back to the spectator area—or maybe it was the safest spot to watch when arrows were being shot.

Theo would need more than luck to hit the target, or even come close. Testing the weight of the bow in her hands, she moved to the square directly in front of the closest target and took an arrow from the quiver propped up by a wooden stand. The projectile's tip was not pointed but flat, reducing the chances of injury if a perilous shot resulted in a stray arrow. The shaft was made of a flexible wood with feathers connected to the end. She combed through her collective memories in search of a diagram she'd seen that featured an archer in a readied stance for a shot.

It was necessary to place her feet at shoulder width and slightly angled from the target. Placing the split end of the arrow against the string, Theo positioned her hands as best she could, sure to keep a firm hold on the arrow while adjusting her fingers.

The position felt highly uncomfortable and unstable, but was a mirror image of the illustration she'd seen.

Not a sound could be heard as she pulled the string back approximately fourteen inches to create the force and trajectory necessary to at least have the arrow fly as far as the target, though if it penetrated the circle was anyone's guess.

Theo's arm shook from the strength needed to continue holding the bow high, string pulled back with the arrow aligned and ready to shoot.

One final calculation and adjustment and Theo was satisfied with her angle.

She released the string and sent her arrow flying— straight toward the target.

Theo closed her eyes, she couldn't bear to see if the arrow landed in the lawn before the target or soared past it entirely. It had been the best attempt she could muster, having never handled the equipment before.

A loud gasp erupted from the spectator's area, and Theo kept her eyes tightly shut. Had she hit an unintended target? Had the shot gone wild after leaving her bow? Would she be made to leave the field in disgrace?

Maybe she'd have no need to write her mother, but be loaded into a carriage this very night and sent back to London.

Applause sounded behind her with several calls of "fine shot" and "she's a natural archer."

Theo opened her eyes to see her arrow protruding from the exact center of the target. She heard someone say, "It seems you have competition, Adeline."

Turning back to face the crowd, two blonde-haired girls stood next to Josie. One girl's arms were crossed, and a frown marred her delicate face. The other smirked. The displeased girl must be Adeline—and she did *not* look happy.

16

The group broke, and Josie, along with another girl, rushed to Theo's side, offering their congratulations on a perfect shot. Even Adeline, the most accomplished archer at Miss Emmeline's hadn't executed a shot as flawless, Josie crooned, only to gain another nasty look from the girl.

The urge to confide that she had never picked up a bow before today was strong, but Adeline had finally decided to put her sullen manners aside and approach the group.

"This is Georgie and Adeline," Josie introduced the two girls. "It is clear that Headmistress will assign you to our room."

"It is lovely to meet you all," Theo said when Josie took back her bow and returned it to its peg on the half-wall.

"Come," Georgie said, her voice far deeper than Theo would have imagined for a girl so tiny. "It is mealtime, and if we do not arrive soon, all the candied desserts will be gone."

"She does not look the sort to enjoy sweets," Adeline snapped. "But, nonetheless, Georgina is correct. If we don't hurry, there will be no table left except the one next to Headmistress's…and I do not wish to have her lecture me again on my mealtime manners."

"If you hadn't exchanged her sugar for salt, she would not keep such a close eye on you," Georgie laughed.

"That was some time ago," Adeline muttered. "For a woman of her advanced age, she certainly has a stellar memory."

Josie returned and slipped her arm through Theo's, pulling her after Georgie and Adeline as they advanced back through the double doors of the school. "That was a fine shot, Lady Theo. I know we will be bosom friends, all four of us."

Theo allowed her new friend to lead her to the dining hall—all the way chanting silently to herself that she would enjoy her time at Miss Emmeline's School of Education and Decorum for Ladies of Outstanding Quality—it was either that or return to London and a future under her mother's thumb and careful watch. Even at the young age of twelve, Theo knew she was not destined to live the tedious life of a sheltered London debutante.

Chapter One

London, England
October 1825

Alistair Alexander Price entered his father's townhouse—for all intents and purposes, *his* townhouse since his father had taken ill the year before and was unable to travel. Alistair was responsible for the care and well-being of his siblings—he was to tend the account ledgers, he was answerable to all his father's tenants—and it seemed, Alistair was also solely accountable for the funds needed to fulfill all of those obligations.

"Your coat, Mr. Price?" Donavon, the family butler, held his arm out, prepared to take his over garment.

Alistair shrugged, allowing the coat to fall from his shoulders and into his butler's waiting arms. "Thank you. I will be in my study, please make sure I am not disturbed."

"Of course, Mr. Price." The servant gave him a faint smile.

Alistair was fairly certain the staff was delighted to have the Melton horde in residence—and agreeable to Alistair filling his father's vacant shoes, though he had not inherited the Melton Viscountship as yet.

With a nod, Alistair continued on to his father's study. He shook his head. *His* study. It was highly unlikely his father would ever journey to London again.

Alistair needed a quiet place to think, and if it took drinking himself into a stupor to figure out his family's problems, then so be it. With eight younger siblings in residence, a quiet room was hard to come by; however, he knew his three brothers were at their fencing lessons, and the female part of his household avoided his study as much as possible—unless summoned. Alistair had made a point of using the room when doling out lectures on inappropriate behavior, as well as when imparting bad news.

Anyone who invaded his private space was subject to one or the other—and on many occasions, both.

His footsteps sounded as he walked down the corridor, past his sisters' receiving room—not that the five Melton females were used to receiving guests beyond family—and beyond to the study.

The day had not gone as planned, to say the least. His father's longtime solicitor, Mr. Adams, had shared with Alistair the dire conditions of the many Melton estates. Since the viscount had begun his downward spiral and his illnesses finally took his ability to walk, not a single tenant issue had been addressed, no roofs had been mended beyond what the villagers could do themselves, and no upkeep to the estate gardens had been done. And their family coffers were continually drained from the expenses of supporting nine children and a full-time physician to care for the aging viscount.

Alistair's father had once been a very hands-on viscount, not trusting estate business and tenant concerns to anyone. That left Alistair to fumble his way through things once his father was unable to leave his sickbed—and his mother unwilling to leave her husband's side.

Alistair rounded his desk and fell heavily into his chair—the chair he'd seen his father occupy for all of Alistair's twenty-five years. It had remained vacant for nearly two years before Alistair and his mother made the decision to remove the children to London to avoid them witnessing the viscount's worsening condition. His mother was to join them before his sister, Adeline, was presented to society.

The news had arrived yesterday—two short weeks before Adeline's first ball—that Viscountess Melton would not be joining her children in London. At least, not this season.

Certainly, Alistair could handle depositing Adeline at her dress fittings, consulting with her on which invitations to accept, and accompanying her on outings to Hyde Park, but he did not enjoy any of those things, and as a rule, strictly avoided any excursion that would result in meeting marriage-minded females. There was an overabundance of those to contend with in his own home without seeking them out about town.

And Alistair hadn't the time or the patience for any of it.

Thankfully, he only need present one sibling to the *ton* this season, Adeline—next season would be Adelaide and Amelia, and after them, Arabella the following year. Lastly, Ainsley. It was all too much to wrap one's mind around. The viscount's coffers would be empty long before Alistair inherited the title. And what to do about his brothers: Abel, Alfred, and Adrian? They were remarkably unconcerned with their future paths. None of the three wanted their father to purchase them a commission to serve their country—though Alfred and Adrian were much too young to be burdened with such thoughts as yet. Not a one had an interest in any trade, but Abel did enjoy spending his spare time assisting at the British Museum, without pay, of course; however, at the age of twenty and one, he should be focusing on something more suitable to support a family.

Alistair would see his duty through: ensuring that all of his siblings were wed and taken care of. And then, if there were still time for him and he hadn't been beaten down by the strain of it all, he would think about his own future.

There were many years ahead of him before he had the luxury of pondering what he wanted for his life. Little Ainsley was only ten, after all, and with eight years until her introduction, Alistair would have no rest until then.

What had his parents been thinking? Nine children with his father already close to fifty when the first was born. It was irresponsible, to say the least. At this point, Alistair would be close to the same age when he had the time to focus on finding his own wife. Never would he burden anyone with supporting his offspring.

As he stared toward the open door, a flash of green flew past, catching his attention. He had glimpsed a trail of blonde curls before the girl was out of sight, her slippered feet making no sound.

He was out of his chair and following, a lecture on the inappropriateness of running indoors on the tip of his tongue. It was necessary for him to hurry to the entryway as his siblings were fast to disappear, especially if they suspected he was in pursuit.

Adeline stood, ready to enter the receiving room when he called her name, his displeasure clear in his voice.

Her hand paused on the door handle but did not turn it.

"Adeline," he chastised. "What have I said about running in the house?"

"It is only necessary to run faster than the person chasing you?"

"Do not play feebleminded with me," he sighed, knowing he had, indeed, said those exact words many times, but that was before he and his sister had reached adulthood—and he'd been forced to take his unofficial place as head of the Melton clan. "What did I say about running in the house *yesterday*?"

"That it is highly inappropriate for women who've left the schoolroom and expect to be accepted in ballrooms," she mimicked. "Women who have turned their cotton pinafores in for silk gowns should refrain from such uncouth behavior."

"And…" Alistair prodded. He shouldn't have to lecture Adeline on her decorum. Hadn't he spent enough coin on her tutelage? For a woman of eight and ten, she could use a healthy dose of maturity.

"If such young women do not agree, then they are free to pack their trunk and return to the country."

He smiled with pride at her ability to recite his lecture from the day before. "Very good. Miss Emmeline's School of Education and Decorum for Ladies of Outstanding Quality has at least taught you one valuable skill. Now if only you could follow the sound advice you memorized."

Adeline stuck her tongue out at him as she turned toward the door once again.

"Adeline!" Again her hand froze on the knob—knowing her luck would only get her so far with her eldest brother. "You must put your childish ways behind you if you favor a successful season."

"Of course, my dearest, most loving, and wise brother." Her talent for charming others—all the while mocking them—was a gift all of his siblings shared, though her sweet words never fooled him. "Now, if you do not mind, it is discourteous to keep guests waiting."

"Not many are informed we are in London. Who is calling on you?"

And why hadn't he been informed there was a visitor in his home? It was not only his aging parents but also his servants who'd taken a liking to his younger siblings, often doing their bidding without realizing it.

"It is only Theo, Alistair." She said the name as if it should be familiar to him. *Only Theo?*

He wanted to demand she tell him who the bloody hell Theo was and what the man was doing calling on his sister without properly introducing himself to Adeline's eldest brother before requesting an audience with her. True, their parents were still responsible for the lot of them; however, as the eldest male in good health, it fell on Alistair to keep his siblings safe.

And he could not do that if unfamiliar men were coming and going right under his nose.

Instead of ripping the door off its hinges and confronting the man who dared enter his home without an invitation, Alistair took a deep breath. Far different from the deep breath he'd taken earlier in his study as he'd allowed the pressure of his responsibility to settle. No, this deep breath was giving him time to gather his words to use as his weapon instead of his fists.

Many—especially his female siblings—called him domineering and imperious when it came to his family. But his father had trusted him to lead well in the viscount's stead, and no matter the difficulty of the task, Alistair would do exactly that.

Adeline looked at him as if he'd grown a second head with five eyes. "Are you experiencing a decrease in memory, dear brother?"

His temper rose at Adeline's reference to their father's diminished mental capacity, and his sister knew she'd gotten to him. She was most successful at finding every little thing that irritated him and drawing his annoyance out. And since her return from boarding school, he'd realized she hadn't changed. Not even the smallest bit.

The viscountess, Lady Melton, had hoped that separating the two siblings would ease their lifelong discontent and competitiveness with one another, but while Alistair had been made to mature far quicker than most, his sister was still the hellion she'd been since birth.

"I assure you, I am in full capacity of my senses, Miss Adeline," he spoke the words slowly, pronouncing each as if she were the one who was struggling to grasp his meaning. "Why do you not introduce me to your *friend*, Theo?"

Maybe he was the boon Alistair had been praying for—a man to take his wayward sibling off his hands before the season had even begun. Alistair's only regret was that he'd paid the modiste's note the day before. He need push this *Theo* to announce his courtship quickly and have the betrothal papers drafted as soon as the man hinted at the possibility—before he discovered that Adeline was not the demure miss he assumed her to be, but a sharp-tongued, quick-witted, infuriating debutante who knew exactly how alluring her blonde hair, fair skin, and pale blue eyes were.

Adeline made no move to join her guest, most likely suspecting her brother had some plan contrived—and she would be correct.

"Come, dear sister," he hissed. "Let us not keep *our* visitor waiting."

"But—"

"Do you not want me to greet our guest?" he asked. This Theo gentleman must be highly unsuitable if Adeline were working this hard to keep Alistair from entering the room. Again, he searched his memory for any mention of a Theo—or, more likely, Theodore—who'd made his acquaintance. There was that elderly earl, Lord Bays. His given name was Theodore if Alistair weren't mistaken, but he was far too old for his sister's liking and, he gulped, wedded going on three decades. Certainly, Adeline hadn't lowered herself to consorting with men who were spoken for. "Allow me to open the door."

Adeline scrutinized him before shrugging. "Very well, let us greet *our* guest. Do not embarrass me before my friend."

"Embarrass you?" Alistair asked, stunned. "Why ever would you think I would do something so juvenile?"

"You have been known to make me look awful and think it is comical." She released the knob and crossed her arms. "Or need I remind you of how cruel you and Abel have been to me?"

"Must I remind *you* what a nuisance you were as a child?" he retorted. This was the way of things for them: bickering, bantering, and arguing—with no end in sight. "You would follow Abel and me around constantly. It was improper for a young girl of quality."

"You lost me in the woods!" she shrieked. "I was only ten, and the sun was setting."

"But you never followed us outdoors again, did you?"

"*Humpf.*" She tapped her foot, waiting for him to agree that he would not mortify her. When he made no move to agree to her request, she continued, "And the pie?"

Alistair couldn't help but chuckle at the reminder. "The pie dropping over the railing from the landing above the main hall was Abel, and you very well know that. We could not have known you'd be walking below at that precise moment."

"My new frock was ruined from the berry juices."

"Again, that was many years ago, Adeline," he said. "I have grown—matured—as I hope you did as well during your time away at school. Now, please allow me to escort you to greet this Theo gentleman."

A smirk landed on Adeline's face, and her brow rose. "Of course, dear brother. Let us join our guest."

He set his hand on her arm to halt her before she entered the room. "Do not think I take kindly to men calling on my sister without my express permission. This will not go unmentioned."

"Oh, I certainly hope you do reprimand Theo." Adeline giggled, a sound Alistair hadn't heard in many years. Actually, he hadn't heard it since she'd slipped a dozen pond frogs into his trunk before he'd left for Eton. The carriage had been made to stop only two hours' journey from their country estate to free the trapped creatures; however, they'd already done the intended damage to his entire wardrobe, and Alistair had spent an entire week wearing the same set of clothes until new ones could be sent. "It is only what is deserved."

Alistair had had enough of his sister's irksome banter, so he stepped around her, pushing the door wide. "After you." Alistair bowed mockingly as she flipped her hair over her shoulder and preceded him into the room.

Entering, he immediately scanned the room looking for the man who dared enter his home with no regard for proper etiquette, putting his sister's reputation in question before her first season was underway.

"I do not appreciate hearing that someone dares cross the threshold of my home without suitable cause to do so." Alistair's voice thundered through the small receiving room. He wanted the man to be aware his actions were not agreeable to Alistair—Adeline's guardian while in London. "You are certainly fortunate I am in residence to rectify the situation."

He paused, glancing around the room for his intended target, but no man stood by the open hearth, nor by the windows, their drapes held back with a simple tie to allow the warm sunlight in.

A small gasp brought his attention to the delicate sofa his mother favored when in London.

"Lady Theodora Montgomery," Adeline said, rushing to stand before the sofa. "I have missed you ever so much. I am happy to see you have arrived safely in London."

After bending down to give the woman a quick hug, Adeline cast a smirk in her brother's direction—knowing she'd successfully redirected the embarrassment to him. "I do apologize for my brother's abominable greeting."

The woman's eyes were rounded with fright at his callous tirade as she stood abruptly, ready to flee.

"As you can see, he is as dreadful as I've told you all these years," Adeline confessed, squeezing Lady Theodora's hands before turning to Alistair. "Have you terrified my dear friend enough for one day, brother?"

The poor woman was so startled she hadn't managed a single word in greeting—Alistair regretted any alarm he'd caused her; however, she must understand Adeline had misled him. She was certainly a gently bred woman, unlike his hoyden lot of sisters.

"Lady Theodora," Alistair started, attempting to mend the dismal situation. "I am Mr. Alistair Price, Adeline's eldest brother—and I assure you, I am not the horrid man my sister claims."

The woman looked wholly unconvinced by his proclamation, but offered her own greeting nonetheless. "It is nice to make your acquaintance, Mr. Price, but please refrain from dropping a pie on my head while I'm in your home. I fear my mother would be quite vexed if I ruined my new gown."

Alistair took a step back at her brazen comment as his sister doubled over in laughter.

"My dear, Theo," Adeline said, a giggle on the fringes of her words, "I have missed you so."

Why did he feel as if he'd walked into a trap set up by his most cunning sister?

Chapter Two

Theo stifled the urge to glance over Adeline's shoulder and take in the fearsome man she'd heard stories of for the last six years. He was the epitome of everything his sister had said of him...and so much more. His fair hair and glaring blue eyes matched his sister's, but that was where the similarity ended, at least for Theo. Alistair was tall, far taller than anyone in her family, and his skin had seen much sun—unlike Adeline's delicate features. Many would not believe Theo's friend spent many hours a week outdoors honing her skill with a bow.

But this man, he smelled of adventures far grander than those Theo and her friends were determined to have in London. His shoulders and back held a rigid, mature pose one attained from years of hard work—and a bit of arrogance.

"It is very nice to meet a friend my sister met while at Miss Emmeline's School." He took the chair across from the lounge Theo had sat upon before they entered and nodded for her and Adeline to sit. He bent his large frame to occupy the chair so glaringly designed for a woman—and not a full-size man. She and Adeline followed his lead, with her regaining her position on the sofa and Adeline next to her. "How did you find your experience away at school?"

The man's quick temperament change confused Theo as he likely expected and intended. Mr. Price had entered the room, furious, with a tirade meant for his target. Then she'd seen a hint of remorse from the man, which then quickly turned to unmerciful teasing of his sister—and lastly, Theo had seen his shock at her words. It was as if he sought to keep both Adeline and her off guard and on the defensive while in his company. But not Theo, no, she conversed with great intellects and free thinkers—such as her older brother and his dear wife, Jude—therefore, a bit of sarcasm wasn't enough to tie her tongue.

"The instructors were adequate, the library extensive, and the weather in Canterbury was as expected." Theo folded her hands primly in her lap and crossed her legs at her ankles as she had been taught by both her mother and also, later, in her class on decorum. "The accommodations were rather more than I'd expected from a boarding school, though they are in need of some repairs after these many years and so many students. Our tuition is being spent on learning aids and not on basic grounds upkeep and maintenance. It is something I brought to Headmistress's attention before departing. I certainly hope a means for rectifying the situation is found."

Theo kept her gaze solidly on Adeline's brother, refusing to share a conspiratorial glance with her friend.

She'd thrown him off with her candid response to his question. He'd likely thought her addle-minded and uninterested in what actually went into making an education a successful one.

"That is very good to hear, Lady Theodora," he replied. "And how would you go about rectifying the lack of upkeep for Miss Emmeline's School?"

Theo had the sense he was toying with her once again, to gauge her true understanding of estate management—and likely, her knowledge of business ventures and such. Thankfully, she'd taken great care to study this exact question, and was why she and her dear friends—Josephine, Georgina, and Adeline—had a plan. "It is quite simple, really."

"Oh, do tell." He leaned forward a bit. Theo feared the chair would collapse under his weight, spilling him to the ground.

"I have not all the answers, but I believe it is within Headmistress's right to request donations and sponsorships from successful women who've attended her school in the last fifteen years."

"And how does one define 'successful' for women who are meant to parade before society to make the most favorable match possible?" he inquired. "A rich husband? An extensive dowry?"

She hadn't come to debate the merits of educated women, nor droll on and on about the high demands of a prejudicial society. "There are many more things to consider than the advantageous marriage of a woman. For example, Lady Evangeline, now the Marchioness of

Dovenshire, is currently working in the sciences and has made great strides in the study of the human brain."

"I was unaware she attended Miss Emmeline's." He tapped his forefinger to his chin in thought. "Adeline, were you aware that Lady Evangeline—a marchioness, nonetheless—attended your alma mater?"

At her friend's perplexed expression, Theo continued, "Yes, she graduated over a decade ago." Theo wasn't certain what shocked her more, Alistair's lack of knowledge about the high quality of women attending Miss Emmeline's, or the startling fact that he knew of the marchioness and her work. "She is a very kind woman. And I think upstanding members of the *ton* would be more than willing to give back to such a magnificent school."

"Your family must be extremely proud of your dedication to your academic success, Lady Theodora," he said, turning to Adeline. "I am looking forward to seeing such accomplishments present themselves as my dear sister adjusts to town life."

Adeline glared at Alistair, the unveiled criticism of her sibling having obviously disconcerted her. It was something Theo had never dealt with in her home—at least not directed toward her. Cart was overly supportive of any endeavor Theo undertook, encouraging his only sibling to strive for as much knowledge as possible.

"Alistair," Adeline huffed. "Can we not speak of something else?"

Theo was in agreement—she and her dear friends had concocted a plan to help Miss Emmeline's School with the much-needed building repairs, but to do that, Theo did not need attention drawn to herself.

"Certainly." Alistair sat back, the chair giving a loud protest at the shift in weight. "Tell me, Lady Theodora, do I know your family?"

It was a harmless enough question. "My brother is Simon Montgomery, Lord Cartwright."

She watched Alistair closely to see if he recognized her family name. It had been years since her family was left destitute by her rascal of an uncle, and Cart had worked tirelessly to restore their family name and increase their coffers. Yet, many in London were still hesitant to associate with anyone holding the Montgomery name—much to her mother's displeasure.

"It does sound familiar, but where have I heard it before?" Theo remained silent as Mr. Price continued to ponder the name. A smile lit his face as something dawned on him. "Yes, I know. My brother, Abel, fancies himself a position at the museum one day. Your brother, he is the curator, am I correct?"

"*Almost* correct," Theo said, unsure if Mr. Price was in favor of gentlemen earning a wage much like a commoner. "He is the acting curator while his dear friend is away in Scotland in search of a long fabled church made entirely of gold. Normally, he is in charge of new acquisitions—and donations from private citizens to the museum's collections."

"And likely where you garnered your vast knowledge of contributions, am I correct?"

"Just so, Mr. Price." Theo had come to Adeline's with a purpose, a reason better left unmentioned before her friend's brother. She gave Adeline a soft nudge with her elbow. "In any case, it is certainly lovely to have Miss Adeline so close, though we are not blessed to share lodging anymore. It is odd to have a room to myself again, the nights are overly quiet and the mornings subdued. I find myself wandering my townhouse halls—boredom barely kept at bay."

"I would not know that feeling," Adeline said. "I am now required to share a room with Amelia and listen to my other siblings bickering all day and long into the night."

"We are a large family, Adeline," he chastised his sister. "Many feel blessed to have a roof that doesn't leak and food that isn't moldy." He stood abruptly and gave the women a curt bow. "It was lovely to meet a friend of Adeline's. Now, I will allow you time to visit."

"Dear brother," Adeline called as he strode toward the door. He paused and turned back toward the women, his eyes landing on Theo briefly before moving to his sister. "Lady Theo is having a garden picnic at her home tomorrow. If it suits, may I attend?"

The puzzled look on Mr. Price's face said Adeline was not one to ask permission before doing something, but more of the type to beg forgiveness after the deed is complete. "And who will be attending?"

He directed the question to Theo, not his sister. It took a moment for Theo to respond, as she was unaware of a garden picnic at her home on the morrow—and certainly, she was unsure whether her townhouse even had a garden as she and her brother favored the study and the library far more than the outdoors. "Oh, it will be my sister-in-law, Lady Cartwright." She searched her mind, unsure who else Adeline wished to be in attendance. It needed to be simple, not too many people who could dispute their claim at a later time. "And Lady Georgina and Lady

Josephine. I believe that is all. My mother has other obligations and will not be joining us."

Mr. Price looked between the pair. It was a simple request, a quite proper outing with a chaperone in good standing to watch over them.

"Georgie will come round to collect me and bring me back after," Adeline rushed. "Or, you may bring me to Mayfair. Mayhap you would enjoy attending with me?"

The last place Theo could picture Mr. Price was sitting upon a blanket-covered lawn, eating tarts and tiny sandwiches, speaking of fashion and suitable hats for the season to come. At least that was what Theo imagined women at picnics spoke of, not that she'd been to one since she was a very young girl.

Mr. Price shuddered as if an afternoon picnic was the same as being bid to attend Almack's. "Heavens, no," he said. "You may go, Adeline, as long as you return in time for your afternoon fitting at the modiste. I have many business engagements tomorrow. Plus, I am certain I will attend my fair share of womanly gatherings once you are presented to society. I bid you both good day."

"Of course, dear brother. One does not miss a fitting with Miss Cleo," Adeline called to his retreating form. "Good day, Alistair."

Adeline broke into a fit of laughter as soon as the door closed behind her brother. "I knew he would balk at the thought of a picnic with a horde of females."

"Since when am I hosting a picnic at my brother's house?" Theo hissed. "I am certain Jude will not object, but truly, this is short notice."

"We are not going to your townhouse tomorrow, silly." A mischievous smirk settled on her friend's face—one Theo had learned meant the woman was up to something and she'd be better suited not to know what it was. Unfortunately, Adeline continued before Theo could voice her objections to hearing her friend's plan. "There is a tourney in Whitechapel tomorrow afternoon, and Georgie and I will compete."

"Whitechapel? That is a most dangerous part of town."

"Do not fret," Adeline said. "The tourney announcement was in *The Post* this morning, and the entries are said to be over a hundred. The winnings will be enough to pay for my—and Georgie's—entrance into the Grand Archers' Competition of London."

"And when did you plan to tell me you were using me and my home as an excuse for your absence?" The fact that Adeline made so many decisions without consulting Theo was irksome in the extreme, but Theo reminded herself that Adeline, Georgie, and Josie had befriended her on her first day at Miss Emmeline's, and for that, Theo would be eternally grateful to them. "And what time shall I be ready tomorrow?" At Adeline's puzzled expression, Theo continued, "So, I am not to come?"

"Who will serve as our alibi if you are not at home on the morrow?"

"What about your dress fitting with Miss Cleo?" Theo asked.

"There is no appointment," Adeline chided as if it were obvious, and Theo was too inept to see the whole of the ruse. "It was my backup plan in case you did not receive my letter to come for a visit today."

Theodora

Theo should feel left out, the outcast who was the last to arrive in their small group, but while Theo dreamed of adventure, gallivanting about the less savory parts of London was a bit more than she was prepared for. Though she was undoubtedly the best archer in their group, Theo was unsure whether she was ready for such a public display of her skills. Besides, she could not chance anyone recognizing her, for the scandal would no doubt affect her brother's position at the British Museum, one he longed to assume and had worked towards for many years.

"Very well," Theo said. "Have you both been practicing in my absence?" When Adeline avoided her question, Theo prodded. "Adeline, you know how important it is to keep up with your marksmanship exercises."

"I know, Theo, I know," Adeline said. "But I have been ever so busy preparing for my season; dress fittings and the like, not to mention gloves, shoes, and hats. I will do better starting after this competition."

"Where are you gathering the coin for your entry fee?" Theo knew Adeline was allotted no allowance by her parents or her brother. Her friend's financial status was well known among the girls at school. "I can ask Cart for an advance in my allowance—"

Adeline forced a smile. "No, that is not necessary. Georgie has enough for both our entry fees—at least that is what she says. The new duchess hasn't completely cut off her allowance as yet. And if we win, the money will more than cover the entry fee for the larger tourney in a week's time."

Theo longed to believe they could fulfill their scheme to help Miss Emmeline, but without practice, there was little chance of Adeline and Georgie besting anyone. And if they lost, they would have less money than when they started.

Their sworn promise the eve before they departed their beloved school—the place they all found one another—would be for naught. They'd stayed up late that night spending their final night at Mrs. Emmeline's planning their futures; but they all understood they'd be in far different circumstances if they hadn't met one another. How could they deny that to future generations of girls—sent away from their homes and families to a foreign part of England? She, Adeline, Josie, and Georgie were eternally grateful that Headmistress had placed them all together. It had made the last six years of Theo's life not only tolerable, but enjoyable. Presently, they were charged with finding a way for the school to go on. To provide a refuge for all manner of young girls to come; hopefully one day, their own daughters.

"Promise me you will send word when you arrive home tomorrow?" Theo begged. "I will not feel a moment's peace until I know you and Georgie are safe—no matter the outcome of the tourney."

They were only young women. They could not make the necessary repairs Headmistress needed to keep her school open, not to mention the safety of everyone who lived on the property. That left only the money necessary to make the repairs. They'd all agreed it was something they could help with, though none of them were in a position to request it of their families.

"I promise, and do not fret, with your tutelage, there is not a man—or woman—who stands a chance against a member of the Lady Archer's Creed."

"Friendship, loyalty, and honor above all," they chanted in unison.

And there was one specific thing they were all adept at—or at least three of them. Though, it was something Theo hadn't expected to happen so quickly.

"I certainly hope your instincts are correct, Adeline, for if not, we all have much to lose." Not only them but their families, as well. And Miss Emmeline especially. The school—the place they'd called home for six years—was in dire need of repairs, repairs their headmistress could not complete and also afford to pay her instructors' salaries. "Now, please tell Georgie to remember her breathing."

"I will." Adeline stood. "And you have no need to remind me to keep my arrogance under control for overconfidence leads to the downfall of man."

Those were not Theo's exact words, but the meaning was there. "I wish you both the best of luck."

# # #

"Are you certain your calculations are correct, Theo?" Lord Cartwright asked, surveying the many hand-drawn maps before them, spread haphazardly around the room. "Because if they are accurate…"

There was no need for Theo's brother to finish his statement—they both understood the magnitude of her research. It was gratifying to know the countless hours she'd spent at The King's School library weren't for nothing. Cart had taken her to the school, a short walk from Miss Emmeline's, on his first visit to Canterbury. Theo had instantly fallen in love with the grandness of the ancient buildings and that they included both girls and boys in their educational development. The school was far too expensive for her to attend, but their library was open to all—if you were willing to read, study, and research everything without removing the books.

"I spent my final month in Canterbury going over and over every book I could locate on the matter." Purported as a grammar school, the grounds and facilities were far more than anyone would expect from a school almost two-centuries-old. She'd even convinced Josie to accompany her on occasion, which suited her friend. The library had an extensive collection of medication references as well as an entire wall filled with nothing but old maps and other geography tomes. "My calculations are accurate. Over the next five hundred years, the world's oceans will continue to rise, taking over what was viable, inhabitable areas of land."

"Have you established what is causing the rise?" Cart looked from the papers spread before him to Theo, his eyes narrowed as he read her notes once more.

"I believe it is due to the melting ice in the colder parts of the world." Theo held a book out for him to see. "Here you can see that the lower elevations will be affected far more than areas of higher elevation."

"Remarkable."

Theo suppressed her smile. "With Cassini's help and extensive knowledge, we should be able to pinpoint which areas in England—and the world—may very well be under water in the next thousand years."

"Have you told Cassini of this yet?"

"When I requested an audience on his next voyage to England, I did mention a bit of what I'd studied over the last several years; however, I was not so foolish to tell him all." No serious person in academia was imprudent enough to divulge all their research before the time was right. "At the time of my letter, I was still researching a few theories for the increased water levels along the English coast. I am fairly certain I have established the cause."

"Your thorough research certainly speaks to that point." Cart gestured to the piles of books, papers, and maps littering his study. "I cannot believe you spent this much time at The King's School—I expected you to revel in your time away from home, meet friends, and discover who you are, away from Mother."

He'd said the exact same thing to her on each of his visits. "Yes, to have the educational experience you were not afforded due to Uncle Julian's betrayal and misuse of Father's estate."

What her brother failed to understand was that she'd delighted in every minute away at school. She had met friends, had been given the luxury of studying what she found most compelling, and she had discovered what set her apart from others of her age.

Theo set her book aside and stared hard at her brother. "Simon." She affectionately used his given name, though most addressed him by his shortened title. Theo didn't reach for his hand as he'd always shied away from contact, but she gave him her most reassuring grin. "I spent my time at Miss Emmeline's School wisely. I did meet new friends, as well as receive a superior education. That The King's School library was so close was a grand surprise, and my time there was worth every moment. Your sacrifice—and Jude's—has been a most blessed gift to me."

"And what of your future?"

"My future?" Theo asked. She'd labored over the subject for years, discovering where exactly her fate lies. "Well, I plan to take things as they come. I will attend this season, as agreed upon by you and Mother before I left for boarding school. As for past that…well, I sent my letter to Cassini, asking for an internship of sorts, though I am unsure how Mother will react."

Cart's stare softened. "Leave the Dowager Countess to me, but I want you to understand that there is no hurry for you to wed—unless you settle on a man who truly suits. There are many life paths open to you: continued education, travel, and any number of hobbies."

Theo envisioned her dear friends in Whitechapel at the archery tourney. Certainly, she loved the pastime— took great pleasure in her skills—and even enjoyed teaching the perfect technique to others, but beyond that and the plan they'd developed to help Miss Emmeline, she hadn't seen any future in the sport beyond garden and country parties.

She'd considered the other two: education and travel. Possibly even combining them and journeying to France to visit the grand museum and attend lectures, all while working with Monsieur Damon Cassini, a man whose family had dedicated generations to developing topographical maps.

"Do tell me you will not make any decision—even agreeing to consult with Cassini—before completely exploring all your options." Cart worried for her, that much had been obvious since her birth, over a decade after his. Her brother had always stood up to their mother, demanding the dowager release her stifling hold on her only daughter—giving Theo a chance to know life beyond London proper.

Tears threatened at the depth of his love for his only sibling; in truth, she felt the same affection for him.

"I have no plans at courtship this season. As far as Cassini is concerned, the man agreed to meet with me to discuss my theory. That is all. He may very well have already discovered all I have, and be uninterested in my research."

"Even so, Stanford and I have agreed your knowledge is well suited to lectures at the museum." His faith in her never ceased. "In only a few days' time, my baby sister will be speaking before some of the most enlightened minds in all of England."

"I am looking forward to my lecture, Simon." Several years ago, Theo would have rather fled the country for Siberia as opposed to standing before a crowded room and speaking. Alas, her time at Miss Emmeline's had taught her that presentation—of any subject—was important. A woman who could assert herself with poise, grace, and knowledge before a gathering was a woman who would not soon be forgotten. This did not always lessen Theo's nervous habits, but it did give her solace. Headmistress was a wise woman, and her first day's task for her pupils was meant to teach a lesson, and show growth over time. "But do not hope for too much from my first foray— speaking before a group of schoolgirls is far different than lecturing a room of intellectuals. Besides, many will wonder what you and Stanford were thinking, allowing a girl just out of the schoolroom free rein in the museum's lecture hall."

He chuckled. "When did you gain the skill of comedy, dear sister?"

Theo hadn't tried to jest. Her fears were real and in no way imagined.

"You are well-known at the museum," he confided. "Years ago, I shared our calculations on trajectory and how it could be applied to archery with Stanford and several other men. I could not understand if they were more fascinated with our discovery, or that a mere twelve-year-old female had been part of something grown men hadn't yet considered."

The confession brought her up short, stopping her next words. To think that educated minds had spoken of her, known of her work, and were agreeable to attending her lectures was…well…it was nothing short of astounding.

Theo focused on her clasped hands to hide her smile.

"In fact," Cart continued, "we have over sixty attendees scheduled to attend your lecture. Sixty! We have not had such a grand turnout since Richard Trevithick visited the museum in 1804 to discuss his steam engine—and that was long before my time with them."

Pride beamed from her brother, and Theo only hoped her lecture was worthy of his patronage.

"Theodora! Where have you gone, child?"

The study door flew open, crashing against its casing as the dowager rushed into the room, Jude, Cart's wife, fast on her heels.

Her mother stopped short, pressing her hand to her chest as if something had frightened her into stunned shock. "My heavens, Simon. What is all this nonsense?"

Cart jumped to his feet. "Mother," he said by way of greeting, his tone cool and unaffected. "We were discussing Theo's time at Miss Emmeline's."

The dowager eyed the stacks of books and papers littering every available surface. "This drivel is behind her, Simon. Presently, she should be focusing on her presentation to society, not senseless books and other worthless notions. And her name is Theodora." The dowager pronounced every syllable. "You must stop with that silly nickname. She is a lady, certainly a diamond of the first waters this season, and I will not have anyone referring to her by a man's name."

"Cart, I tried—" Jude attempted to speak.

"*Trying* and accomplishing are two very different things, Judith." The dowager faced her daughter-in-law, her lips twisted into a scowl. "You would be wise to learn that if you ever hope to fill my shoes as Lady Cartwright."

Theo didn't need to inform her mother that Jude had already usurped her place as countess, relegating their mother to dowager status. Anastasia Montgomery knew her place, but refused to accept it; though Cart and Jude didn't seem to mind. The dowager did dote on Samuel and Olivia, and obviously relished the thought of having another girl to present to society—maybe one who actually took interest in pretty frocks, ribbons, and gloves.

"Certainly, Mother," Cart conceded, but threw a wink in Theo's direction. "Jude and I will endeavor to reach your high standards for the Earldom."

"That is correct, you will," the dowager huffed, bringing her fan forward and whipping it rapidly to and fro before her. "Now, Theodora, Judith, and I have an appointment with the modiste. Let us be off." Her skirts flared about her when she pivoted toward the door, almost colliding with Jude, who stood a few paces behind her. "Judith, you are quiet as a mouse—do inform me of your continued presence, will you."

"Quiet as a mouse," Cart repeated with a laugh. "I do believe that is a great compliment to my dear wife."

"Seen and not heard is only preferable to children, Simon," their mother chided as she hurried from the room.

"I dare say it is also preferable for dowagers," Theo mumbled as she stood to follow Jude and her mother from the room.

"I tell you, Theo," he chuckled, the papers he held shaking in his hands from his merriment. "You certainly did not obtain your wit from Mother."

"Thankfully, not her sense of entitlement either, brother." Theo flared her skirts and lifted her chin, following their mother from the room—her stride and stance matching the dowager's.

Masking her amusement with a serene smile as she headed toward the foyer, Theo had to fight her grin as the echo of Cart's riotous laughter followed her the entire way.

Chapter Three

Alistair should have known Adeline could not be trusted to arrive home in time to depart for her fitting—a missed appointment that would no doubt cost him dearly. No one missed an engagement with Miss Cleo. The modiste prided herself on booking fittings months in advance, and Adeline's lapse in timing would certainly affect the delivery of her new wardrobe. There were less than two weeks until the season officially began, and his sister was taking the responsibility of her preparation far too lightly for Alistair's liking.

The embarrassment of his needing to track down Lady Theo's residence to collect his hoyden of a sister was infuriating and embarrassing. Adeline had agreed to return home in time for her fitting, and Alistair had misguidedly believed her—the thought of her lying before her friend was something inconceivable to him.

Alistair had to settle his account with Miss Cleo, and he'd decided to attend with Adeline, see for himself all the garments worth the king's ransom he'd been billed. Luckily, he had, or he would have never known she'd missed the fitting. And unluckily for his sister, she wouldn't be allowed out of the house again without him or Abel to escort her.

The shock on the butler's face when Alistair had pounded upon Lady Theo's door had been one of utter bewilderment that had swiftly turned to unease. Alistair had been shown to a drawing room quickly enough, and it was only then that he saw the irony of his calling on Lady Theo without Lord Cartwright's permission—or so much as a proper introduction.

His fury at Adeline was too great to care at the moment.

The fire in the hearth blazed, causing Alistair to grow uncomfortably warm as he paced the room. He needs must calm himself, or he'd frighten Lady Theo…again. And, truly, he was angry at Adeline, not her friend. It would be beyond impertinent of him to take his aggression out on the innocent woman whose only misstep was befriending Alistair's wayward sister.

Alistair removed his jacket and slung it over his arm as he moved to inspect a shelf farthest from the fire and view several obscure items set carefully upon stands. One was a scroll, tightly bound. An odd thing to display, as one could not see what words it held within. Another shelf held several books—in no discernible order to Alistair, though they all seemed to focus on geography, one about the great desert plains in Africa, and another about the rich soil found in the New World. Certainly not subjects he was prepared to find in a lady's receiving room.

"Mr. Price?" Lady Theo squeaked behind him. "How may I help you?"

He turned toward her, not having heard her enter the room—his demand caught in his throat. She wore the simplest day gown of pale blue, making her ordinary brown hair seem a much deeper brunette as it fell about her shoulders.

He swallowed, shaking his head softly to banish the thought of what her silken waves would feel like against his cheek. "My apologies for calling unannounced, but I am looking for Adeline. She did not arrive home from your picnic to attend her fitting. By chance, is she here?" he asked, but Alistair hadn't the slightest clue where his sister would be if not with Lady Theo. His siblings were new to town, and they were not acquainted with many people as yet.

She took a step back, her shoulders tightening as she avoided his stare, almost as if she sought to hide the answer he'd clearly seen in her eyes. Lady Theo was not adept at lying—likely never having the need until her acquaintance with Adeline. He felt a bit responsible for that burden.

"She...well..." Lady Theo stuttered. "She departed with Georgie and Josie in time to arrive home for her fitting, Mr. Price."

Her claim was about as convincing as Adeline's too fair skin—Alistair being aware she applied powder to give the illusion of a fairer complexion. But what did Lady Theodora have to hide from him?

And why was she willing to risk his anger for Adeline?

"And she was headed directly home?" If she insisted on lying, then he would push her to say the words aloud.

"I would assume so." She still hadn't met his intense gaze.

"Let us say she did not, indeed, go home. Where would you presume she went?"

"I would not wish to guess or assume anything, Mr. Price. Should I know more than I do?"

Answering a question with a question—a tactic she'd likely learned from Adeline. Lady Theo must have been warned of his extreme aversion of others answering his questions with other questions. "I would suspect that since you and she are so close—"

"We are not *that* close," she said, cutting him off.

"Close enough to have shared a room at school for six years and dined together this afternoon." He dared her to deny him once more.

"I am sorry, but I am unaware where Miss Adeline went when she departed my home," Lady Theo said. "If by chance I hear from her or the other women, I will send word immediately."

"Very well," Alistair gave in, allowing Theo her secrets. "I will do the same. If she arrives home, I will send word that she is safe."

"That is much appreciated," Theo said. "Now, if you do not mind, my mother and I are expecting visitors shortly."

"I thought your mother had plans that would not allow her to attend your picnic." He raised a brow.

Obviously stunned, it took Lady Theo a moment to get her thoughts in order before she spoke—and Alistair would be lying if he said he didn't enjoy catching her off guard as she had him the day before. "Yes, well, she arrived home not long ago, and we have guests arriving any moment. As I said, I will send word if I hear from Adeline. My butler can give you Lady Georgina's and Lady Josephine's directions if that would help." She turned to walk toward the door, signaling their visit was at an end. "Squires will see you out. Good day, Mr. Price."

"It was a pleasure seeing you again," he called. Lady Theo's shoulders tightened at the word "pleasure," and he watched the sway of her hips as she led him into the hallway.

"Theodora?" a voice called. "My heaven's, what dress are you wearing? It is certainly not suitable for our esteemed guests."

Alistair retreated several paces into the room to hide his presence. His calling on Lady Theo was not entirely proper as she hadn't been introduced to society. That she was friends with Adeline did not rectify that fact.

"Mother," Lady Theo said, her footsteps speeding up—along with the sway of her backside—as she moved down the hall toward the other woman. It was as Alistair had suspected, she'd kept her footsteps light when entering the room to speak with him. "I had a surprise visitor, but I am finished now and was coming to find you."

"Well, I suppose there is not enough time for you to change. At least Marianne was able to tame your wild locks this morning." The women's voices receded as they moved away from Alistair and Lady Theo's receiving room. "Mr. Oliver Gladstone will arrive any moment. I know you will find him to your liking."

Gladstone? That holier than thou scoundrel who owed money to every gaming hell and bordello in London? That man was to no one's liking.

Alistair would feed his sister to a horde of hyenas before giving her over to a rascal such as Gladstone who called himself a *gentleman*.

However, Lady Theo's suitors—and her future in general—did not concern Alistair any further than where it pertained to Adeline's current whereabouts. Convinced Lady Theo and her mother had retreated far enough away, Alistair made his way to the foyer to depart, Lady Theo's butler nowhere in sight—Lady Josephine's and Lady Georgina's directions forgotten.

Unfortunately, his good luck did not last for a knock sounded at the front door, and the butler appeared.

The butler eyed Alistair, silently wondering why he was still there Alistair was sure, but the man's manners kept him from speaking out of turn.

"I was showing myself out, my good man," Alistair commented when the butler made no further move to answer the door.

Alistair grasped the knob and opened the portal wide, coming face-to-face with Gladstone.

"Mr. Price," the man hissed. "Whatever are you doing here?"

"Gladstone," he replied. "I would ask you the same thing. There are no card tables within these walls—nor scantily clad women."

"I am here at the dowager countess's behest, to meet her daughter, Lady Theodora." Gladstone looked down his pointy nose at Alistair, which was a feat as the

54

man was almost a foot shorter than he. "Though, I cannot ascertain any reason *you'd* be here."

Alistair was uncertain whether to admit he'd come to see Lady Theodora, himself. "I came to speak to Lord Cartwright. Unfortunately, he is away from home at present."

"Ah, well, I had heard Abel was looking for a post at the museum. I guess my sources were correct." Gladstone stepped around Alistair and allowed the butler to take his jacket, Alistair's own still draped over his arm. "It must be quite taxing being the spare heir." The man visibly shuddered, and Alistair took yet another calming breath to suppress his retort.

"But do we all not wish for a bit less responsibility and the ability to live a *carefree* life?" Alistair emphasized the term, knowing that Gladstone was close to having his massive amounts of debt called in and his townhouse seized. "Perhaps I will see you at the tables shortly—maybe at my club?" At the man's outright venomous glare, Alistair continued, "Oh, that is right. White's does not take kindly to members who are unable to pay their bills. I guess I won't be seeing you at White's anytime soon—though Abel is looking forward to his sponsorship being approved shortly. I suppose being a spare isn't as bad as it appears."

Gladstone's face flushed a bright red, although Alistair was unsure if it was his anger or humiliation that cause the heat. Gladstone was the only son of a merchant. His designs to marry into the *ton* were well-known.

With a sense of accomplishment, Alistair strode out the front door.

He must call on Lady Theodora's brother presently to dissuade the man from entertaining any type of offer from Gladstone to court or wed Lord Cartwright's sister—that was, as soon as Alistair located Adeline and locked her in her room until the season was underway.

Chapter Four

Theo entered her mother's salon while the dowager countess hurried to the foyer to collect Mr. Gladstone. Theo's mind was on one thing: escaping her house to search for Adeline. She needed to warn her of Mr. Price's fury over his sister's failure to arrive home as expected. The Whitechapel tourney would be starting in an hour's time—with no hope for her friend to return home before the sun began to set.

Adeline's plan had been flawed from the very beginning, and her friend hadn't needed Theo to point it out.

Theo sat heavily in her favorite chair by the window. A part of her knew Adeline's troubles were not her making, but that did not alleviate Theo's guilt over Mr. Price's irritation with his sister. If only she'd been able to concoct another lie quickly—something that would have appeased Price and kept Adeline from further trouble. Her friends would never trust her again with anything.

She stood when Mr. Oliver Gladstone entered the room, taking in his roundish figure—more suitable to an aging vendor outside Hyde Park than a gentleman on the fringes of the *ton*. He would certainly do himself an enormous favor by taking up fencing or even horseback riding to counteract the structure he'd clearly inherited from his mother, Mrs. Eugenia Gladstone, the daughter of a baron who'd married a wealthy merchant. Even his jet-black hair lay oily across his forehead as if his mother had given him a haircut before he'd arrived to meet Theo.

Theo had had occasion to meet Mrs. Gladstone several times when the elder woman came calling at their townhouse. From what Theo could remember, it was highly likely the mother and son shared a lady's maid for their hair and fashion styles.

After entering the room, Mr. Gladstone continued to speak with her mother, the Dowager Lady Cartwright, and did not spare Theo a single glance. It gave her ample time to take stock—the way he smiled, his lips pulling back in a harsh slash across his face with his teeth yellowed and crooked. His skin was pale to the point of appearing as discolored as his teeth. He would certainly benefit from a dusting of white powder— mayhap when they were better acquainted, she'd send the gift round to his home.

Mr. Gladstone stood with his shoulders squared, likely thinking it made his less-than-average height appear taller, though all it succeeded in doing was highlighting his protruding paunch.

Theo could scarcely believe the difference between the man who'd just departed her home and Gladstone. Where Mr. Price stared at her intensely every moment they shared space, Gladstone could not be bothered to make her acquaintance or even so much as nod in her direction. Possibly he was hampered by poor sight and truly couldn't see her standing only five feet from him. Surely that was the only plausible excuse for making such an uncouth first impression.

"Mr. Gladstone," the dowager countess finally said, cutting off their talk of—heavens knew what; Theo hadn't been listening. "May I present my daughter, Lady Theodora Montgomery."

Gladstone turned to face her as Theo stepped forward. As he appraised her, she noted his beady eyes inspecting her as if she were a piece of livestock at the auction house. Everything her brother and Judith had instilled in her shouted this man was not right for her— and most certainly, no intelligent woman of the *ton*.

"Lady Theodora Montgomery." He gave her a slow, unsteady bow, and she feared for a brief moment he would topple to the ground before her. She even had the good sense to take a small step back in case he did careen to the floor. It would not do for them to find themselves entangled on the rug; however, he righted himself with a little less grace than most men. "Our mothers have spoken of this day for many, many years. It is an honor to meet you."

Theo got the sense it was anything but an honor. "And you, Mr. Gladstone."

"Do have a seat, Oliver, dear," Theo's mother chimed in, ushering them back toward the lounge. *Dear?* She'd never once heard her mother speak in such a soft, endearing tone. The dowager stood before the only chair, making it necessary for Theo and Mr. Gladstone to share the lounge. It dipped precariously as he sat next to her, his thigh brushing hers before Theo scooted the few inches away. "I am sorry to hear your mother was unable to accompany you, Mr. Gladstone."

"Yes, well." Gladstone used the guise of clearing his throat to move closer to Theo once more. "She is overly occupied by her charitable deeds. My mother hopes to visit someday soon."

"Very good," her mother said. "I will see where Olivia is with our tea. Do speak amongst yourselves, I will return shortly."

She shot a scolding glare at her mother's retreating form. It was all a bit too contrived for Theo's liking. She'd arrived in London from school only a fortnight ago, and proper entertaining dresses had been delivered only the morning before—and now, Gladstone was calling.

Even more suspect was his calling at a time when Cart and Judith were out with the children.

Her mother could not possibly think they would make a favorable match. It had nothing to do with his birth as a merchant's son or his lack of title. It had everything to do with the lecherous stare he'd given her when they'd been introduced.

"Lady Theodora," he started, shifting his body slightly to face her. "I was told you attended Miss Emmeline's School of Education and Decorum for Ladies of Outstanding Quality in Canterbury. How did you fair?"

"Very well. Thank you for asking." She'd spoken of this topic only the day before with Mr. Price, yet

Gladstone's question seemed a nicety to elicit no information deeper than that her stay had been agreeable. She decided to test the depth of his interest. "Headmistress has done a fine job of hiring adequate instructors in all subjects ranging from the sciences to arithmetic to literature."

His brow rose in shock. "All of those subjects? I fear your mind must have about burst from all the useless knowledge. I am certain a woman of your standing favored tutelage in decorum and etiquette far more than the likes of which men study at university."

Useless knowledge? Theo routinely visited the British Museum with Cart and attributed far more time to her studies in geology and literature than learning the dances popular in London's ballrooms or which hat and gloves suited which dress.

"I, for one, will not push such high expectations on my daughters," he confided in a whisper, leaning ever closer to Theo, his knee rubbing against the fabric of her blue gown. "It is not necessary for their delicate minds to be weighed down by learning anything past basic reading and arithmetic for keeping the household ledgers."

Theo only nodded, unable to voice how drastically her views differed from his.

He must have taken her silence to mean she was enthralled with all he spoke of. "It is also my belief, as well as my family's—and dare I say, yours—that females be learned in child care and serve as proper hostesses for their families. It is a far more valuable trait for a woman to learn obedience to her father—and later, her husband—than notions of science, do you not think, Lady Theodora?"

"Obedience, Mr. Gladstone? In what regard?" she asked, her left eye twitching at her annoyance with the man, her clasped hands tightening in her lap at the thought of what he could mean.

"My mother and father were betrothed at a very young age—my mother only one and ten years." He paused, a faraway, blissful look entering his eyes. "My father, being almost at his majority at the time, was able to guide my mother's learning. She was schooled in all things domestic. My father credits her proper upbringing for his continued success in business."

Theo's jaw tightened at the mere thought of the elder Gladstone perusing a child for his bride.

"How is that?" She shouldn't be insisting on further answers as it only delayed her departure for Whitechapel. "If you will forgive my forward questioning."

"Very worthy inquiry, my lady," he said, his hand coming forward to settle on hers. She stilled the urge to pull her hand back. "She was raised a submissive girl who honored a man's wishes; therefore, allowing my father to aim all his efforts toward his business, not worrying about a wayward wife."

"Yes, your father is a lucky man," Theo agreed, though her heart went out to his mother—for all she'd been deprived of in her life.

"Now, do not hear me incorrectly, I am progressive in many ways—take that I do not see the need for women to sit before the hearth and work at their needlepoint for hours on end." He chuckled at his self-proclaimed radical view. "I have found an inventor in Scotland—but you are not interested in the history behind this all—but he has a machine that not only sews, but also embroiders, making darning and needlepoint unnecessary."

Theo wanted to scream that hearing of his man from Scotland was the first interesting thing to come out of Gladstone's mouth.

Instead, she smiled, acting as if the revelation were agreeable to her. She had no intention of pushing him to start a formal courtship. His requirements for a suitable wife meant naught to her.

The dowager viewed her only daughter as the quiet, timid mouse that had departed for school six years before—a girl who did her utmost to please her mother. Little did the dowager realize, Theo had never been that girl. Her brother and his wife knew that, and they'd never force Theo to marry a man not to her liking, especially since their marriage was one of mutual love.

Her mother hurriedly entered the room, Olivia on her heels pushing a cart heavy with tea and sandwiches. Theo could not think of a worse way to spend her day than continuing her time with Mr. Gladstone.

"Mother, I—" she started.

"Thank you ever so much for allowing me to call on Lady Theodora," Gladstone gushed, standing. "But I must be going. My father is expecting me shortly."

If Theo didn't despise the man so much, she'd hug him. Hopefully, he'd seen much in her he didn't favor and would move on to another innocent miss to court—hopefully one of an acceptable age.

"May I call on your daughter again in the near future, my lady?" he asked Theo's mother, ignoring her once more.

It was galling when others acted as if she weren't present—or in possession of the ability to speak for herself. No, she did not favor a future call from Gladstone. In fact, she'd far more favor a swim in the River Thames, stark naked, than endure this man's droning on and on about his ideal wife.

"I, and my daughter, would enjoy that very much, Mr. Gladstone," her mother replied, dashing all hopes of being rid of the man for good. "If you are certain you cannot stay for tea. Do give my best regards to your mother and father."

"It pains me gravely to say I cannot stay," Gladstone said, placing his hand—his fingers fat as holiday sausages—over his heart as if it seized. "I will certainly pass on your good tidings. And I look forward to visiting with your daughter again."

"I will show you out." Her mother bustled to his side, slipping her arm through his as they departed the room. Gladstone did not so much as glance in her direction when he left—similar to when he'd arrived. It appeared he favored a wife seen but not heard, or likely never seen *or* heard except when he deemed he was in need of a meal.

After the love her mother and father had shared, despite it being cut short, Theo was highly disconcerted by the notion that her mother would doom her to a life devoid of such mutual affection.

However, Theo did not have time to dwell on that fact—she had a friend to warn and a room to depart before her mother returned.

She was in no jeopardy of being betrothed to Gladstone before her season officially started.

Though she did fear her dearest friend would not make it to *her* first season if Mr. Price found her before Theo did.

Theo heard the thud of the front door closing as she slipped from the room and ran towards her brother's study—and the drawer he'd set up for his mother and sister's pin money. She took only enough for the hackney fare and fled through the double doors and around the side of the house—only pausing for a moment to consider leaving a note about the missing funds.

Their alleyway led to a busy street on the border of Mayfair—the perfect place to hail her first London hackney driver.

Chapter Five

Alistair fought his baser instincts—to return home and badger all his siblings into confessing where Adeline had run off to and demand to know who was in cahoots with her, but his bid for patience was rewarded when Gladstone slunk from Lady Theodora's townhouse only a brief twenty-five minutes after his arrival. If Alistair had wagered correctly, Lady Theo would shortly send word to Adeline about his fury.

It would leave him only the need to follow the servant directly to his errant sister.

A slip of pale blue caught his eye as it flashed out a side door and disappeared down the alley bordering the back of the row of townhouses.

"What in the damn hell..." Alistair's words trailed off as he spurred his horse from the shadows across the street and into action, traversing the lane that ran parallel to the alley used to deliver goods to the many houses on her street. His sister must be close if Lady Theo had departed on foot. He needs must keep her in sight, for if he lost her, there was little chance of him tracking down Adeline and bringing her home. Passing another long drive, he caught sight of her once more as she continued down the rutted alley. There were only three more homes on the street before intersecting with Piccadilly towards his own townhouse on St. James.

"On, Saber," he pushed his mount.

If she made it to the main street, he would likely lose sight of her in the crowd.

Alistair reached the end of the byway where Lady Theo emerged from the alley and waved her arms wildly. A moment later, a hack pulled up beside her. Holding her gown high, she climbed aboard without assistance. He was too far away to hear what was said, but he pulled his horse back a few steps as the hack picked up speed and entered traffic once more, passing in front of him on Piccadilly.

She didn't spy him as the hack moved past, her hair whipping in the breeze.

Alistair allowed several carriages to pass before following her onto the busy thoroughfare. He could not risk following too closely, for she'd likely spot him trailing her and keep moving in an attempt to lead him astray.

However, the fashionable part of London turned to less desirable areas as they approached the River Thames, continuing outside the city wall. It was an area that even Alistair avoided as the streets were rife with pickpockets and those not against harming another for their own gain—and here Lady Theo was, risking her safety in such a brazen manner. This was far more disconcerting than her association with Gladstone, and another subject he'd bring to the earl's attention when soon they spoke.

Not that Alistair was one to criticize another man on his methods of raising his siblings—at the moment, Adeline was missing and very likely the one leading Theodora into the East End of London.

Navigating around a cart piled high with vegetables and being pulled by a horse not long from expiring, Alistair kept the hack in sight as they entered Whitechapel. The driver turned down several streets, cutting off pedestrians and almost hitting a man on horseback. All the while, he watched Lady Theo careen from side to side.

Alistair was utterly useless to aid her.

The many carriages, horses, carts, and people on foot intensified as they traveled deeper into Whitechapel, the hack slowing to a snail's pace before pulling to a halt before a crowded field, the closest thing to a park Whitechapel had.

A sign proclaimed, *Archery Tourney—Open to all!*

Lady Theo handed the driver his fare and jumped down from the hack. She spoke with a man at the park entrance before sliding past him into the crowd beyond. The park was not so large he worried about locating her inside.

Dismounting, Alistair nodded to a young boy sitting against a dilapidated building bordering the park. "What is going on here?"

"Can ye no' read?" the boy responded, smiling to reveal two missing front teeth. "It be a bow tourney. Gonna be a good one, me thinks."

"Why are you not inside, then?" Alistair asked, holding Saber's reins at his side.

"I doona have the coin, m'lord. So I be listen'n from 'ere."

"Would you like the coin to enter and watch from the stands?" Alistair said as the boy's eyes lit up but quickly turned skeptical.

"I doona reckon I know, sir." He stood from his place against the wall. "No one be jus' giv'n away shillings."

"Oh, certainly not," Alistair confided with a chuckle. "If you hold tight to my horse until I return, I will give you the coin to enter the park."

The boy smiled once more. "I can be do'n that. How long ye be gone?"

"Not long, I promise." He held the reins out to the boy. "My friends call me Alistair, and this is Saber."

"I be Alger, sir."

"Noble spearman?" At the boy's look of confusion Alistair continued. "Your name means 'noble spearman.' With a name as such, you cannot be anything but trustworthy."

"Me mum thinks so," the boy answered. "I keep good watch on Saber while ye be gone."

"Thank you, Alger. I will hurry so you do not miss much of the action." Alistair patted the boy on the shoulder before walking the short distance to the entrance Lady Theo had gone through—her driver waiting.

"Mister?" Alistair called to him, struggling to be heard over the growing crowd moving down the walk.

"Fare's paid, and I be wait'n for me customer," the driver responded without so much as a look at Alistair, but the man's comment was all he needed to hear.

Lady Theodora did not plan to be long within the tourney before departing once more. If his sister were within the park, Theo was either collecting her or giving her fair warning. He needed to locate them both before something untoward happened. The area was certainly not safe for any woman, chaperoned or not.

He tried to slip past the man who'd allowed Lady Theo entrance only a few moments before.

"Ye be enter'n the tourney?" the man asked, blocking Alistair's entrance.

"Yes," he replied without thinking, only knowing Theo was beyond.

"Where ye equipment be?"

"Ummm—"

"View'n people go round ta the other side."

Alistair needed to enter here—it was his best chance of finding Lady Theo quickly. "My companion entered with my equipment earlier."

The burly man eyed him from head to toe, most likely noting his less than suitable attire, but eventually stepped aside. "Very well. First round starts soon. Practice area be that way."

"Thank you, my good man." Alistair didn't wait before entering, fearing the guard would change his mind.

His hope of finding Theodora—along with Adeline—quickly and departing before they were recognized was dashed as soon as he entered. Hundreds of people milled about the grassy area beyond, raising bows and aiming at various targets. It was a wonder no one was injured by a stray arrow—it was utter chaos. How was he to spot anyone—especially a woman he'd only known for a day—in this horde of people?

Chapter Six

Theo paused, rising to her tiptoes once again to search the many tourney competitors. The smell of unwashed bodies had invaded her nose the second she entered the park—there were certainly more people present than the small area could allow, making practice far more dangerous in such close quarters. Nevertheless, men—with a few women mingling—pulled their bowstrings taut and released, sending their arrows flying toward a row of crudely made targets—unlike the expertly crafted targets provided to them at Miss Emmeline's. Many arrows whizzed right past their intended mark, landing on the ground beyond, either due to a horrible shot or poorly constructed arrows.

Men shouted and laughed, teasing one another. Others called for quiet as they prepared to release their arrows. Vendors moved in and out of the crowd, offering their foodstuffs and wares for sale to anyone who'd stop long enough to listen. The drone of the shouting and cart wheels upon the hard-packed ground echoed in Theo's head.

It was evident from the piles of discarded waste that many had arrived before sunup to ready for the competition—and to guarantee themselves a spot in the tourney. The grand prize, while not large by upper-class standards, was enough to draw archers from all over London. Theo had located *The Post* advertisement for the tourney after Adeline had voiced her intention to attend. There was said to be an entry all the way from France.

A man carrying a longbow collided with her, almost causing her to stumble to the ground.

"Watch it, miss," he barked, continuing on his way without another look her direction.

Her unease grew as she cast her gaze across the vast park, knowing she should return to her waiting hack and journey back to Mayfair. There was little chance of her finding Adeline and Georgie in the crowded area. Let the women learn of their trouble when they arrived home. That would be the safest way to handle the situation, but Theo wasn't the kind of person to forsake a friend in need, no matter how much bother they were to her.

Truly, Adeline and Georgie should never have entered the tourney to begin with. They needed practice and time, or they would lose what little money Georgie had been able to scrape together. They should not have risked being outshot in the first round. Taking in the caliber of sportsmen around her, Theo knew *she'd* need practice to best some of them—and she was by far the superior archer of their group. The chance to speak with Georgie hadn't presented itself since yesterday, and Theo feared the girl's nerves would get the best of her long before it was her turn to compete. If Georgie were in trouble, then Adeline was wasting her time entering the competition.

Theo searched the crowd once more for her friends' hooded frames. They'd agreed to conceal their identities to reduce the chances of being noticed. It was a smart decision as Adeline pointed out it would also draw merriment from the crowd, happy to cheer on a masked archer—and not only that, but a *female* masked archer. The mystery in itself would be enough to keep the crowd's attention. Theo only feared their ruse would incite the crowd's need to unmask Adeline and Georgie—that was if they were not bested and cast out in the first round. A voracious crowd's attention would wane quickly if they deemed the mystery not grand enough.

"Ye be look'n for me, sweetie?" a voice hissed in her ear as a strong hand latched on to her upper arm, squeezing until she winced from the pressure. The putrid smell of alcohol assaulted her nose as his hold on her tightened further. "Let us be seek'n some privacy, me little lassie."

Theo felt the burly man pulling her toward an open doorway leading into a warehouse that bordered the tournament grounds.

"Unhand me this moment, before I sound an alarm," Theo shouted, turning toward the man attempting to accost her.

Her warning only served to cause him to pull her closer, his leering smile daring her to try and break free or call for help.

Theo glanced around the tourney quickly, hoping someone was paying attention and would come to her rescue; however, not a single person made eye contact with her, each busy with his or her own task.

"Come now, ye a might pretty thing." He pulled her a few feet closer to the doorway, the darkness beyond leaving no doubt about her chances of escaping once within. "Jus' a few pecks in the dark."

Her heart pounded as everything around her began to spin. Theo was unable to focus on anything as she frantically searched the crowd. A bead of sweat slipped down her forehead, over her brow, and into her eyes, causing a blinding pain. Theo blinked away the sting and strained to focus on the many faces around her, but they all blended into one.

Her skin felt as if a thousand tiny bugs bit at the spot where he grasped her arm, her terror causing her knees to buckle as he dragged her ever closer to the darkened building. She should not have come, she should have awaited word from Adeline and hoped she'd fared well, she should have told Mr. Price where to find his sister—she'd had so many options, but Theo had chosen the wrong one. Maybe her mother and Mr. Gladstone were right: education was wasted on feeble-minded females.

How could she have put herself in such a situation?

The stranger's hold became ever stronger as they approached the doorway. "Ye go'n ta like a few minutes with ol' Donnie-boy, ye see."

His breath washed over her, assaulting her senses with the stench of alcohol once more. Her eyes watered, and her arm throbbed as her feet tried to gain purchase and stop him from dragging her the remaining distance.

Cart and Jude would never find her. Her mother would wonder what had happened to her. And her friends…they wouldn't even know she'd come—to help them. On a positive note, she needn't worry about being in Mr. Oliver Gladstone's company again, though that fate did not seem as dire now in her moment of need.

"Help," Theo called to a man, grabbing his shoulder with her free hand, but he only shrugged from her grasp and turned away.

She must do something, anything, or she'd be another casualty of the East End, a place where no proper woman should venture. An area that, if she'd confided in her brother, Cart would have argued against her traveling to.

The darkness was getting closer, and Theo was still unable to break free. In only a few more feet, any further fight would be unnecessary for she'd never be able to see in the dark to find an escape. She stumbled, attempting to throw the brute off balance and slow his pace, giving her a moment to think. To flee.

It worked well enough that she regained her footing somewhat. She raised her foot and slammed her heel down, hoping to make contact with his toes, and she was surprised when the man let out a yelp as her heel solidly struck the top of his foot. Donnie-boy—as he'd called himself—released her arm and lifted his injured appendage, hopping on the other leg as he cried out in agony.

And still, no one paid attention. At least it was satisfying to know even though no one came to her rescue, they also paid no mind to his shouts of pain.

It took Theo a moment to realize she needed to run, and fast, before he recovered and made another grab for her. It was unlikely he'd allow her an easy escape once more.

Frantically, Theo searched the crowd for a place to hide or at least an area where people would help her. A lock of the fairest blonde hair escaped a cloaked figure only a short sprint from where Theo stood. It could be Adeline—or some other female, but there wasn't enough time for Theo to ponder her decision.

She grabbed her skirt and lifted the fabric to avoid tripping and ran.

"Adeline," she shouted, weaving through the horde of people, unsure if the woman would hear her or if the man were close on her heels. She slowed when a woman carrying a tray of oranges stepped in her path, but quickened her pace once more when she saw the blonde woman flanked by another hooded figure. It had to be them. "Adeline…Georgie!"

Relief flooded Theo when the pair turned, revealing their familiar faces partially hidden under their hoods.

The reprieve didn't last long as she slowed, thinking she was out of danger, only to have an hand grasp her once more.

Adeline started toward Theo, only to freeze. Her hood fell back to reveal her look of utter terror.

It was as if the entire crowd stopped, captivated by the sight before them as Georgie let out an audible gasp.

A part of Theo knew her time was limited—help was not coming, and her dear friends would be of little assistance against the man holding her arm so tightly it was certain to bruise.

If anything, her friends shrank back in an attempt to escape.

It was up to Theo to free herself.

With a shriek, she turned on the man who held her, her nails raking down his face to his neck as she kicked out at him once more; though the man was smarter this time, and he sidestepped her assault, brushing her arm away from his face before she could do any real damage.

Theo only saw red as she allowed her anger and indignation to consume her at the physical attack levied on her by this stranger—a man who cared nothing for her, or who she was, or what her future held.

He released her arm and grabbed both her hands, pushing them to her sides as he pulled her around once more to face him.

She didn't want to see the man, didn't want the last image in her mind to be of him.

"Theodora," her spoken name cut through the terror and fury that filled her. Her eyes focused, and relief flooded her—only for panic to return and take its place when she spied the man who held her close, their bodies pressed together, not an inch separating them. "Theodora, stop fighting me."

"Alistair?" she almost cried. Tears burned the backs of her eyes, brought forth at her indecision of whether she should embrace him or continue fighting for her freedom. "How did you find me?"

Chapter Seven

Before Alistair knew what was happening, Theo slammed her foot into his shin, and he couldn't help wondering what drastically incorrect decisions he'd made in life to find himself in the middle of a crowded park in Whitechapel, holding his shin in pain—felled by a slip of a woman. In the next moment, he saw her elbow heading for his gut. Maybe it was his parents' need to bear so many children, especially the petite, hooded blonde scurrying away from him—or more likely his insistence he could handle all eight of his siblings for one season in London to afford his parents a bit of privacy during his father's illness.

Certainly, it was not his rash choice to track down Lady Theodora's residence this morning in search of his missing sister. No, his intentions had been pure, born of his protective nature—something ingrained in him as a gentleman and an older brother.

A crowd started to gather as he released Theo, who immediately rushed toward his fleeing sister, flanked by another hooded female.

His life was spiraling out of control, and he was helpless to do anything to right it—let alone keep the fall from being so steep.

"Lady Theodora," he called, resignation in his voice. "Please, halt. I mean no harm."

At first, he did not think his plea was heard over the boisterous crowd as their interest waned and they went about their business, forgetting the scene they'd witnessed the moment before. Theo would run farther into the crowd, and Alistair would have little choice but to pursue her—and his sister.

She had almost reached his sister when he called, "Adeline!"

His wayward sibling sent a brief glance his way before looping her arm through Theo's and dragging her until the crowd swallowed them.

A loud trumpet sounded, and a man shouted, "All archers to their posts—Round One is about to begin!"

Had Adeline come to watch the tourney? Maybe she'd snuck away in hopes of seeing a man she was smitten with, or she'd come to…he was unsure what he hoped she'd been attempting when she'd lied to him; however, when he pushed through another grouping of spectators, the sight that greeted him was anything but what he'd expected.

His unpredictable, combative, precocious sister was armed with a long archery bow and was in line to take her place among the other competitors, her hooded companion behind her.

A spark of unease filled him as he searched for Lady Theodora, spotting her on the fringes of the crowd, farther down from him.

He started toward Adeline to stop her before she took her place on the field. Whitechapel—and archery tourneys—were no place for a proper debutante, especially one as young and naïve as Adeline. Any chance he had of securing favorable matches for his other siblings faded as Alistair pictured someone in the crowd—or another archer—recognizing his sister among the participants. The scandal would spread through society faster than a wildfire, taking his entire family down with it.

The crowd parted to allow him through as the line of archers, bows and quivers slung over their shoulders, marched to their places. He watched as Lady Theo tapped Adeline's companion on the shoulder, taking her bow as she took a place behind Adeline in the procession, blocking Alistair from reaching her.

"Ye cannot go any farther without a bow, sir," a man called, halting Alistair.

He glanced around in search of...of what, he did not know, when an elderly man held a bow out to him. Alistair eyed the offering. The weapon looked a century old, and he hadn't so much as set eyes on his archery gear since before he left for university.

This entire debacle was maddening—and likely to turn embarrassing if he chose to compete.

"Take it," the old man prodded. "Ye look ta be a fine shot. But know ye be split'n da prize with me if'n ye best all these other men."

"Kind of you, sir." Alistair accepted the bow, took the man's offered number for the tourney, and entered the field. With only one spot left, Alistair took it and leaned forward to see Adeline and Lady Theo several places down. The other hooded woman had moved back to where Theo had waited with the other archer's companions.

Lady Theo seemed overly focused on the tourney as she counted out the paces to her target. She looked up to the sun and returned to her post. Licking her finger, she held it high to test the wind strength—or lack thereof, as Alistair was becoming very aware of. The gathered crowd, boxed in by buildings on three sides, allowed no breeze through. Within a few hours' time, the heat would be unbearable, even for this time of year.

The hooded robe Adeline wore would cause her to overheat—he only prayed she lost in the first round and he could take her home—where she belonged.

Another trumpet blared, and a man strode onto the field between the archers and their targets then turned toward the gathered spectators. "There are fifty archers to complete. The first round will consist of five lines of ten. Each archer will have one arrow in each round. Ten advance to the final round. There is only to be one winner."

The line of archers surrounding Alistair all called out their agreement to the tourney rules.

"Archer number one!" the announcer called after he'd safely departed the field. "Loose your arrow when ready!"

The crowd went silent as the man who'd taken the field first removed an arrow from his quiver and raised his bow in salute to the audience.

Alistair noticed the archer's feet were spread far too wide, and his back was arched—his arrow would hit the top of the target, far from the red center.

The crowd applauded as the man sent his arrow flying through the air—the tourney officially underway.

As predicted, the arrow hit the top of the target, slightly to the left, and quivered but held its spot.

Another round of cheers and clapping erupted from the spectators' area.

The archer gave the crowd a quick wave before departing the field to wait for his place in the second round, confident his shot would secure his advancement. The next three men aimed and released their arrows in quick order, two sticking to the target and one missing it completely. The crowd issued the appropriate cheers or calls of displeasure as the round moved on.

Too quickly, it was Adeline's turn—and Alistair wondered how long she'd studied the sport. It had been years since she'd sat and watched him and Abel with their bows, begging to have a turn. She'd been far too small at the time, her arms not long enough and her strength to slight to pull the string back far enough to launch the arrow.

Alistair watched in amazement as she took a deep breath, her figure and face still shielded by her cloak, and hefted her bow—his bow!—to position. Where had she acquired his old bow? Her feet were set solidly at the appropriate width, with her dominant foot in front and her shoulders squared. It was the exact stance he and Abel had spent months learning from their father—her confidence was something unteachable, though. Even Abel had given up the sport after injuring his fingers several times.

Alistair inhaled sharply, holding his breath in until he thought his lungs would explode from the force.

After another breath, Adeline released her arrow, and it soared—hitting the red, outer circle on the target.

The crowd screamed in merriment as the announcer informed the crowd that Lady Archer Number One had struck in a better position than the previous four men. His sister, ever the showwoman, held her bow high to the crowd, inciting another round of applause.

Next was Lady Theodora, her face exposed to the crowd, the only other woman in the tourney besides Adeline. He watched her set her feet, much like his sister had, but her fingers held the arrow to the string in a far different fashion—a feat he'd never seen before. She shook her head, her loose hair falling from her face and down her back. From his vantage point, Alistair could see only her side profile—her lips compressed in concentration and her eyes tiny slits of focus.

The fragile, innocent-looking debutante he'd spoken with only hours before had turned into a woman utterly at ease with a bow. She was far more adept in her method than he—but how had she and his sister gained such skill?

"Lady Archer Number Two, proceed!" the announcer called.

Lady Theo gave the smallest of nods and adjusted her aim slightly—and released her arrow.

Alistair held his breath once more as the projectile flew through the air. The crowd jumped to their feet, recognizing it was a shot worth cheering for. Unfortunately, Alistair was incapable of taking his eyes off Lady Theo. Her hair hung over her shoulder in dark waves, and her skin—ever so lightly sun-kissed—glowed, her compressed lips breaking into a smile and then a smirk as she pivoted to face him. Her chin lifted, challenging him to best her shot.

The minx had no idea the gauntlet she threw.

Alistair missed the next archer altogether as he continued to stare at Lady Theo and Adeline as they departed the field. Glancing to her mark, Alistair saw that she'd hit the target square in the center of the red circle.

A perfect shot.

A feat most accomplished archers struggled to attain.

He'd misjudged the delicate Lady Theodora, written her off as nothing but another debutante— newly arrived from the schoolroom—in London to secure a husband.

The draw of friendship between Adeline and this woman became clear. Though Lady Theodora was far more reserved than his dear sister, they had a strength about them that most men would envy, a confidence lacking in most women of their age—and innocence.

And Alistair was helpless to look away, or forget what he'd seen in her, as much as he knew there was no other option. The weight of his burdens could not be made any heavier by the draw of a female. He already had five he had no idea what to do with.

"Archer number ten, please ready yourself to shoot," the announcer called, pulling Alistair from his thoughts of the intriguing Lady Theodora. "Release at will."

Alistair quickly took in the few targets before his, another two men had completely missed with their arrows. One held on at the very edge of his target.

So far, Lady Theodora had the best shot.

This round would only secure two spots in the final—Adeline being the second best at this point; however, Alistair had been an accomplished shot in his youth. He'd practiced so many hours, he'd eventually bested his own father, though the man had blamed it on his failing eyesight.

The arrow the elderly man had offered Alistair was of fine quality, likely handmade by the man himself—the stock crafted precisely and the weight between tip and end balanced perfectly as it should be. He'd expect the shaft to be made of ash, a flexible, less expensive wood, but this one was made of yew, far more lightweight than other woods: a wood not normally used by the lower classes due to the expense of procuring the material.

His first observation of his bow was that it was older than he. Under closer inspection, he noted the fine quality of the gear. It was debatably superior to his bow—the one Adeline had shot with.

Alistair glanced over his shoulder to Lady Theodora, who watched him intently from the side of the field, scrutinizing his every move, with Adeline and the other hooded girl flanking her.

He needs must win this tourney—or at least shoot well enough to knock his sister from the competition. If she were to win—or Lady Theodora—their identities would be made public. *The Post* was certainly in attendance, and if a woman won an archery tourney, they would not stop until they'd exposed the hooded female's name. The story would not halt there either, as they would find some scandal attached to the lady and write damaging articles to that effect. His sister—or Lady Theodora—could be ruined before their season officially began, crushing any hope Alistair had of attaining suitable matches for any of his sisters.

The notion of journeying back to his family estate with all eight siblings in tow was terrifying.

His body moved of its own accord, taking a stance he hadn't practiced for many years; his muscles hadn't forgotten though he'd forsaken the sport for pugilism and fencing in recent years. London proper did not afford the necessary practice areas to hone one's skills in archery without the risk of inadvertently injuring a bystander. As Alistair shot with a right-hand bow, he placed his feet shoulder-width apart in a square stance parallel to the shooting line, and his left foot in front.

Alistair lowered his shoulders from the fencing position he'd become accustomed to and tucked his hips in to flatten his back.

The mental checkpoints his father, Viscount Melton, had hammered into his head all those years ago returned. The technique and practice had developed not only muscle memory and increased his endurance, but it had also taught him focus at a very young age.

Now it returned out of necessity.

Finally, Alistair raised his bow, his fingers securing his arrow on the string, ready to fly. His shoulders remaining at ease, and his chest relaxed. He pulled the string back as he adjusted his line of sight for his shot.

The air was still—stagnant and hot—decreasing any chance the breeze would catch his arrow and alter its course.

Alistair released his string, and the crowd gasped before erupting in cheers.

He'd hit the center, only a hair above where Lady Theodora's arrow had struck.

Theodora

Turning to where the previous archers gathered, Alistair found Lady Theodora in the crowd, her mouth slack with shock over his impressive mark. Next to her, Adeline stamped her foot and crossed her arms before turning and walking back to the practice area. Her brother had knocked her from the tourney—bested her.

A bit of remorse flared, but Alistair was unwilling to allow either woman to win—their ruination, and his family's name—hung in the balance.

Chapter Eight

Theo waited as the final round of archers took their places in their shooting order. The time had dragged by as she'd done her best to keep her stare anywhere but on Alistair, who'd been pushed to wait farther down the line of competitors who'd already taken their turn. Adeline had returned to watch the following round, despite her anger over being bested by Mr. Price.

"I am sorry," Georgie whispered. "My hands were shaking something fierce, and I worried my arrow would miss the target altogether."

Her dear friend was timid to begin with, but finding Mr. Price had followed Theo to the tourney had been enough to send the girl into hysterics, rendering her unable to compete. They'd used their last coin as their entry fee for two archers—Theo was left with no other option but to take Georgie's place in the tourney or risk losing any chance they had at helping Miss Emmeline if Adeline was outshot.

That precise thing had happened, being Theo's fault for unwittingly leading Mr. Price to his sister. The man had tricked her into rushing to Adeline—all along planning to follow her. She hadn't expected her actions to be so predictable.

"Do not blame yourself or feel bad, Georgina." Adeline did enough casting of blame and spreading negativity for the three of them, Theo would not do the same. "My arrow held true, and I will move on to the final round. I still believe not a soul in attendance can best me."

"But Mr. Price?" her voice quivered.

"What about Mr. Price?" she demanded a bit too forcibly, causing Georgie to recoil.

"His arrow was nearly better than yours."

"But it wasn't—and you must remember, I have mathematics on my side: the correct calculations needed to hit the target dead center with each shot." Theo gave Georgie a reassuring smile as another round ended, and Adeline huffed. "Do not be so upset, Adeline. We will continue to practice, and you shall do better in the Grand Archers' Competition—it is the only one that matters, after all."

"May I speak with you, Theo?" Adeline's crossed arms did not bode well. "In private?"

"Of course." Theo had little option but to follow Adeline as she paced away from Georgie. Coming to a stop, Theo crossed her arms—prepared to do battle with Adeline, as had been the case many times in the past. "What have you to discuss?"

"Why did you lead my brother here?" The venom in her voices cut and her eyes narrowed on Theo. She was caught in the trap that was Adeline's fury. "I specifically told you not to come. To remain home and I would send word when the day was done."

"Alistair came looking for you—I was worried." It was true; however, Theo was far more anxious about Georgie. Adeline was callous enough to take care of herself. "I wanted to warn you. That is all—I promise I had no intention of him following me to Whitechapel."

"I should have known better than to think you would not ruin everything." Adeline adjusted her hood and pivoted to re-join Georgie, stopping at her side.

Theo bit her tongue to stop the retort that would only cause Adeline's vexation to increase. If Theo hadn't come, their chances of winning the purse prize would have been almost zero.

Both women remained silent as another archer released his arrow.

It had been a great risk for Theo to take Georgie's position in the tourney, but one she was unwilling to dwell upon until after she'd won. The repercussions could be severe or, with any luck, no one was present who recognized her—besides Mr. Price.

Her arm still ached from where the unknown man had grabbed her, but Theo's terror had quickly been replaced by surprise at Mr. Price's appearance, and then focus as she'd taken her place on the shooting line. There was no room in her day to worry over what harm could have come to her—it hadn't, she'd held her wits about her and freed herself with no one the wiser. Not even Adeline or Georgie had seen the man attempt to accost her. Though she was certain the man's face would be forever burned into her memory, haunting her in sleep for many nights to come. She—along with her friends—would practice safer methods for attending tourneys in the future.

Theo glanced toward where Mr. Price had been standing only a few minutes before, but he'd vanished.

"Looking for me?" he asked, his lips brushing her ear.

"Certainly not, Mr. Price. On the contrary, it appears *you* cannot stop looking for *me*." Theo glanced over her shoulder to where he'd moved to stand directly behind her—so close, his chest nearly pressed into her back. Georgie inched away in alarm, though Adeline acted as if her brother were not present. "Is it proper to stalk women who fail to give you what you want?"

"I only came to collect what belongs to me—my sister," he replied, a deadly edge to his words. "You are nothing more than a means to an end, Lady Theodora." Her heart skipped a beat at her name on his lips.

Theo scoffed to cover her reactions and laughed at his chosen terminology. It was something she and Cart had spent many years debating. Means can be followed without the intended end coming to be.

"Do you find our situation laughable?" he asked.

"Do you not mean, *your* situation, Mr. Price?" Theo responded. "My situation is exactly as I intended it to be." *Exactly* may be a bit overzealous because, truthfully, Theo hadn't had any intention of attending the tourney, nor competing, but she would not admit that to him. It was also not in her best interests to confess her fear of being recognized.

"I would have preferred it greatly if you hadn't dragged my sister into this farce."

Theo swung around. "I am tired of your high-handedness and inaccurate assumptions."

Theo's bow knocked Adeline when she turned, making it necessary for her to acknowledge her brother's presence.

"Oh, you!" Adeline screeched. "It is your fault my arrow was off."

Being faced by two angry women should invoke terror in a man, but Theo did not catch the slightest hint of fear from Mr. Price.

Instead, his arms crossed, and his eyes narrowed in annoyance as he turned to Adeline. "You will collect your things and depart with me as soon as the final round is over."

"I will do nothing of the sort," Adeline argued, mimicking her brother's stance and narrowed-eye expression. "I arrived with Georgie and will depart with her."

"The three of you are lucky I am not dragging you all out of this tourney kicking and screaming." He turned his intense stare to Theo and then Georgie. "Do your families know your whereabouts?" he demanded.

Georgie peered at him, but refused to answer this question.

Theo offered instead, "We do not answer to you, nor are you responsible for us, Mr. Price."

"I will take that as a no, they are not aware of your outrageous behavior."

Again with his assumptions, but Theo would not back down.

"Maybe after I deposit Adeline at home I will pay a social visit to Lord Cartwright—and your home," he paused, turning to Georgie. "Is it Lady Georgina?"

Georgie refused to meet his stare, but Theo suspected the girl worried about the punishment certain to come and her stepmother's wrath if her whereabouts came to light. It was never a physical punishment, but more what was kept from Georgie when the duchess was irked by something—the girl would go days and weeks without seeing her father.

Theo saw exactly where Adeline had inherited her overbearing and dictatorial nature. It was a fair conclusion Viscount Melton's children were used to getting everything they wanted, and if not, they took it by force.

With Adeline, it was an admirable quality when witnessed in small doses, but with Mr. Price, it was highly off-putting, domineering, and more than a bit vexing. He hadn't inherited the Melton Viscountship as yet, but that did not stop his entitled behavior.

"It would be in your best interests to explain to me why you are here, risking your futures, all to play some silly sport." He glared between the trio. Adeline looked away, refusing to speak, and Georgie's gaze landed squarely at her feet. "Maybe I could be persuaded to forgo calling on your guardians if someone shared the reason behind this all."

He was allowing them a way out; however, Theo would not admit they were only competing to earn the money needed to enter a far grander tournament that would be held in London's Greenwich Park and attended by hundreds of archers from all over the known world. If he suspected this was not the end of their risk taking, he would surely go to Cart and demand he take control of his sister.

"You are only angry because I bested you—a *woman* outdid the great Mr. Price at archery," Theo challenged in hopes of distracting him from his course of action and away from their true purpose for entering the tourney.

He laughed. "You think I am envious of your skill with a bow and arrow, Lady Theodora?"

"There is no other conclusion that makes your attitude and demands justified, sir." Instead of distracting him, Theo saw his hold on his temper slipping at her accusation. "Besides, Adeline and Georgie were well shielded and have gone unrecognized."

"And what of you?" he countered. "What if you win in the final round? *The Post* will demand to know your name, and seeing as you did not shield your face, they will find it, and your illustration will be spread around London. You and your family will be without recourse to stop it, and you'll be branded a hoyden—a woman of questionable values—who gallivants about London unchaperoned. Is that what you want?"

Theo shook her head, knowing the grievous injury would befall not just her, but also her brother and Judith—as well as their children.

"What of you, miss?"

"It is Lady Georgina." Her friend spoke in the aloof manner bred into her as the daughter of a duke—unwilling to cower to anyone.

"Very well, what of you, *my lady*?" His reasoning was compelling, but his manner in imparting it left much to be desired. "I can assure the lot of you that I do not wish this for Adeline or my other siblings."

Their heated conversation collected stares from the crowd surrounding them.

"Can we not discuss this later, maybe with a small amount of privacy?"

"Certainly," he responded. "I suggest we all depart now, and we can talk of the dangers of your actions on the way to deposit each of you to your respective homes."

"Maybe we should leave—" Georgie started.

"Absolutely not," Theo said, silencing her friend. "I am in the final round and aim to win this tourney."

"If I do not win," Mr. Price said. "If you seek to continue this foolhardy escapade, I at least implore you to borrow Lady Georgina's cloak. If you haven't already been recognized, that will lessen the chances in the next round."

Theo wanted to rebuff his demand; unfortunately, his words had merit. She would not cast off his words only to spite him.

Georgie removed her cloak and handed it to Theo without any further prodding needed.

"Final round is to commence," the announcer called. "Archers, take your places. There is to be only one shot by each archer. If you miss your target, you are disqualified and should depart the field immediately. If your arrow finds the target, please remain at the shooting line until all ten archers have taken their shot." A loud cheer issued from the spectators, and the archers clapped in agreement, calling out that they approved of the terms. "Take your places. Round five finalist will shoot first, round one winner may select her position first."

Theo donned the cloak and secured her hood, refusing to face Adeline's brother and give him the satisfaction of gloating over her compliance with his demand. Next, she retrieved her bow from its peg on the rack and took her place on the field. She felt, rather than saw, Mr. Price follow her. His presence was not only demanding, it was also compelling—calling to Theo and drawing her notice.

She needs must calm herself, take the advice she normally gave Adeline and breathe deeply, releasing the air and lowering her shoulders. Any tension in her posture would adversely affect the trajectory of her arrow—and she could not risk Mr. Price being the reason she lost the tourney.

Adeline and Georgie had given Theo no say when they'd made the decision to enter the tourney. Theo hadn't expected anything different. When she'd met Adeline, Georgie, and Josie, they'd been at Miss Emmeline's for nearly a year. In that short time, they'd developed a strong friendship—one Theo knew she'd never break nor completely be a part of.

She had made peace with that fact. It did not make their closeness any less special, for every person sought something different from friendship. The women gave Theo a sense of kinship she'd never had before arriving at Miss Emmeline's. Before departing for school, her only friend had been her older brother. A sad fact, indeed.

"Good luck, Lady Archer Number Two," Alistair called. The crowd echoed his words of encouragement, unknowingly passing on his sarcasm. "Do enjoy your second place win this day."

Theo turned a pointed glare on him, refusing to respond to his attempts at distraction. She would not allow him to anger her, to riffle her focus, or diminish her confidence with a bow.

The archers took their shots, only two missing the target in this round as they moved down the line, closer to Theo's turn. The expertise of the archers was less than she'd expected, and with a bit more practice, Adeline and Georgie should do well in the larger tourney if these same men entered.

Theo longed to compete against the top archers in England, to take her place among the elite sportsmen. Alas, it was not to be—at least, not this year. Her brother had scheduled a meeting for her at the museum: the chance to sit down with the descendants of Giovanni Domenico Cassini, the inventor of the topographical map. She hoped to offer her suggestions for improving their ideas and putting the maps into mass production to distribute along plains areas with prevalent flooding regions. It was a lofty aspiration, but it was hers alone. Something more important to her than any archery tourney. With the prize purse, they could save Miss Emmeline's livelihood and ensure that young girls had a safe school to attend, but improving the quality of maps and allowing for better foresight before heavy rains and flooding could save millions of lives.

"Lady Archer Number Two. Ready your arrow."

Theo set her stance, knowing the square was favored by all archers, but her calculations deemed the position could be improved on by adjusting her back foot slightly, enabling her to draw her bowstring back a hair farther, which added to the force behind the loosing of her arrow—enabling her tip to drive further into the target and hold. Since her discovery, Theo's shots had stuck with a resounding thud, no chance of losing purchase and falling to the ground. It was this that increased her odds of besting all other competitors. Many were burdens with not only finding an accurate aim but attaining the force to match—Theo hadn't this concern. She would never admit to hedging her bets on the odds or anything resembling luck. Cart would insist she only put her trust in tried and true facts, proven by continual testing and resounding proof to the affirmative.

She stilled herself in an attempt to feel the breeze against her face. The overcrowded park made it impossible for even the slightest breeze to cool her heated skin. The lack of wind worked to her advantage and made one calculation unnecessary.

Due to her less than average stature as compared to targets mounted with men's heights in mind, Theo tilted the tip of her arrow slightly up. Most would not notice the adjustment, but if her aim were correct, the arrow would soar a bit high before dropping in to hit the red center of her target.

Theo released her bowstring, confident in her aim, and her arrow flew through the air, steadfast in its course.

Odd that so much rested on this one shot, and Theo felt no apprehension. She felt completely at ease with the feel of the arrow leaving her bow and the trajectory of its flight. It would hit the target in the same spot as her first round shot.

The resounding explosion of applause confirmed that Theo had indeed made the best shot of the tourney so far, with only Mr. Price left.

She glanced to where Georgie and Adeline had stood to watch—but neither woman remained to behold her victory.

Chapter Nine

Alistair followed Lady Theo's line of sight. Lady Georgina and Adeline had disappeared...vanished into the crowd. He shouldn't have allowed his sister out of his sight, even to continue in the tourney. The right thing would have been to lead her directly back to his horse and tie her to the pommel—paying the boy, Alger, to keep watch over her. Alas, Alistair doubted he had coin enough to exchange for the trouble Adeline would cause her young guard.

Alistair's blood boiled at his sister's audacity, her gall to flee his watch once more. The pounding in his head kept the noise of the park at bay as his mind whirled with the consequences he'd face shortly.

Adeline's behavior was as maddening as Lady Theodora hitting her target dead center for the second time in one day. Even with months of training, Alistair doubted he could hit two such shots in a row. And it wasn't that he needed to release another consistent arrow, no, he needed his final shot to be better than the last—or Lady Theodora's identity would come into question as the victor.

It would have been far wiser if he'd collected Adeline when he'd first arrived and departed immediately, instead of being manipulated into competing. Though, he wondered if he'd truly been influenced or if he were enjoying the bout of rivalry despite his annoyance at his sibling's improper behavior.

"Archer Number Ten. Release your arrow."

The time had come, and no amount of agonizing over his stance, posture, or aim would help at this point. He double-checked his shot line and drew back his arrow, the yew bending at the force.

Alistair's arrow drove hard and fast toward its target—hitting dead center of the red circle.

His grin could hardly be contained, and the urge to lift his bow high toward the crowd—much as Adeline had done—was not easily suppressed. Instead, he focused on the two targets to hide his elation.

His arrow had hit the exact spot Lady Theo's had.

If there were a definitive winner, Alistair could not see it from his vantage point.

The spectators inhaled sharply. He could only attribute their stunned silence to the closeness of the competition.

"Lady Archer Number Two and Archer Number Ten," the announcer shouted as he ran out onto the field. "Your arrows are too close. I must inspect them before announcing the champion."

This satisfied the crowd, for they stomped their collective feet and clapped at the judge's proclamation.

Alistair moved toward Lady Theo as the bested archers left the field. "Where did you learn your skill with a bow?"

She took her eyes off the judge just long enough to send him a triumphant glance, as if she knew they'd determine her the victor. Thankfully, her face remained hidden from the crowd, only on display from his position next to her. "In my brother's library."

"Your parents allowed archery within the house?" His brow rose at her unexpected reply. Her family must be wealthy indeed to have a library large enough to practice with a bow—and have room and little concern for the damage it would cause. "You have a family most peculiar."

"Heavens no, my parents did not allow sporting games indoors, Mr. Price. That is preposterous," she said. "You asked where I learned my skill—and it *was* in my brother's library. I never held an actual bow until arriving at Miss Emmeline's." She must have noticed his confusion because she explained. "Archery can be reduced to a simple equation to summate the force, trajectory, and angle needed to hit the target by an arrow of specific weight and length—also factoring in airflow, obviously."

"Obviously," he agreed, but nothing about her explanation was in any way obvious to Alistair. In fact, he only partly understood the words she'd used, let alone assign meaning to them. He rubbed his hand across his cleanly shaven jaw. "You are very impressive with a bow, Lady Theodora. I commend you on your skill. If you win, it would be a great honor to celebrate your victory."

He was astounded to realize he meant it. He hoped she did well, just as he longed to compete admirably. Though he had nothing hinging on the tourney, Alistair suspected she, and her friends, had a great deal invested in the outcome. Although it made little sense why a group of properly born and bred women would seek to compete in such a basic way.

Lady Theo's brow furrowed. "Celebrate my victory? Only moments ago, you threatened to drag me off the field. Tell me, good sir, what has changed?"

His earlier words had come from a place of anger—and fear—for his sister's safety, all of their well-being. He still worried over her identity being revealed and her reputation being in jeopardy, but thankfully, Adeline was nowhere to be seen. If Lady Theo had no aversion to bringing disgrace upon her family, then why should he worry overmuch about it?

"Nothing has changed." He leaned his bow against his hip. "I am adjusting to the situation at hand—a state of affairs you pointed out is not within my control. So, I have decided to enjoy myself instead of remaining cross."

"That is a wise decision and far healthier for you," Lady Theo said, watching as the judge made his way toward them. "I see he has made a decision. May the best archer win."

"I certainly plan to," Alistair said with a slight chuckle. "I do hope you are gracious in your defeat."

His intent was to make up for his boorish behavior thus far. He'd taken his irritation at his sibling out on her, which was uncalled for, and spoke to his need to mingle among society more. His mother would have been mortified at his conduct toward a gently bred woman, especially one of marriageable age and status—and a sister to an earl. He pushed the wayward thought from his mind—any woman, whether proper or not, held no interest to him, let alone Adeline's dearest childhood friend.

His throat closed and his chest tightened, banishing his jovial mood.

Alistair was in no need of a wife. His brothers were in need of wives, just as his sisters would be seeking husbands, but Alistair was not looking for another person to care for. He had his hands full, and with little Ainsley barely ten years of age, he had the better part of eight years before he'd have the liberty to think of himself, and that was if Ainsley made a match in her first season. Heavens, he'd heard of some debutantes taking the better part of three to four London seasons before catching the eye of an eligible, acceptable man.

Alistair could very possibly have three unwed sisters on the marriage market at one time.

A sharp pain assaulted his head at the mere thought.

The man judging the tournament stood before them and turned to address the spectators. The eyes of the gathered crowd were wide, rounded, and very few blinked, showing they were eager for word on the victor—possibly more than Alistair.

"Ladies and gentlemen," the announcer called, holding his arms wide, palms facing up. "I have favorable news, and not so favorable news. Which does the crowd seek to hear first?"

Alistair silently chanted bad news, bad news, bad news to himself, the spectators unwittingly shouted his choice.

"Very well, the bad news it is." The man shook his head, projecting a forlorn, dramatic air as if they were dealing with news far worse than he'd originally let on. "In all my many years at the helm of this tourney, I have never seen anything the likes of this. I am heartbroken to announce that the archers' arrows are too close to the same spot to proclaim a victor—but the fortunate news is that Archer Number Ten and Lady Archer Number Two will have another chance to best the other…which means, this tourney is not yet over!"

A thunderous round of applause and shouts of gaiety were heard from every corner of the park.

It could not be correct. Alistair wagered requesting another opinion—knowing he'd be hard-pressed to shoot another stellar arrow. His challenge of the judge's ruling would only serve to extinguish the revelry of the crowd.

"Archers, please depart the field while replacement targets are placed at a distance farther than the previous rounds." The audience cheered once again at the mention of a tougher competition, though Alistair was confident in his skill at any distance within reason.

"Shall we?" Alistair took his bow in one hand and held his free arm out to her. When she made no move to take it, he continued, "I do not bite."

"It is not your bite I worry about, Mr. Price," she said.

Then what do you fear, Lady Theodora? But her apprehension did not concern him. All he need do was secure his victory and save Lady Theodora the burden of hiding her face long enough to collect her winnings and depart, while every spectator salivated to know the hooded female's identity. As a gentleman, Alistair told himself he was doing this for her brother, Lord Cartwright, who would seek to keep his sister's reputation free from scandal.

The man would thank him, even though Lady Theodora's current stare resembled daggers sharp enough to slice through any armament. She could give him any attitude she wanted, for he was only attempting to save her reputation.

Alistair cleared his throat and gave his offered arm a shake—reluctantly, she set her hand lightly upon his elbow, and they proceeded to a sparsely populated area to the right of the practice grounds.

Her rebellious streak had escaped his notice that morning—and if he were honest with himself, he admired her gumption. Yes, she'd been forthright with him on both occasions they'd met, but she'd seemed the typical London miss, schooled in decorum and etiquette, bred to take her place as the wife of some wealthy, arrogant English peacock. She'd live her days attending midday teas, taking walks in Hyde or Regent's Park, spending nights at the opera, or attending soirees. And when her husband grew tired of her always being underfoot, he'd banish her to the country to raise their horde of children, only to return when the time came to introduce her daughters to society. The cycle would continue—perpetuated by decades of ritualistic human offerings to keep the peer's lineage going. Keeping those with unsuitable blood from sullying their esteemed ranks.

It was a cycle he was perpetuating by thrusting Adeline into the marriage market—but what other choice did he have? It was either send his father's

Viscountship into complete poverty or feed his siblings to the ravenous wolves known as the *ton*.

"You need not scowl, Mr. Price," Lady Theo whispered, leaning so close he could smell the lavender soap used to wash her garments. "You will scare the spectators."

"If that will keep notice from you, then it is what needs done." Alistair attempted to banish the scowl from his face, for no other reason than to return her to ease.

"Why are you so concerned with someone recognizing me?" she asked, turning to fully face him. "I can assure you, no one knows who I am, not even before donning Georgie's cloak."

"If you win, that will all change," Alistair said, nodding toward the crowd. "See that gentleman over there?"

"The man standing apart from the crowd?"

"Yes. That is a writer for *The Post*. Do you see his notepaper and nub?" He knew she had when she hastily averted her gaze and pulled her hood lower. "If you win, he will demand you lower your hood and show yourself. A female archer—not only an archer but also an accomplished one. He will not stop until he knows the face and history hidden under your cloak."

"You say that as if it is highly scandalous, Mr. Price."

"It is!" he fairly shouted, causing her to stiffen at his outburst and her pace to slow. "My apologies, but if you are unmasked as the archer who won this tourney, your face and name will become news to everyone. People will wonder what other improper behaviors you have dabbled in."

"I have never—"

"That does not matter," he cut her off, his admiration of her spirit waning at her continued combative nature. "You will be ostracized in every London ballroom. Your suitors will be limited to only money-hungry lords and social climbers."

"And if marriage is not so important to me?"

"Marriage is important to every young debutante," he argued. *And most intelligent men*, he wanted to add but kept the thought to himself least she misunderstands him.

"It is not to me," Lady Theo challenged. "I have other aspirations outside of becoming a wife and bearing children. One day, yes, but not for many years. And by then, any scandalous gossip will have faded from the *ton*'s memory."

"Society has a long memory, indeed," he said with a chuckle, meaning to lighten his reference but his tone was far too deep. "What will you do then? Hang about the fringes of society until you are securely on the shelf and then wish you'd taken my warning far more seriously?"

"Mr. Price," Lady Theodora raised her voice to match his. "You are the most domineering man I've ever had occasion to meet. I certainly agree with Adeline's assessment of your overbearing nature."

"You do not take your future seriously, my lady," he rebutted. "That I am heavy-handed or overbearing has nothing to do with it. I am responsible for securing a favorable future for my siblings, just as your elder brother is charged with your well-being. I do not take the duty lightly, especially since Adeline is determined to thwart my efforts at every turn."

"Marriage is not the only thing to determine the success of one's future."

"What do you mean by that?"

"I mean that while some see marriage as their definitive goal in life, I do not."

The woman was maddening and made little sense. What woman did not seek a wealthy husband, children, a home, and pretty things—certainly Adeline did. "Are you saying that Lord Cartwright would be amendable to you gallivanting about unsavory areas of London without a proper chaperone? Wait—even a proper chaperone would not rectify this situation."

"You are here with me—and before you scared them away, so were my two dearest friends."

Alistair remained silent. He saw no point in arguing over the inadequateness of three female friends journeying to Whitechapel to compete in an archery tourney.

"Are you not a proper chaperone, Mr. Price?" she persisted with a smirk.

"That depends, my lady." He scrubbed his hands over his face and moved a few steps away from her before immediately returning to her side. "But my escort means little if a woman is found in Whitechapel at an archery gathering."

"Archery is a perfectly acceptable pastime." Her hands settled on her hips, awaiting his reply.

"Your archery interest is *perfectly acceptable*, except you fail to consider the place in which you are determined to practice your preferred pastime." He paused when his jaw tightened. "If you, Lady Georgina, and Adeline where—let us say—in the Melton family gardens or even at a country house party, your activities would be considered above reproach. However, you are in the East End. A very unsavory area, I might add. And surrounded by unfamiliar men of indeterminable scruples."

His tirade came to an end, and he sucked in a deep breath, his lungs burning for his never-ending lecture.

Alistair was tired of their heated debate—it was getting neither of them anywhere and was causing curious glances from the people who walked past them. The last thing he needed was to draw more unwelcome attention their way. "Now, I would be a most proper chaperone if you allowed me to escort you home after I am proclaimed victor." He attempted to direct the conversation back to the light-hearted banter from moments before.

"So confident. Possibly bordering on arrogance." Lady Theo's face reddened under her hood, and she allowed her hands to fall from her hips.

"What happened to the quiet, timid miss I met yesterday in my home?" Alistair couldn't help but wonder if it was a facade she used to her benefit often—and how many others she had used the tactic with.

She glared, but her tone softened when she answered. "Is it hard to believe that woman never existed?" Theo glanced at the ground quickly as if debating the merits of saying anything further in her defense. "You saw what you wanted to see, as many people do, sir."

Her words—an accusation of sorts—cut him deeply.

Alistair had never been a man to judge another so harshly, but he could not deny the validity of her retort.

Chapter Ten

"...you saw what you wanted to see, as many people do, sir." Theo noticed the hurt her words caused as the tourney master called them back to the field for the final round. It seemed difficult for people—her mother being one—to understand a woman was more valuable than the match she made. She thanked the heavens above Cart was not aligned with Mr. Price—or Mr. Gladstone—on this subject.

The draw to follow her harsh comment with something to soothe the wound she'd inflicted would not overtake her common sense. Mr. Price's high-handedness deserved her stern criticism.

The spectators stood and cheered when she returned to the field, her quiver slung over her shoulder—a comforting familiarity she'd miss once she dedicated all her efforts to her mapmaking passion. With her free hand, Theo confirmed her hood was in place, shielding her face from view. While she wanted to deny or ignore all of Alistair's warnings, it was difficult knowing her actions could impact her family—and friends. A knot formed in her throat. It wasn't something they'd thought about or discussed before agreeing to do what needed to be done to help Miss Emmeline. They were a group of unknown women who wanted to assist someone they cared for—why must there be serious repercussions to worry over?

Her brother had lived through two scandals during his short time as earl. First, he'd been linked to the theft of a valuable vase and his integrity called into question. His position at the museum had even been withheld until the situation was resolved. And then, he'd married Judith Pengarden, a wonderful woman, loving wife, and admirable mother to Theo's niece and nephew, but ultimately, the true thief responsible for stealing the vase.

This did not take into account their uncle's betrayal and misuse of their family's estate fund, nearly causing Cart to face debtor's prison shortly after his majority or sell almost every piece of property not entailed to the estate. He'd done what needed doing—and rescued them from poverty, as well as convinced their mother to allow Theo to attend school away from London and the scandal surrounding Cart and Jude's marriage. It was something Theo would forever be grateful for. It had taken several years for Lord Cartwright and his new countess to change society's opinion of their ignominious match—now viewed as it had always been, one of great mutual love and affection.

Theo was desperate to believe her brother would not be vexed by her interest in archery. But she was unwilling to risk her future alliance with the British Museum and the French mapmakers due to her scandalous diversions, no matter how needed the prize was for Miss Emmeline's School—or how important the money could be to her own future.

She would not share with Mr. Price that this was to be her one and only tourney, or that she hadn't planned to participate at all but to guide her dear friends. Theo was not foolish enough to disregard the risks of being recognized. She'd agreed to help Adeline, Josie, and Georgie hone their skills at archery. That was to be all— lessons. Theo never meant to compete herself.

"Good luck, Lady Archer Number Two," Alistair shouted above the cheering crowd as he took his position next to her. "May the best bowman—or woman—win."

"I look forward to the challenge, and I will gladly accept your offer to see me home—after I've won the prize purse." Theo hadn't planned to stay, only to warn Adeline; however, after the man had grabbed her, nearly dragging her into the abandoned building bordering the party, Theo would be content to allow Alistair to deposit her safely at home. Then he would be on his way to track down Adeline.

He nodded at her compromise. "We leave immediately following. No speaking with anyone— collect our prize and depart."

It thrilled her to think of a carriage ride—alone— with Alistair.

Mr. Price, Theo corrected her thinking.

She'd never been unattended in a coach with a man other than her brother.

In fact, until Mr. Price's arrival, and then Gladstone, Theo hadn't occasion to be alone anywhere, with any man.

"Archers," the man shouted again. "Archer Number Ten will cast the first arrow. Lady Archer Number Two will follow."

They both shouted their understanding, and the crowd jostled one another and settled in for the final round. Their cheers quieted, and they held their breaths once more in anticipation.

"Archer Number Ten, you are free to release your arrow."

The tension was evident in the air, and Theo could feel Alistair's nervous energy beside her as he prepared his arrow. There was no time to spare thinking on Mr. Price's technique and shot, she need only be concerned with *her* final arrow.

She trained her gaze on her target, assessing what was needed to hit her mark again. They'd shifted the targets back about ten paces, but thankfully, the wind had remained nonexistent. There was not much adjustment necessary, she need only alter her aim a fraction higher and pull her string back a millimeter farther.

Mr. Price released his arrow with a whoosh, and Theo heard the arrow fly through the air and stick in the target. He had no lob in his shot—his arrow always seeking a straight line to its mark with no concern for degree of descent or wind gusts.

Theo smiled in triumph. He'd hit a half-inch from the center of the target. He might as well have missed it completely, as it left Theo the opportunity she needed to sink her arrow dead center and win.

"Admirable shot, Archer Number Ten," she called mockingly. "Please seek me out if you ever realize your need for lessons."

"I believe it is you who is in need of a lesson, Lady Archer, but not with a bow and arrow." She enjoyed their banter until she noticed the crowd listened to their every word.

Laughter broke out from the audience, and Theo gasped at his suggestive comment. The crowd was enjoying their back and forth more than the competition, though it was impossible they heard every word over the chatter of the people around them.

"And you are the man to teach me?" Theo refused to cower under his wit or the embarrassment that flooded her as she pondered the promise behind his comment.

"There is not another man more fitting for the task—and certainly, not another who'd commit to making an honest woman of you," Mr. Price shouted to be heard over the growing noise from the spectators.

How dare *he* suggest *she* was anything less than honest? The chuckles from the audience told her they enjoyed the accusation immensely—no matter if it were true or not.

"Ladies and gentlemen," the announcer shouted for order—and silence. "Quiet yourselves until the final archer's arrow has found its mark."

A shiver ran through Theo as she felt, rather than saw, Alistair's intense stare settle on her as she raised her bow and pulled the string back. Without any further thought, she released it. It was only then that she allowed her nerves to overtake her calm external demeanor as her shoulders tightened and her lips compressed into a frown. Her bow, crafted to fit her size, felt unusually heavy in her hands.

Her arrow stayed on its intended course, soaring higher to meet the raised target and passing nearly completely through the red center.

She'd done it—she'd bested Mr. Price and won the tourney.

With a squeal of delight, Theo hopped up and down as if she were a babe given a stick of sugary candy. Her hood wavered slightly on her head, causing her to halt her celebratory dance.

The prize purse exceeded the amount needed for Adeline and Georgie to enter the Grand Archers' Competition.

Elation flooded her. Theo made no attempt to hide her smirk at her own skill.

The judge was by her side in an instant, offering his congratulations and requesting to know where she'd gained her superior technique and altered archery stance. It all happened so quickly. He held her purse of coins before her and requested a name to give the crowd. His intense stare told Theo the audience members were not the only ones captivated by the mysterious, hooded, female archer.

"You may call me Lady Archer," Theo replied, slipping the prize money into the deep pocket of Georgie's cloak.

"And where did you study archery?" he inquired.

The question had her floundering for a response. "I mastered the sport under the Lady Archer's Creed in Canterbury, sir."

"An honor, indeed, to witness your skill, Lady Archer." He gave her a curt bow before turning to the crowd.

"That will do." Mr. Price stepped to her side.

She hazarded a sideways glance at him. If he were upset over losing the competition, he showed no signs of it.

The spectators started to take to the field, quickly moving in her direction, their voices raised as they called congratulations to the tourney winner.

"A word in private, Lady Archer?" Mr. Price spoke loudly for all to hear. "I would seek a rematch—at a time and place of your choosing—but I will have my chance."

His dramatic demand had the crowd halting, their breaths held once more as Mr. Price slipped his arm through Theo's and pulled her away from the growing spectators—all eyes followed them, ravenous to witness the coming spectacle.

"My good people," Alistair called over his shoulder as he and Theo moved away. "I will return your victor shortly, but I must speak with her about offering me the opportunity for a rematch. Do forgive my wounded male pride."

The crowd cackled at his mention of his damaged sensibilities.

To her, he whispered, "Let us depart without further delay. The crowd will not allow you to escape without revealing yourself—and angering a mob this large is not in either of our best interests."

Theo took in the advancing crowd. Alistair was correct, as much as she dreaded admitting it. Their only recourse was to flee the park, out the entrance near where the hack had dropped her off—all without giving him the satisfaction of admitting he was right.

Alistair held his bow out to an elderly man who stood by the rope holding back the spectators, before nodding to Theo—it was time they left.

No one stopped them as they pushed through the milling crowd, all eager to depart and arrive home before the sun fell below the horizon.

"Sorry for the delay, Alger. Here is a bit extra to make up for missing the tourney." Alistair flipped a young boy several coins and collected his horse before signaling her hackney driver who waited not far from them.

"It be a'right, sir," the boy called, shoving the coins deep into his trouser pocket.

Theo's fingers searched the folds of her cloak for her own pocket and the purse pouch hidden within. Its hefty weight and warmth satisfied her.

Theo should resist Alistair's domineering manner, insist she could arrive home without his assistance, but his scowl told her he would not allow her out of his sight until she'd entered her family home. And she'd already agreed to allow him to accompany her.

At his insistent stare, Theo clamored into the hack, placing her bow in the open boot behind her as Alistair tied his horse to the back and climbed up next to her. "Keep your hood up until we reach Mayfair, my lady. People are watching and will likely come in search of us once they realize we've fled. Driver, to Mayfair, as quickly as possible."

Nodding, she kept her head lowered as the hack took off. The wind from their movement made it necessary for her to securely hold her hood on her head as they hurried around slow carts and pedestrians on foot. The farther they journeyed away from the East

End the dress of the lower class increased to middle class, and finally to fine brocade as they reached St. James Street and the elite of society finishing their day of luxury on Bond Street.

Mr. Price's breathing grew deeper as they got closer to the Cartwright townhouse.

"Turn here," he commanded. The driver immediately obeyed—much as his siblings likely hurried to follow their eldest brother's wishes. All except Adeline, that is.

He glanced over his shoulder repeatedly as they fled Whitechapel, returning to a more respectable part of London. "I do not believe we were followed, Lady Theodora."

She pushed back her hood and patted her hair into place. "Thank you, Mr. Price."

Alistair shifted in his seat to stare at her, his eyes penetrating. "You can thank me by not doing such a senseless thing again. The risk that you and Adeline—as well as Lady Georgina—took was reckless and foolish."

"None of us were recognized, Mr. Price," Theo argued.

"Do call me Alistair, and stop with the pompous 'Mr. Price.' My father is 'my lord,' and older men are Mr. this or that. I am only Alistair, Mr. Price in public, if you insist upon formalities." He took a calming breath, something she'd noticed he did quite often when he was angry or irritated. "Your brother would do well to keep a firm hold of you."

"As you do with Miss Adeline?" Theo risked asking, her throat tightening on the words, almost keeping them within. It was crass to question his skills at presenting—and guiding—Alistair's sister.

"No, as I *attempt* to, but as we both can see, I haven't succeeded in doing so," he snapped.

"Maybe if you were not so demanding and overbearing, Adeline would heed and consider your advice."

"I do not give advice, Lady Theo," he said. "I am in charge of all of my siblings while we are in London. It is my responsibility to keep them safe and their reputations intact—as well as my family name beyond reproach. I am unable to do that if they lie to me and sneak from the house on fool's errands."

"All I am saying is that if you worded your demands as requests, maybe they would not fall on deaf ears." The carriage hit a deep pothole, causing Theo to career into Mr. Price—Alistair. "My apologies." She pulled herself back to an upright position.

"Deaf ears? You think my siblings do not hear a word I say?"

"I think"—Theo swallowed before continuing, selecting her words carefully—"I think your siblings, Adeline especially, are very much like you. How would you react if someone shouted orders at you continually? Spent their days telling you what to do and when to do it? I am certain you would not take kindly to that."

"That is neither here nor there," he responded. "It is a great undertaking to present a debutante to London society, especially when it is your sister and she is beautiful and captivating and cunning—and she is well aware of all those things. I am completely unprepared to rein her in."

"She is not a horse," Theo laughed. "Maybe a whip and lead rope are not the way to guide her."

"And what am I to do if a particularly loathsome man takes a liking to her—or worse yet, she finds herself in love with a rogue?"

"I cannot speak to that, sir," Theo responded. "This is to be my first season, as well."

"What if your brother—or mother—found a man favored you, but was not worthy of your hand?"

Theo thought for a moment. It was not a situation she expected to be in—certainly her mother had designs for her future, but nothing would come to pass without her agreement, and if her agreement were lacking, then Cart would never allow the match.

"What of you and Mr. Oliver Gladstone?" Alistair asked when she remained silent.

"What of him?" His question brought back the time she'd spent in his presence earlier in the day. Alistair must have seen the man entering her home.

"He is courting you, is he not?"

A shudder went through her at the loathsome question. "He most certainly is not," Theo responded in denial. Gladstone may think to have a vested interest in her, but the man was detestable. "We only met today."

"And you do not favor his courtship?"

"I have not decided on the matter." Theo had no intention of allowing any courtship between her and Gladstone to develop, but that was none of Alistair's concern. "My mother thinks we will suit, though we hardly know one another, and I have not assessed his suitably yet."

"He is not suitable in any way," Alistair growled.

Theo's eyes widened in surprise. "I was unaware you were acquainted with Gladstone." Alistair's high-handed reaction was in line with all she'd witnessed of him, but the venom in his tone was too harsh, even for the likes of Gladstone.

"I would not say 'acquainted,' Lady Theo. I loathe the man and everything he stands for."

There was more Alistair wanted to say, but he kept quiet as their carriage turned into Mayfair. Theo only had a few brief moments to find out all she needed to prove to her mother Gladstone was not a favorable match. "And what, may I ask, does he stand for?"

"Come now," Alistair said. "He did not regale you with all of his charitable contributions and holier than thou views on society and their immoral transgressions?"

Theo shook her head, remaining silent, but shifted her position to face Alistair more directly. It was an invitation for him to continue.

"He speaks of the evils of society and debauched upbringing, and all the while, he seeks a title of his own—as his gaming debts increase and his collectors hound him at every turn."

"How do you know this?" Theo knew London's tendencies for latching on to a man's worse qualities and spreading the news far and wide. Her own family had known disgrace at the hands of society's gossip rags. "Sometimes, things are not always as they appear."

Theo knew firsthand the unjust light the *ton* cast on any man—or woman—at the slightest hint of scandal. Cart had sent Theo to Canterbury to keep her from the rumors swirling around his marriage to Miss Judith Pengarden. And the simple fact was no one took the time to listen to Cart, nor meet Jude. If they had, then they would have seen through the malicious gossip.

"Do you not believe me?" He didn't allow Theo time to respond. "I was at my club not long ago and witnessed him being cast out due to his unpaid debts."

"That is very troubling, indeed." Theo nodded in agreement. Being thrown from your club did certainly appear very damaging.

"How do you know him?" His stern demand alerted her to the gravity of the purported situation.

"My mother is involved in several charitable groups Mr. Gladstone's mother coordinates." Her muscles tightened, and she sat up a bit straighter.

"You would do well to stay far from the man." His jaw clamped shut as if he hadn't meant to issue the warning with such force. "Lady Theodora, it is only—"

"As I said, I have not made any decisions about him or entertained any interest he may have in courting me." Theo should explain Alistair had nothing to fret over. She had no intention of encouraging Mr. Gladstone in his endeavor to court her. "But I thank you for your...concern." She cast her eyes to the clock, fearing what he'd see in her eyes.

"Your decision is clear, is it not?" he asked.

"There you start again. You would do well to learn that a forceful approach to every situation is not the most favorable way to gain what you seek or the best way for your advice to be heard."

"You would risk your future on a man I've told you is unworthy?" he asked. "For what, Lady Theodora? To spite me and teach me a lesson about my deplorable methods for handling situations and people? It would be far easier if my siblings—and others—found value in my words and ignored my way of communicating them."

Mr. Price was in no way listening to her—yes, he was hearing her words, but he was making no attempt to process and listen to what she was actually saying. Never in her life had she occasion to discuss a topic of such great import with a man who could not move past his own pride and arrogance to truly understand what she said. "Be that as it may—and I do take your warning seriously—it is my duty to take all available information and make my own decision for my future."

"A future tied to a scoundrel does not sound appealing."

"I agree, Alistair; however, my future is *my* decision to make. And I assure you, I will think through everything before making any determinations. Besides, I am uncertain marriage is something I am meant to do at all."

At this, he fully turned toward her, his knee resting against her thigh. His body heat seeped through her skirts and the heavy cloak. "Does not every woman seek marriage?"

"Most do, yes," Theo admitted. "But I have much to experience before conceding to marry and start a family."

"This is very forward-thinking of you," he commented, turning back to face forward, the pressure of his knee against hers disappearing. Theo yearned to make another shocking statement that would cause him to turn toward her once more. "Not many fathers—or brothers, in your case—would agree with that course of action."

"I am very grateful to have a brother who is as forward-thinking as I. In fact, it is one of the traits I learned from him." How to tell a man such as Alistair the wonderfulness of knowing her future was not predetermined or in the hands of anyone but her. "For now, I will attend my first season in London while helping my brother at the museum—after that, I may travel before deciding where my future will be spent."

Theo was unsure why she shared so much with him—maybe it was to help him understand there were other options open to Adeline that did not consist of a hasty marriage to the first notable man who requested her hand. Maybe it was to show him women were capable of determining their own future—and could succeed at it.

Though she sensed he was not as close-minded at Mr. Gladstone, Alistair would benefit from listening to Theo's beliefs about a woman's place in life.

"Coin!" the driver called.

They were parked in her drive, and the hackney driver stared at them from his perch, anxious to collect his coin and be on his way to the next patron.

Theo scrambled to withdraw her purse with her prize money and counted out the correct amount before flipping it to the driver.

"Lady Theo," Alistair said, attempting to halt her. "I will pay the fare."

"Certainly not," she countered. "It is you who did me the favor of making sure I arrived home before a scandal erupted—not to mention besting you before a crowd of a hundred archers, irrevocably wounding your male pride. The least I can do is pay for the transport home."

She smiled when he made no further move to dissuade her.

But he did reach behind them and collect her archery gear before hopping down and offering his hand for her to depart.

The man confused Theo—one moment, he was all indignant over some inconsequential subject; and the next, he was giving orders as if he were her guardian and not Adeline's. And still, in the next moment, he was the perfect gentleman, helping her down from the hackney. It would be far simpler to put him—and his demands—from her mind if he were consistent in his demeanor instead of continually drawing her attention.

Once she stood next to the hackney, he handed her the bow and quiver. Theo slung them over her shoulder, her string catching on her cloak. "Thank you for seeing me home, Mr. Price."

"It was my pleasure, Lady Theo." He inspected her. Neither turning away nor breaking eye contact. His horse remained tied to the back of the hack. The driver huffed, attempting to get their attention. "Please call on me if you are in need of assistance."

"What could you possibly help me with," she asked. "I am more than capable of taking care of myself."

"Of that I have no doubt, my lady." He took a step closer, his hand touching hers. "But it is not only your reputation and safety that concern me, it is also my sister's. Do send for me if you need anything. It would behoove you—and your friends—to avoid trouble, at least until you are all well and married."

Alistair leaned forward and placed a kiss to her lips before Theo knew what he intended.

His mouth pressed firmly to hers, yet didn't seek to overpower her. Theo breathed in, allowing his scent of sandalwood and musk to envelop her.

It happened so quickly—she was ever so unprepared for the intimacy—that she hadn't any time to react more than that, and she wondered if she had imagined it. But no, her lips still tingled from the heat of his mouth against hers, much like the warmth she'd felt through her cloak when his knee had rested against hers in the carriage.

Her hand flew to her lips, pressing against the spot his lips had touched.

"My lady," he said, stepping back and issuing a quick bow before turning to untie his horse from the hack. The driver spurred his horses into action as soon as Mr. Price had untied his reins and started back toward Piccadilly Street to find his next fare.

Theo kept her eyes on the hack as it disappeared, scared to look back at Alistair—afraid of what she'd find there.

"Good day, Lady Theodora," he called, forcing her gaze back to him. "I certainly hope to never meet you again on an archery field."

She had no notion what the proper farewell greeting was for a man who'd just stolen her first kiss. Righteous indignation should flare, and she should chastise him for taking such liberties—especially in her drive where anyone could witness the intimacy. But…

She quite enjoyed the kiss—more than enjoyed it truth be told. A tingle flooded her body at the mere thought of his lips pressed to hers.

Instead, she stood silent as he mounted his horse, gave her a final farewell wave, and rode off in the same direction the hack had gone, leaving Lady Theo frozen in front of her townhouse, wondering what was to come next. Would she act as if he hadn't kissed her? Should she inform Adeline immediately about what had transpired?

Theo was unsure she wanted to share this with anyone, least of all Mr. Price's sister.

Chapter Eleven

Alistair should make his way home—confirm Adeline had arrived safely, but he found himself navigating his horse in the opposite direction towards White's Gentlemen's Club. He needed a drink...and time to clear his mind before going home to handle his wayward sibling.

He was in no mood to deal with Adeline and her foolhardy ways. His anger would no doubt get the best of him. After mounting his horse, his only focus was Theodora—and her advice. He was not fool enough to think his sister was a horse in need of whipping and reins.

Had he actually planned to arrive home and address her behaviors with punishment similar to a horse needing a firmer hand?

It was imperative he handle his sibling's rebellious streak—curb her inappropriate behavior—but not while he still seethed at her calculated actions to outmaneuver him.

The time may not arrive until the morrow. By then, he hoped to have a clear handle on what he would say to her, what her punishment would be—should be…for certainly a riding crop to her hind quarters was not justified.

No amount of calming breaths or counting to ten was helping Alistair as his horse moved through the congested evening London streets. His mind was heavy with thoughts, though he was uncertain what caused him greater pause…his sister or…

What in all that's holy had he been thinking?

Kissing Lady Theodora.

His sister's dear friend—and sibling to a very influential earl, Lord Cartwright.

He was no better than that scoundrel, Gladstone, who he'd attempted to steer Theo away from. Possibly more of a rogue, for he'd accompanied her home under false pretenses—not that Alistair had planned to kiss her. No…he'd only meant to warn against accompanying Adeline into any further perilous activities; however, he hadn't gotten the chance to fully broach the subject or issue his warning. She'd distracted him with talk of Gladstone and her plans for the future—or had it been he who'd led them to the more intimate nature of their discussion?

He had no right to offer unsolicited advice regarding her association with Gladstone, nor lecture her on her future prospects, especially when he'd failed so completely with Adeline since her return from school.

Was Lady Theo correct, were he and Adeline more similar than he recognized?

Certainly, she'd posed a thought-provoking inquiry when she'd questioned his ability to listen and surrender to the demands of another.

Alistair pulled sharply on his reins to lead his horse around a cart that had stopped in the middle of the street after its crates of fruit had fallen.

It had never happened before—anyone questioning his demands, besides his own siblings. His father had already been of an advanced age when Alistair was born—past his prime, and already starting to decline when Alistair was old enough to start his education in preparation for taking over the Melton estate and Viscountship. Alistair had received no formal training from his ailing father. Everything he'd learned had been imparted during his short time at university, gained from his steward, imparted by his solicitor, or learned from many hard hours poring over the account ledgers and meeting with his servants. Even his mother had found herself too busy tending to her aging husband to take much interest in Alistair's—and her other children's—upbringing.

He spurred his horse to a faster pace as the road before him cleared. The hour was close to mealtime, and the more fashionable members of the *ton* were safely at home, preparing for their evening entertainments.

Maybe Alistair was not so different from Gladstone—obvious from the liberties he'd taken with Lady Theodora. And then he'd ridden off without further thought to his actions. He hadn't seen her to her door nor looked about to see if anyone had witnessed their kiss.

Truly, it wasn't *their kiss*.

Alistair had set his lips to hers and taken something he hadn't realized he wanted—all the while, Theo had stood frozen and unmoving.

He'd realized his mistake and withdrawn, not giving her time to push him away—or react.

Would she have kissed him back if given a moment to move past her shock? Certainly, it was dismay at his unwelcome action that had kept her frozen and not repulsion. If it were the latter, it would wound his pride far more than losing to her at the tourney.

Alistair shook his head to push the thought from his mind, and the wind caught his hair, moving it into his eyes.

He had no right to ponder what her reaction might have been if he'd announced his intention to kiss her—maybe even begged for her permission—before setting his lips to hers.

He would expect their paths to cross during the coming season in a crowded ballroom or at the opera, though the opportunity for a few moments alone would not present itself, nor would Alistair seek her out.

He would keep his distance. If she hadn't been recognized at the tourney, *he* would not be the cause of scandal for her. He'd made no attempt to hide his face from the crowd, and there must certainly have been someone in attendance who sighted him.

Alistair pulled his horse to a stop outside of White's and dismounted, a livery rushing to take his reins.

"Good day, sir," the stable boy called. "I will have your horse brought round to the stables."

"Thank you." Alistair didn't pause further, needing to seek solace within the club and find clarity at the bottom of a glass. A drink—or two—would serve him well and push any remaining thoughts of Lady Theodora from his mind.

Her thick, dark hair…her brown eyes with flakes of gold about the edges…her confident demeanor…her proficiency with a bow…her ability to assess where Alistair lacked in his own duties…

It would all fade away with enough quiet—and bourbon.

Pushing through the doors, it took a moment for Alistair's eyes to adjust to the dim interior as the warmth of the room surrounded him. It was one of the only places in London—besides his father's study—where Alistair felt completely at ease. The main room was sparsely inhabited, many men not venturing to their club until later in the evening. It was exactly as Alistair had anticipated. And precisely what he needed.

No one to invade on his quiet moment. No siblings arguing. No one demanding his attention for a situation he was embarrassed to admit he didn't know how to handle. Adeline's behavior and Theo's words of caution faded as the familiar scent of cigars swirled about him.

He'd reassured his mother that he and his siblings could undertake a season alone, leaving Lady Melton free to tend to her ailing husband, Adeline and Alistair's father—but he had been wrong.

Though, how wrong was not entirely apparent as yet.

He'd known Lady Theodora for less than two days, and already, his priorities were shifting. Spiraling out of control was a more fitting phrase. Alistair had charged himself with securing his siblings' futures, but since meeting Lady Theo his focus and duty had gone awry. The importance of his responsibilities dulled, overshadowed by images and feelings of a woman he had no right to long for.

He took a seat in a vacant armchair, tucked into a corner, out of sight from the main entrance. A drink appeared at his elbow within moments, the servant departing without a sound.

Maybe Alistair should pack up his brothers and sisters and return to the country—or send word, begging his mother to journey to London.

"Do allow me entrance," a male voice demanded across the room, close to the front doorway. The hair on the back of Alistair's neck stood on end. "I am meeting someone here."

"Sir." The doorman remained calm, likely dealing with arrogant men of the *ton* on a regular basis. "You do not have membership and Lord Cartwright is not here. You may wait outside for him to arrive."

At the mention of Lady Theo's brother, Alistair suspected his unease was correct—Gladstone had arrived. It seemed he could not journey anywhere and escape the woman…thoughts of her, thoughts of them, together.

A simple evening enjoying a tumbler of exquisite spirits was obviously far too much to ask for.

"You expect me to await Cartwright at the curb…as if I am a livery servant waiting to take his mount?" Gladstone blustered.

"My sincere apologies, Sir," the servant continued. "Rules are rules, and you must be a member in good standing or be accompanied by a member to gain entrance."

Alistair chanced a glance over his shoulder. Gladstone was fuming—his face scarlet red and his eyes wide. His paunch thrust forward as if his rotund frame spoke to his right to enter White's without accompaniment or membership.

Turning back to his drink, and the fire roaring before him, Alistair felt a tick of satisfaction. He would not put it past Gladstone to be so obtuse as to demand Alistair vouch for his entrance.

There was not a chance of that occurring; however, there was a high likelihood Alistair would drink enough for the pair of them.

"I will have you without a position before the night is over," Gladstone yelled, disrupting the quiet of the inner sanctum White's provided its members. "You will allow me to pass—immediately—and fetch me a drink while I wait."

Alistair rubbed the back of his neck, his head beginning to pound at the mere sound of Gladstone's whining. If Alistair didn't intervene, no member would have the respite they'd come for. Their evening would be ruined, though not everyone in attendance need have a horrid night when Alistair could return the relaxing atmosphere with only a quick conversation.

Standing, Alistair pasted a smile on his face, despite his feelings of disgust and dislike for Gladstone.

"Oliver," Alistair said, making sure his voice was in line with that dictated by White's rules. Gladstone's fury transferred from the servant and landed on Alistair as he placed his tumbler on a table and strode toward the main entrance. "What is the problem?"

Gladstone narrowed his eyes, leery of Alistair's intent—as he rightly should be. "I am meeting Lord

Cartwright here this evening and this…" He paused, giving offending servant an indignant once over. "…servant is denying me entrance." His voice grew more intense, louder, as he spoke, catching the attention of several other members.

Reaching the man, Alistair set his hand on his shoulder, gently turning him toward the door. "Allow us to go outside and await Lord Cartwright's arrival. I am certain he will rectify the situation with all haste." He glanced over his shoulder at the bewildered servant. "Sorry about the disturbance, Edgar. I will remain with Gladstone until Cartwright arrives."

The doorman sighed in relief as the door quietly closed behind them.

The evening air pushed against Alistair, chilling him through due to his lack of overcoat.

"Price." Gladstone rounded on Alistair, pulling away from his hand that still rested on the man's shoulder. "I can handle my own affairs."

"The disturbance you were causing speaks to the contrary," Alistair said, pinning Gladstone with a stare that told the man any argument was unnecessary. "I think you should be on your way. Do not return again and keep your vexation far from me, or I will—"

"You will what?" Gladstone taunted, his lip rising in a sneer. "Are you threatening me?"

"Just looking out for your best interests, old boy." Without another word, Alistair turned and walked back into White's. Edgar held the door wide for him and shut it before Gladstone could issue another protest.

Returning to his seat, Alistair grabbed his drink from the table before sitting. A servant appeared at his side, a crystal decanter of bourbon at the ready.

"Thank you, Mr. Price," the servant muttered.

"Not a problem, my man. I only wish he would have attempted a swing at me. It would have been extremely satisfying to knock the man off his high horse."

# # #

Alistair stumbled ungracefully to his townhouse doorstep. No light shone from any window, and he hoped everyone was abed, deep in slumber…and that the door was left unlocked. Either luck was on his side, or someone waited up for him. It was too much to think it was his butler.

Pushing the door open slowly, he slipped in and removed his jacket to reveal his rumpled shirt beneath. Hours spent in his chair at White's had made the linen appear the worse for wear. Alistair glanced down, noting the evidence of his evening meal—consumed in the same chair—clinging to the white fabric. The shirt was likely now rubbish—useless, similar to how Alistair felt about himself. With each tumbler of bourbon, his sense of inadequacy grew until he pondered ordering his servants to pack up all their belongings and prepare the family to journey back to the country.

His mother would certainly be available next year; Adeline was young, could wait one more season to be presented to society without causing undue speculation.

There was no doubt they'd all make a fuss about his decision; however, his parents had given him control while they were in London. If he chose to ship the lot of them back home, then it was his prerogative to do so.

Alistair had even spent a spell daydreaming of his remaining in London, unencumbered by his horde of siblings. Free to travel about town without worry for what commotion and trouble were going on at home. It was only that, though. A moment of woolgathering that had come quickly to an end when he noticed the decanter at his elbow had been emptied.

Just as quickly, his obligations and responsibilities crushed down on him once more.

He must seek his bed, gain a deep night's sleep; the morning would dawn clear and on a positive note—he was determined to see it so.

"Brother." A candle floated down the main staircase held aloft by Adeline, gowned in a nightshift of the purest white—certainly costing the Melton estate a fine price. "You are home."

"And you should be in bed." Alistair straightened his shoulders, infusing his words with the authority bestowed on him by the viscount and viscountess. "Now, return to your room—we will speak in the morning."

She continued down the last several stairs, stepping into the foyer in her slippered feet. "I most certainly will not."

"Unfortunately, I have no intention of participating in any discussion this night." He made to move toward the stairs, but she stepped before him, her eyes glaring daggers. "Move aside at once."

"Not until I have said my piece."

"I am uninterested in *your piece*, Adeline." Again, Alistair tried to push past his sister, but she grabbed his wrist with her free hand, the candle swinging precariously in her other as he attempted to pull from her grip. "You are a selfish, petty girl, unconcerned with the damage and scandal you are causing this family."

She glanced at the floor between them. "Competing was not my idea; it was Lady Theodora's. I agreed because I suspected you would not find out."

However, Alistair had long ago learned not to fall into his sister's coy traps; her attempts as remorse were always ungrounded in actual contrition. It normally only lasted until she'd gleaned Alistair—or his parents— weakening to her ploy.

"You think to blame Lady Theodora for your part in this scheme?"

"It is true, brother," she insisted once more. "When I arrived in London, Lady Theo and Lady Georgie already had their plan set in action. I did not seek to upset them."

"If you keep this foolishness up, you will not only ruin this family, you will also lose the few friends you have."

Her eyes hardened as she realized he would not be buying into her ruse to place all the blame on another's doorstep, leaving her to play the victim in it all.

"You stole my bow from our country estate. *Before* we journeyed to London," he said, taking a step toward her, challenging her to not back down, to continue with her lies and deceit. "Do you know what my limited studies in law tell me?"

She shook her head, wisely remaining silent.

"It shows intent. You intended to participate in tournaments once you arrived in London, or there would have been no reason to secret away with *my* bow. There is no denying that fact."

"Alistair—"

"Enough, Adeline," he shouted, slicing his hand through the air to quiet her protest. "I am done here. I will seek my bed, just as I recommend you do. And do not attempt to push this blame on your friends. You are just as culpable as they." He moved past her as she finally stepped aside. "Good night, Adeline. Sleep well."

Chapter Twelve

Lady Theodora sat on the blanket she'd spread on a grassy expanse in Regent's Park, allowing the slight breeze to whip her hair about her shoulders. The fresh smell of early morning air filled her senses and pushed from her mind all that had transpired the day before. She was determined to focus her energy and thoughts on Georgie's and Adeline's archery lesson, not the tourney in Whitechapel and her near discovery, the fleeting intimacy of Alistair's lips against hers, or the longing to have him take her in his arms once more—not that she'd ever actually been in his arms to begin with—that had plagued her all night long.

Mr. Price was high-handed and tyrannical, demanding everything be as he deemed it—something Theo was unaccustomed to. Her brother never demanded anything of her, and while her mother, the Dowager Lady Cartwright, had expected proper decorum and etiquette in Theo's younger years, she had moved on to more interesting subjects. Namely, her charities.

Theodora

Theo was left to live life on her own terms—at least to a certain extent and within the confines of what was proper among society. Her years at Miss Emmeline's School of Education and Decorum for Ladies of Outstanding Quality had taught her to be independent and responsible for her own needs. Taught her to reach for her dreams with the freedom to study what interested and inspired her. She'd been happy there. She missed her peaceful days of studying, afternoons on the archery field, and evenings spent laughing with Josie, Adeline, and Georgie. She'd been content, and in many ways, fulfilled.

Pulling her shawl tighter about her shoulders, Theo watched the trees swaying in the wind.

It had been a simpler time, when her only concern had been which subject she'd commit to memory next, what map she'd dissect after supper, and what outlandish hairstyle Adeline would concoct—throwing the rest of the girls into a dither, trying to replicate the 'latest fashion in London.'

The days ahead, once the season began, would be filled with dress fittings, society get-togethers, the opera, plays at one of the several outdoor playhouses, and endless social calls. But it was only one London season—and then Cart had promised her time to discover what she wanted for her own future, that was if she didn't meet a man and fall head over heels in love, giving up any hope of a future outside society's norms. That was her mother's greatest hope; however, Theo took no stock in the notion.

She still had her appointment with the French mapmaker in a few days—the same day as the final round of the Grand Archers' Competition of London, actually. She'd be forced to forego attending, and giving support to her dear friends. They'd spoken of Theo's love for maps over the years. She'd even received a highly coveted 1324 map detailing England's fiefdoms from her friends for Christmastide several years before. Though, Theo was unsure how to explain her future plans to three women whose main goal in life included marrying well, having a family, and taking their place among society. Theo feared they would drift apart in years to come, but she was not willing to allow the ocean between them to start forming so soon.

"Theo?" Josie said, standing beside the blanket with her bow raised. "Are you not listening to me?"

Theo looked up from her seated position, raising her hand to shield her eyes from the sun. "My apologies, I was daydreaming. Has Adeline arrived yet?"

"No," Georgie called from several paces away. "But we cannot dawdle all day—I am expected home for afternoon visitors, and it will not do to anger the duchess by arriving late."

"How is your father's wife faring?" Theo had neglected to inquire earlier after sensing that the topic was off-limits, the duchess not being a favored person to Georgie. "I suspect the babe will arrive soon."

"She is in the final weeks of her pregnancy, but refuses to take to the birthing room as my father requests." Georgie's tone conveyed her hatred for the woman who'd stolen her father's love and attention, and in a final act of treachery, had become pregnant, giving the duke hope for a male heir. "But she is as big as the cows that roamed the property bordering Miss Emmeline's. I find extreme comfort in that."

Theo and Georgie laughed while Josie only allowed a slight grin at the jest, her demeanor turning serious. "It is unbecoming to voice such crude comments about your mother."

"She is not, nor will she ever be, my mother," Georgie seethed. "Can we find another topic, please?"

Theo knew well the ill content that overtook Georgie each time her father's wife was mentioned. It seemed the young, beautiful duchess knew it, as well, as she'd sent weekly letters to Georgie at school while Georgie's father hadn't sent a single one.

Theo turned to Josie. "You sent word to Adeline we'd meet here instead of Hyde Park?" It was the only correspondence they could guarantee would not be intercepted by Mr. Price after he'd witnessed Georgie and Theo the day before at the tourney.

Hyde Park, even at such an early hour, was frequented by hordes of people—any of which who could stumble upon the four women practicing with bows and link them to the article in *The Post* published that morning. "If she is serious about competing, then practice is necessary, or she will be bested in the first round."

"She is a wonderful archer, Theo," Josie said in her steadfastly positive manner. She dropped her bow and sat beside Theo on the blanket. "She will do what needs doing."

Theo raised her brow and asked. "Truly?" She immediately regretted her harsh rebuttal at Josie's injured expression. "You did not see her at Whitechapel yesterday. Her aim was off—and all due to Mr. Price's appearance. She must learn to handle her anxiousness and the pressure of so many people watching her, no matter if it is strangers or her vexing brother."

"Mr. Price was visibly furious with Adeline," Georgie said with a shudder. "He was prepared to drag all three of us off the tourney field. I must admit, if he were my brother, I'd have likely fled the park at his unexpected appearance. I was terrified for Adeline. I think she did well, given the circumstances."

Theo longed to share with her two friends that while Alistair was overbearing and difficult, he was not what he seemed at all. From their short talk on the hack ride to her townhouse the previous day, she'd learned of the great responsibility he'd undertaken with Adeline and his other siblings. It was a task most men would shy away from or outright refuse. However, he hadn't. He'd taken on the duty without properly knowing the challenges ahead.

His actions, as impulsive and overbearing as they were, came from a place of love—for his family and their future. It was a trait Theo had admired in her own brother following his return from Eton to find his estate embroiled in scandal.

"He was not overly frightening," Theo mused aloud. "And his skill with a bow was commendable."

Theo assessed the knowing look cast between Georgie and Josie—the same expression she'd seen the pair give one another several times over the years. Normally, it was in response to Adeline finding a new hobby or professing an attraction to a handsome boy who worked near their school. It had never been given to Theo. She did not relish the knowing glance her friends shared, mainly because she was unaware what startling discovery they'd made.

Deciding to ignore her friends' light giggles, Theo shielded her eyes once more and scanned the expanse of Regent's Park that could be seen from her vantage point. Adeline was nowhere in sight. It was possible Mr. Price had not only forbidden her from leaving their townhouse but also sat as her personal guard to make certain she did not disobey his command again. It was his right to do as he saw fit to protect against any scandal.

He'd certainly seen the article in *The Post* detailing the grand mystery behind the hooded female archers— though one had been disqualified early in the competition—and outlining that the remaining lady archer had won the tourney and quickly vanished, accompanied by the archer who'd placed second. The journalist hinted that the two archers were connected, possibly married, and vowed to uncover the mystery and report his discoveries to all in London.

She prayed no one had taken any particular interest in her during the first round before she'd had the good sense to don Georgie's cloak to mask her face.

Theo's ire at Adeline and Georgie abandoning her at the tourney flared. They'd left her to handle Mr. Price and compete in the final round alone. A note from Georgie had awaited her at home after Mr. Price had departed. Her friend had apologized for their hasty departure, but stated she knew Theo would understand their reasoning. She also stated they both felt confident that Mr. Price would see to Theo's safe return home. Which he had, though he'd left her confused and undeniably excited.

It maddened Theo that her friends were correct. She had greatly enjoyed her time alone with Alistair, as much as it pained her to admit.

"I think I see her," Josie said, waving her arms wildly at the approaching figure. "Yes, it is her—I can see her bow slung over her shoulder."

Relief flooded Theo as Adeline hurried toward them. The feeling was quickly replaced with unease at facing her friend after the kiss Theo had shared with her brother. Was it devious to keep a secret so impactful from Adeline?

The thought needed careful consideration—but at the moment, Adeline was storming toward them, a scowl on her face, and her fists clenched.

Theo suppressed the urge to smile at the similarities between Adeline and Alistair—when they were furious over something, their resemblance was remarkable.

A vexed Adeline was not a woman to cross. And so, Theo stood to greet her and attempt to soothe whatever angered her.

Adeline released a slew of expletives so wicked, Theo found herself blushing before any of the women could offer so much as a simple greeting.

"Can you believe the nerve of that bloody scoundrel who calls himself a gentleman?" Adeline screeched. A leaf hung from Adeline's normally perfectly coiffed hair, and a smudge of dirt marred her cheek. "He tried…he tried…" She was so upset, her words would not come.

"Do calm down, Adeline, or you shall get the shingles from—"

"Oh, a pox on you, Josie, and your silly notions," Adeline ranted, stomping her foot. Josie ducked her head in embarrassment at her friend's callous words regarding her chosen hobby of examining medical texts. "That arse, that despicable man, that nancy of a gentleman…"

All three women gasped at Adeline's excessive use of blasphemous name-calling and language unbefitting a lady, and Theo glanced around to make sure no one had overheard Adeline's tirade.

"Do quiet down and tell us what happened," Georgie begged as Josie turned scarlet red in discomfort.

"The fiend, that scoundrel…Alistair!" Adeline punctuated each word by throwing down her bow and then her quiver of arrows. "He locked me in my room and sat Abel outside my door, promising him an evening at White's if he kept me trapped inside."

Theo was shocked Alistair hadn't installed a deadbolt on every door and window of their townhouse.

"I was made to shimmy down the side of the townhouse, using the window ledges for footings and handholds." Adeline's voice increased in volume, the shrill sound piercing Theo's ears. "And to make it all the worse, the stable master refused to have a carriage readied for me—*me*! I am as much the lady of the house as Alistair is the lord. I had to walk the entire way here—*on foot*. I could have been set upon by thieves. I intend to write Mother and Father about this as soon as I arrive home."

Theo wanted to ask if not *on foot*, what had Adeline walked on to get to Regent's Park, but suspected the question would elicit further screaming and turn the girl's fury toward her. Being the recipient of Adeline's temper was never a pleasant thing.

Josie swiped her cheek as she nodded to Adeline.

"What is it?" Adeline turned to glare at Josie.

"You have dirt on your cheek," she squeaked.

They'd all learned the lesson of hiding until Adeline's fury ebbed long ago.

Adeline brushed at the smudge, but it only smeared. None of them mentioned it again. "I have dirt in other unmentionable places, as well. Did you know there is a bush with pointy branches below my window?"

Theo wanted to answer "yes," judging by the leaf still stuck in her friend's hair and the branch holding tightly to the back of her skirt, but she kept mum.

"Do you want to know *how* I know this?" Adeline continued, though none of the women dared answer. "Because I lost my grip several feet from the ground and fell into its evil clutches! It took several minutes to disentangle myself and my gear—and then, I was made to crouch behind the blasted things for several minutes to make sure the commotion drew no attention."

Theo could no longer hold her mirth at bay, and she let out a bark of laughter.

Adeline rewarded her insolence with a penetrating glare. "Do you think this amusing?"

"You must admit, Adeline, it is slightly comical," Georgie ventured, the only woman in the group who stood a chance against Adeline's venom. "The sight of the stick stuck in your hair is…well…worth your wrath."

"Oh, the lot of you are as bad as my siblings!" Adeline picked the leaf from her hair and made to throw it to the ground, but it only waved in the breeze as it drifted softly to the grass.

"Do not forget the branch stuck to your bum." Josie snickered, proud of her ability to sneak into the conversation.

"I am overjoyed the season is to start shortly as I find myself in need of new friends." After plucking the branch from her skirt, Adeline picked up her bow. "Have you given a lesson without me, Theo?"

"I wouldn't dare," Theo replied, standing. "We were waiting a bit longer in hopes that Josie's missive reached you, and you were able to slip from the house without detection."

"Slip sounds like the appropriate word," Georgie commented, starting a new round of giggling as Adeline continued to scowl. "Now, Adeline, you must find a bit of humor in your situation, or you will burst from vexation. That is a solid medical diagnosis, right, Josephine?"

"Not exactly," the woman commented, sobering at the mention of a subject she alone found fascinating, and the realization Georgie made light of it. "But there are many other possibilities to consider. If your temper does not wane, it can cause a vessel in your eye to burst or your heart to pound so fast you find yourself faint."

"She was making another ridiculous jest—at both of our expenses, Josie," Adeline said. "And I, for one, do *not* find it amusing in the slightest."

Theo looked to the sun, moving ever closer to its midday position directly overhead, signaling afternoon social visits would commence shortly, and the women need return home or be found out, their previous whereabouts questioned. Something Georgie and

Adeline could not risk this close to the Grand Archers' Competition.

"We must begin our lesson." Theo collected her bow and nodded to the women to do the same. She'd arrived early and set out a large target, transported and set up by her coachman, who waited not far beyond a grove of trees that shielded their practice from others who may be taking their exercise in the park. "I must return home shortly, as my mother is in need of the carriage."

"I still do not understand how your brother—an earl—only has possession of one carriage," Georgie commented. "My father's stable house is bursting at the seams with conveyances."

"Not every lord is as rich as the king," Josie said in Theo's defense. "I find myself sometimes lacking even one carriage."

"Yes, well, your family's status is well-known, Josie." Georgie set her hands on her hips. "I do not understand why you cannot enter the tourney. You are the most skilled of us all, and we'd only need one entry fee."

"I do not think she is the superior archer," Adeline rebutted, asserting her leadership over their group—a troop, she delighted in reminding them, Adeline had handpicked, knowing the foursome would be fast friends. "And if anyone implies I cannot best every archer in the coming tourney, it will be taken as a personal affront."

Theo shared a look with Josie and Georgie, realizing it would be highly unwise to mention Adeline's early departure from the Whitechapel tourney the day before.

"However, I will admit that I should apply myself a bit more to mastering Theo's breathing technique and aiming method." It was the closest they'd get to Adeline admitting she was not, indeed, the superior archer of the group and had taken second place—and sometimes even third—since Theo's arrival at Miss Emmeline's. "Let us begin."

At Adeline's command, each took their place. It had annoyed Theodora greatly when she'd first met the trio, but with time and a chance to get to know each woman, she'd decided their relationship suited them all. Georgie—her family overly wealthy and her father a duke—was always willing to share her coin, enabling all four girls to visit the village for sweet treats and new gloves. Josie was content to follow the others, always the sensitive one, and most times, their voice of reason, though that voice was obviously nonexistent when they'd decided to enter archery tourneys to collect money. Adeline was the clear leader of the group, while Theo never quite knew how she fit in with them—she'd been the last to arrive, and had taken her place as the outcast, the one who never fully understood their jests or the meaning behind their whispered words. But the girls had quickly become friends, and Theo wouldn't have it any other way.

All three women took their places, holding their bows aloft, preparing their stance for Theo's inspection. Josie wasn't to compete, but she enjoyed the exercises with her friends, and her sensitive nature had her fretting about being forgotten as the trio bonded without her if she did not participate.

"Do you fear you'll be unable to slip from the house and attend the big competition?" Theo asked as she walked down the line of women. "Would it be best if Josie entered in case you are unable to evade Ali—Mr. Price's watch?"

Georgie glanced over her shoulder at Josie, and they shared the odd look they'd exchanged before Adeline had arrived. Did they know what had occurred between Theo and Alistair? Had he told Adeline of their kiss? Had she written to her friends about her brother's confession?

Her stomach rolled, and a sour taste filled her mouth as she wrapped her arms around her midsection.

Did the trio speak of her behind her back—share tidbits of information between them? She could not expect them to be honest with her when she'd hidden the news of the kiss. Her actions were no better than theirs if her worries were true.

Adeline focused on her stance, unaware of the look that passed between her friends. No, Adeline did not know about the kiss.

Adeline, her long, blonde hair falling tangled down her back, lowered her bow with a sigh. "It is several days away still. He cannot seek to keep me locked away until I've been officially presented to society. His interests will be diverted by attentions more dire, I am certain of it."

Georgie and Josie gave a small giggle, but corrected themselves when Theo turned a hard stare on them. If they knew something, they'd best keep it to themselves, at least until after the tourney. She'd seen how Adeline had been affected by Mr. Price's surprise presence in Whitechapel. They could not risk her being similarly distracted at the next tourney.

"That is good to hear." Theo set her hands on Georgie's raised shoulders to push them down into a more relaxed position. "Exhale and release the tension in your shoulders. It will give your frame more flexibility and allow the bow to work as it should."

"He cannot continue to be vile forever," Adeline continued, not raising her bow again. "I am unsure what he seeks to gain by his obtuse behavior."

"He was worried for your safety," Theo said, adjusting Josie's feet to widen her stance.

"Worried?" Adeline huffed. "Certainly not. It is his need to control me—to assert his dominance as Mother and Father's favorite, and to prove to them he can successfully marry off the lot of us. He is sadly mistaken if he thinks I will willingly agree to any match he selects. I will turn any man away he favors out of spite. We will see who the smug one is then. I can still hardly believe he barricaded me in my room with no other company but Ainsley."

"Ainsley cannot be too bad of company," Josie sighed. "She is a sweet child."

"Her continuous questions about London fashion, ballrooms, silk gowns, face powder, and school are maddening. She hasn't seen her eleventh summer yet, but fancies herself ready to enter a grand ball." Adeline rolled her eyes as she took aim with her bow. "I could not take another second of it. I feigned a headache and asked for a few hours of rest."

Georgie released her arrow, hitting the target just below the red center.

"You are shorter than the average target, like me," Theo said. "Lift your aim ever so slightly."

"Why are the targets so far away?" Josie complained.

"Yesterday, after Mr. Price's and my shots were too close to announce a victor, they began a new round and moved the targets back ten paces," Theo said. "We must be ready for another such possibility."

"But we are excellent archers," Georgie said. "There is little chance of another similar outcome."

"There is likely to be over two hundred archers in attendance, Georgie," Theo chastised. "The likelihood of another archer besting the pair of you is great. I'd have to ask Cart to be certain of the exact probability, but let us assume many of them have skill that is at least equal to ours."

"And if they are both bested on the field?" Josie dared ask.

"Then we shall find another way to help Miss Emmeline," Adeline snapped. "Can you all quiet down? I must concentrate."

Theo continued to move between her friends in silence, adjusting their shoulders, moving their feet, and correcting their aim—all the while thinking of Mr. Price.

His sister proclaimed him a brute, but Theo suspected there was much more to the man than Adeline—or Theo—knew.

However, it was not Theo's place to seek out his hidden attributes.

Chapter Thirteen

"Ainsley," Alistair thundered when the child smiled at him, but made no move to explain herself. "You mean to tell me each morning—for the last, what did you say, 'several days'—Adeline has claimed a headache and requested time to rest?"

"Yes, Ali," his youngest sibling responded, her smile brightening when she thought she was helping him. "That is correct."

He ignored her use of the nickname she'd given him as a babe, focusing on Adeline's vacant bed instead. "Then why, must I ask, is she not abed?"

He despised interrogating his siblings, but there was no way around it. He took in each pale head of hair either facing him or lowered to inspect their meal.

"Maybe she is on the loo?" Adrian chimed in, stuffing a fork loaded with eggs into his mouth. His overly long hair caught in the tines and entered his mouth along with his eggs. "These girls use it more than we do."

"Do not!" Arabella and Amelia protested in unison, their matching blue eyes lighting with indignation.

"You reek far worse than a stable hand after ten hours of work," Alfred said, turning to his twin, Arabella, and prodding her with his elbow for good measure. "And their overuse of the loo is not all, they are messier than we are, too. Adelaide left her ribbons all over the piano in the parlor. I was unable to practice."

"What in heaven's name do my hair ribbons have to do with Adeline's whereabouts?" Adelaide said, giving Alfred her best icy-eyed stare. "Besides, I had good reason to leave my ribbons on the piano keys."

"Oh, yeah," Abel sighed in exasperation. "And what would that be?"

A smile spread across the girl's face, her looks almost as compelling as Adeline's but with an air of innocence that her older sister could not muster. "I had a dress commissioned that matches the ivory of the keys exactly. I needed to select the perfect ribbon to pair with the gown."

"A gown for what?" Amelia whined, her face flushed. "Alistair, why does Adelaide get a new dress and I don't?"

"Silence!" Alistair looked up and down the table, giving each sibling his sternest stare before moving back to Abel. "Please explain to me what you were thinking paying little Ainsley to keep watch over Adeline in your stead?"

"I...well..." Abel gulped, knowing he'd made a grand mess of things.

"I will tell you one thing I know for certain…" Alistair said, setting his fork aside, not having so much as taken a single bite since entering the breakfast room after going to check on Adeline. Imagine his shock to find her chambers deserted and her window open. "You shall not be attending White's anytime soon. Actually, make that until you save the coin to pay for your own membership—*and* find a lord willing to sponsor you."

"That is not fair, brother," Abel called from the far end of the table, his head hanging in shame. Alistair was unsure if he was remorseful or if his actions were meant as a ploy to get on his eldest brother's good side once more.

"What is not fair," Alistair shouted, slamming his hand flat on the table, rattling his fork on his untouched plate, "is that I am responsible—duty bound—to see Adeline and the rest of you married well with a bright future; however, I cannot do that if the lot of you work against me."

Alistair wished he could claim a headache and sleep for the entire season—for it was clearly a disaster waiting to happen. Unfortunately, the opportunity to hide, to bury his head in the sand, did not exist for him. Though he wondered if he'd take the chance if it *were* offered to him.

With a sigh, he retrieved his fork and set his gaze on the meal before him. Cook would think he was displeased with her food if he did not empty his plate.

"I saw a flea-ridden mutt eating Cook's tomatoes yesterday," Adrian said with a snicker, throwing his last bite of toast down the front of Arabella's morning gown. The thirteen-year-old leapt from her chair and hopped around with her hand fishing down her blouse in search of the jam-smeared morsel as her hair came loose from the ribbon at the nape of her neck.

"What in the bloody hell does that have to do with the topic at hand?" Alistair shouted over Arabella's ranting at Adrian's ungentlemanly demeanor, his meal forgotten once more.

"Well, I allowed the dog inside, and he left the half-eaten, juice-dripping tomato in Adeline's dress closet."

"Was Adeline in her room to witness the travesty?" Alistair couldn't help from asking, turning his eyes to Abel, who he'd left to guard his wayward sister's door.

"No," Adrian shook his head. "I followed the beast in and made certain he had a good tumble in Adeline's bed before kicking him from the house once again. I won't have the scabby dog eating my dessert."

Alistair's head dropped to his hands. "But you found it acceptable to allow him to leave rotten fruit in your sister's closet and roll around on her bed?"

"It wasn't my bed, so why should it concern me?" Adrian asked. "You told us to mind our own business."

It was the argument he was destined to have at least three times per day—shouting at one sibling or another to mind their own business and not concern themselves with what the others were doing.

"You told me not to say anything to Amelia when you caught Alfred putting toads in her bed last week," Adrian continued. "And you urged me to look the other way when Arabella knocked over Abel's shaving cream and tried to return it to the jar—along with the dirt from his messy floor."

"Adrian! Close your mouth!" Alistair warned.

"But, Alistair," the boy continued, not realizing the danger of Alistair's flaring temper as his other siblings began to protest the injustices against them he'd attempted to cover up. "I didn't say anything about you telling me that Adelaide is likely to never capture a beau if she doesn't learn a bit about fashion."

He looked to his middle sibling as she looked down at her hideously orange day gown with mismatched blue hair ribbon, and he longed for the floor to open and swallow him whole.

"Good thing you never told Ainsley her hair is the color of rotting straw!" Adrian finished triumphantly, returning to his meal—his work done.

"I have never!" Alistair looked to Ainsley, begging silently for her to believe him.

"Nope," Adrian mumbled around a bite of cheese. "It was Amelia who confided that to me."

There was absolutely no hope Alistair would live long enough to see them all happily married. He'd promised his mother and dying father he could, but in that moment, Alistair realized he didn't stand a chance, especially if all eight ever banded together against him.

If his own siblings didn't thwart his every effort, then surely the higher enclave of the *ton* would. They would be introduced to each of Viscount Melton's children, and for some reason or other, would find them all wanting, no matter the time and energy and years of Alistair's life he dedicated to them.

"You little rat! Why I—" Amelia started at her brother's revelation regarding her aversion to Ainsley's hair color.

"Amelia," Alistair said, standing. "Enough."

He looked up and down the long table once more, making eye contact with each sibling as they attempted to avoid his glare. "No one has any idea where Adeline is at present?"

His tone dared any of them to lie to his face, for he would find out and return with a punishment befitting the crime.

"She is not on the loo? Why does no one take my suggestion seriously?" Adrian asked. "Has anyone checked? I will not, because,"—he paused, pinching his nose and waving his hand before his face—"I learned my lesson on that score."

Abel and Alfred broke into laughter, and Alistair knew he'd be getting no useful answers from his siblings.

No answers would be found within the Melton townhouse.

Thankfully, he was acquainted with one woman who would surely have answers for him—and she lived only a short distance away in Mayfair.

After a strict warning for none of his wayward family to leave the townhouse in his absence, Alistair called for his horse to be readied, and departed for Lady Theo's townhouse—his meal having grown cold.

He had no illusions that he could once again visit Lady Theo's home without a proper introduction to her brother, Lord Cartwright, but Alistair was beyond options, and his patience was wearing thin. Adeline had sworn she would not disobey him again, that she understood the consequences for them all if she brought scandal to their family, yet here Alistair was, riding through the streets of London in search of her whereabouts.

Like an utter fool.

By the time the proper season was underway, he would be known as the laughingstock that was unable to tame his horde of siblings.

Alistair thanked all that blessed him he wasn't in the market for a bride himself, or he'd be avoided by every marriage-aged woman of the *ton* and given the cut direct from their mothers. He'd be eaten alive in society, no differently than at home.

Part of him wondered if his parents hadn't taken the easy path by bowing out of Adeline's debut season. His siblings were a handful, even before Adeline had returned from school.

He guided his mount through the early-morning streets. Servants rushed to do their masters' bidding, and vendors with carts and baskets moved toward the marketplace to peddle their wares. He nodded to an occasional lord in greeting, but kept his pace consistent toward Mayfair.

It was for the best. Alistair spurred his horse into a quick gallop. In just a few hours' time, the speed would be made impossible as the *ton* ventured out of their homes to promenade in the parks or shop on Bond Street.

Turning onto St. James, he noticed no activity in any of the drives he passed, which suited Alistair as he most certainly did not need his name attached to that of Lady Theodora Montgomery, especially in conjunction with a social visit far earlier than was proper. However, his hopes were dashed when he reached her drive to see a carriage departing as her front door closed. Someone had either just arrived or was only now returning home—but from where? He attempted to gain a look inside the enclosed carriage, but the draperies were pulled tightly over the windows, hiding the conveyance's occupants from sight.

Alistair waited on the street as the carriage moved down the narrow lane to the stables behind the townhouses.

He abhorred he'd been brought to this level—seeking out Lady Theo to help tame his sister. Much as it pained him, however, his family and their future came before his pride.

For the second time in as many days, Alistair found himself knocking on Lady Theo's door and being greeted by the same servant.

Behind the man, he noticed Lady Theo handing her bow and quiver to a waiting servant and then removing her cloak to reveal a muddied dress hem and dirt-caked half boots. She'd been practicing—but where in London were women allowed to hone their skills? Except on their own property, most women did not partake of archery. The sport was appropriate as a pleasurable pastime for women, but the *ton* would never approve of ladies gallivanting about to tournaments, or practicing in public locations.

She had clearly been somewhere—very early—and her previous whereabouts would lead Alistair to Adeline.

"Good day, sir," the butler greeted, a slight sense of shock at his presence visible. "Lord Cartwright is not at home."

Alistair assumed his most jovial smile. "I am here to call on Lady Theodora. Is she receiving?" He glanced over the butler's shoulder once more to see if his words had garnered her attention.

"Mr. Price." Lady Theo stepped before the servant currently holding her bow and quiver, attempting to mask their presence as the servant left the room. "How lovely of you to call. To what do I owe the pleasure of this visit?"

"May we speak in private, my lady?" He had no intention of feeding the servants' gossip mill with word of Adeline's disappearance. "It is of a sensitive nature."

Her brow furrowed suspiciously, but still swept her arm wide, "This way, sir. We may speak in my mother's drawing room." She preceded him down the hall, giving him ample time to admire the sway of her backside, her muddied hem moving from side to side with her quick pace.

Neither made any move to close the door upon entering the space.

A fire blazed in the hearth to ward off the last of the morning chill, as if someone had recently occupied the room.

Lady Theo stood before the lounge and turned to him, her arms crossed. "What can I help you with, Mr. Price?"

She was guarded, keeping a small table between them. He'd kissed her—in a most improper place—and then simply rode away without a backwards glance. Lady Theo had every right to be leery in his presence. In fact, he would not have blamed her if she'd refused him entrance to her home.

"It is Adeline," he confessed. "She is missing—climbed out her window and down the side of the house. I am worried she's injured herself." And if he found her in one piece after fleeing out her window, Alistair was tempted to rectify that situation. He'd chain her to the horse post in the stables if need be to keep her from her unmanageable ways. "Have you seen her?"

"I have no idea why you'd think I know where Adeline went off to today."

"I am certain the notion springs from the simple fact that you knew exactly where she was the last time, yet saw fit to lie to me." He made a show of glancing down at her stained hem and mud-splattered boots. "Come now, Lady Theo," Alistair sighed. "Let us be past all this. I attempt only to keep my sister safe until she is properly wed and no longer my concern."

"Again with the topic of being rid of your sister." Theo sat, nodding at him to do the same. "I am Adeline's friend, and I have no allegiance to you, nor do I agree with your barbaric methods for keeping watch over your siblings."

He'd incorrectly thought their kiss—while uncalled for and inappropriate—had created a bond, a truce, between them. It was obviously not the case.

"Barbaric?" Alistair took a seat in the largest chair in the room, directly across the small table from Theo—agreeable to keeping a certain distance between them. He imagined for a moment crossing the few feet separating them and pulling her from the chair and against his body. Would she deny him the information he sought then? "I only called upon my younger siblings to help me keep watch over her. Must I remind you of the consequences the three of you faced if discovered in Whitechapel…at an archery tourney…without a proper chaperone?" He counted out the strikes against them on his fingers as he spoke, his blood pumping hard through his veins with each item.

164

"Would you like some tea?" she asked, changing the subject. "If we are to have a heated debate on the merits of locking one's sister in her room for days on end, then I find I am parched already."

For not the first time, Theo said the one thing that made him want to forget his fury and laugh. His temper gradually subsided as it had during their drive to her townhouse a few days before.

Alistair had never met a person—let alone, a woman—who could so successfully dim his anger and cause the burden of his responsibilities to appear less dire, even comical.

"I only just left my breakfast table, but by all means, ring for tea," he conceded.

"Very well." Lady Theo stood and pulled the bell pull by the door, signaling for a tray to be brought, before sitting again. She folded her hands in her lap, the vision of grace and poise that was certain to draw every marriage-minded man's attention during the season—unfortunately, the frown that settled on her face was not in keeping with the mask. "I assure you, Adeline is safe."

"And how can you possibly know this?" he questioned. "You are here, and she is…well, not where she is supposed to be."

"I am not her keeper, though I will tell you she should be arriving home at any moment."

"I am her keeper, and that of all my siblings," he confessed. "If Adeline is discovered, it will not only ruin her chances at a successful match, but will also do a massive amount of damage to that of her younger siblings. If I cannot discourage her inappropriate escapades now, then the Melton family will not likely survive this season or any future season. Meaning, Adeline is not only dooming herself, but all her younger siblings, as well."

"I assure you, that is not her intent." Though her words were said with bravado and honesty, Alistair noticed the glimmer of uncertainty in her eyes; a moment of hesitation and doubt as her head cocked to one side.

"There cannot be another tourney—" Alistair had scoured every news article in *The Post* for any listing of current archery competitions, and had only seen mention of the Grand Archers' Competition of London in Greenwich Park. It was a tourney held every other year, and drew archers from across the county, and even France. But it was far too public—with archers much superior to his sister's competency—for the foursome to think of entering. It would be rash—and delusional—to enter a tourney of that magnitude and think to claim victory.

"No, not this day," Theo said, waving his comment aside. "We were only practicing in Regent's Park, as we have the last several days."

Alistair didn't know what concerned him more: that they'd been practicing in plain view at a park, or the many times Adeline had ventured out her window and crawled two stories to the ground below, risking injury to her person.

Lady Theo seemed to sense his unease. "Regent's Park is far less crowded than Hyde Park, and I was able to find a suitable area hidden from view behind a grove of trees. I made certain we were not spotted by anyone, and that we returned home long before most of society took their morning meals."

"And what about—"

"Adeline is quite deft at scurrying up and down the side of your townhouse using the window frames for guidance," Theo said, putting to rest his other concern. "She was always the best at climbing trees at Miss Emmeline's. She said it was due to having older brothers who mercilessly tormented her as a child." She shrugged, giving him the opportunity to deny it.

Alistair had forgotten his sister's fondness for climbing and following him and Abel about their family estate. That was long ago, and was not cleverness found tolerable for a young debutante. "I shudder to think if a neighboring servant spied her slipping out the window, or worse yet, her skills for climbing failed her and she was seriously injured. You must understand I care very deeply for my sister—for all my siblings—and seek to offer them the most advantageous future." He leaned forward, hoping Theo saw the sincerity in his words. "I know I may appear a bit—"

"Overbearing?" Her eyes widened.

"We have established that term is favored by Adeline, yes—" His face reddened, and he rubbed the back of his neck, hoping to tamp down his growing agitation.

"Domineering?" She unclasped her hands and fidgeted with the crease of her skirt.

Alistair thought for a moment. "Again, I can see how it would appear that way to others."

"Tyrannical?" Theo outright avoided his stare with her final accusation.

"Certainly not," Alistair rebutted. "I draw the line there. I am not some classic Napoleon figure, I assure you."

Theo smirked, sitting up a bit straighter at his tone.

She was teasing him, as he'd reveled in doing to Adeline in their youth.

Could it be that Theo had forgiven him for—or forgotten altogether—his abrupt kiss and departure?

But no, when she finally lifted her stare to his face, her gaze settled not on his eyes but his mouth. She hadn't forgotten their moment of intimacy any more than he had.

Chapter Fourteen

Theo found amusement in keeping Mr. Price on his toes—unsure of her stance on his plight to rein in Adeline. It was the same apprehension and insecurity she'd felt since he'd stolen her first kiss and ridden away without a backwards glance. Did he presume Theo received such intimacies often? It was not the case, and she knew not what to take from his forwardness—and immediate departure. She wanted to demand explanation of what his intentions had been in that moment, and what they were now as he sat before her, expecting her to betray her dear friend's confidences.

Theo owed Mr. Alistair Price nothing, least of all her promise to help him keep Adeline from doing as she wished and determining her own future.

However, he owed her much—an explanation for his presumptuous behavior to begin with.

And clarification as to why he kept appearing in places she was—both at her home and around town.

For now, his grim expression said he'd be giving her no answers until she conceded to his pleas for assistance.

"And what if I share with you the extent of your loss of control? What will I receive in return?" Theo was confident she'd garner his agreement to her terms.

Mr. Price's brow rose with interest. "What do you want?"

Oh, the man was experienced in ways of barter and trade, though Theo had spent a full month researching the history and methods behind successful trading enterprises since the beginning of modern time. What she'd learned was fascinating—that demand for a product or knowledge was not based on the need or usefulness of the thing to be traded, but on how unattainable the product or knowledge appeared to others. The information she possessed was, at this moment, highly unattainable to Alistair.

"I am unsure what you can offer me," Theo countered. "For betraying my friend is worth a king's ransom, do you not agree, sir?"

Theo squared her shoulders, determined to keep poised before him—and show not a speck of weakness.

"Is it considered betrayal if you are aligned with helping her remain untarnished?"

"You have still given no evidence she is in jeopardy of harming her reputation."

A light knock sounded at the open door, and her housekeeper wheeled a tray loaded with refreshments into the room. Mr. Price turned his overly charming smile on the woman, and Theo could have sworn her housekeeper's knees wobbled slightly as she walked, her hips swaying to and fro a bit more than was necessary.

She'd certainly gotten word of a male caller, for the sheer amount of treats on the plate was overwhelming—and unquestionably wasteful.

"Thank you." Theo's smile wasn't as cheerful as Alistair's. "I will serve us."

"My pleasure, Lady Theodora," the portly woman said before dropping a deep curtsey to Alistair and departing the room—quietly pulling the door closed behind her.

She looked to Mr. Price to ascertain if he noticed they were now alone, a closed door separating them from the prying eyes and ears of her household. It was scandalous, to say the least. The exact thing that fueled the servant's gossip mill. Thankfully, or not so thankfully, he'd returned his gaze to her—his bewitching grin now bestowed upon her.

"Mr. Price, do I have something in my teeth?" Theo smiled widely, allowing him to see her pearly whites, knowing he'd find nothing but the need to distract him from their improper situation—and the odd way he was now gazing upon her. The expression on his face unerringly matched the one he'd donned a moment before he'd kissed her.

He shook his head, clearing his throat. "Certainly not, Lady Theodora."

"Then I would kindly request you refrain from inspecting me so closely," she chastised. "I am not a mare at the stock house, mind you."

Her words hit their mark, and he sat up straighter, keeping his gaze from traveling the length of her once more. "My apologies, it is only that I've never met a woman such as you before."

"And what type of woman is that?" Theo busied herself with her hostess duties as she set two sandwiches on a plate and held it out to him across the table. "A woman who can best you with a bow?"

"No." He accepted the dish.

"Sugar or cream, Mr. Price?" she asked, taking hold of the teapot and gently pouring a healthy portion, not a drip landing outside the cup.

When he didn't answer, she looked up to him, noting he'd set his plate aside, forgotten.

"Pardon, my lady?"

"Would you enjoy sugar or cream with your tea?" The man was easily distracted; though she was at a loss for what had captured his attention so thoroughly he was unable to keep up with the fairly basic social niceties of accepting tea. "It is a lovely orange flavored leaf that goes exquisitely with a spot of sugar."

"Sugar it is." He glanced to the serving tray as if seeing it for the first time. "I will not argue with your fine recommendations."

"Very well." Theo dropped one lump of sugar into the steaming cup and handed it to Alistair. His fingers grazed hers, sending a sizzling jolt through her as he took the saucer she held out. "Now, you were saying I am unlike any woman you've previously met. Is it because I am a female who does not easily give up the secrets of her dearest friends?"

"Well, yes and no." He nervously glanced at his untouched plate as if Theo's question had hit too closely to his true meaning behind the comment.

"Do share, Mr. Price." Theo made no move to pour her own tea. He would not escape her question so easily. "I am most interested to know."

He swallowed before speaking. "A woman with enough intellect and wit to distract me from my familial obligations."

Theo had come to realize a man who valued a woman's mind and individual thinking was a rare thing indeed. Her mother—and Mr. Gladstone, as she'd recently discovered—took no stock in a woman's education beyond how it would benefit their needs. But Mr. Price was certainly different—a polar opposite to Gladstone—and very much in line with her and Cart's opinion on the matter.

"I do not mean to interfere with your duties to your family." Remorse spiked within her at her need to continue leading him on a merry chase for the information he sought. "Adeline, Lady Josephine, Lady Georgina, and I are attempting to collect enough money to help Miss Emmeline make the much-needed improvements at her school. There are many buildings in complete disrepair, and Headmistress finds herself without the funds necessary to patch the roofs or replace the fraying and broken furniture."

He looked at her doubtfully. "My sister, Adeline, the most selfish woman I've met—possibly in all of England—is potentially sacrificing her reputation and future to help another?" He chuckled. "I do not believe it. You continue to jest with me, Lady Theodora."

"Do not hear me wrong, Mr. Price," Theo continued. "Miss Adeline greatly enjoys besting the most accomplished male archers, but her motives are pure and noble, I assure you."

His laugh grew louder, bouncing off the walls and growing in intensity as his cup rattled on his saucer. A drop of tea splashed over the rim and landed on the floor.

Theo's heart skipped a beat at the sound of his merriment, and she found herself fighting a smile despite the fact that his humor was at her expense.

"You do not think Adeline can do something kind and generous?" To be certain, Theo would not have believed it several months ago. However, Adeline had been more than willing to aid her friends on their quest to help Miss Emmeline and their beloved school.

"This is the same girl who caused two younger siblings to wear too-small shoes because she had to have a pair far more expensive than my father had the coin for. And she is so truly cunning, she convinced my father to allow it to happen." He paused, stifling another chuckle. "Oh, and what about the time she stole all of Amelia's, Arabella's, and Adelaide's school primers and threw them in the pond, thinking it would mean she'd be granted a day off from her studies?"

Theo couldn't help but laugh at the image his words brought to mind; it was exactly the Adeline she knew.

"I think that was the final straw, the occurrence that convinced father that boarding school would benefit Adeline." He paused, snatching a small sandwich from his plate and popping it into his mouth before continuing, speaking as he chewed. The sight should repulse her, but she found her eyes focusing on his mouth all the more. "While I was in favor of the idea then, I am unsure the coin spent on her education has benefited her in any way. She is as untamable and unwilling to listen as she was six years ago."

Theo swallowed past the knot in her throat and pulled her eyes back to his. "I can see how you may feel that way. Nevertheless, we are truly only seeking to help Miss Emmeline."

"Then why were you not set up to compete in Whitechapel?" he asked, noticing as she plucked an invisible spot of lint from her skirt. "Do not think I did not note you took Lady Georgina's place in the tourney—which I might add was a clever decision. I have not seen her with a bow, though I doubt her skill rivals yours."

A blush crept up her cheeks at his blatant compliment. "Thank you, sir." His offer of openness was refreshing. "I had not planned to complete, only instruct my friends on how to shoot with increased accuracy."

"But if your skill is unbeatable—and the main reason is to earn money—why would you hold yourself back and not compete?"

He paid close attention as she pondered what information to share, how much of her personal interests she could divulge without fear he would laugh at her ambitions as he had Adeline. Alistair hadn't meant to be cruel or belittle his sister, he was only unaware of the woman who lay beneath the child Adeline once was. Some days, even Theo wondered if the petty child had fully disappeared or was only hiding just below the surface.

Much like others viewed Theo as a meek, pliable, proper young miss—prepared to take her place among the crop of new debutantes.

"I had engagements that prevented me from entering the tourney," Theo said, hoping he'd change the line of questioning and save her the task of explaining her passion for maps. "Speaking of previous engagements, I must depart soon to meet my brother at the museum—and I must change my dress and correct my hair before taking my leave." Heat flooded her again at the mention of undressing. His eyes traveled the length of her, though it did not make her feel the least bit uncomfortable; in fact, something inside her fluttered as if she'd swallowed a butterfly. His scrutiny was quite satisfying, indeed.

Setting his tea aside, he slowly unfolded himself and stood. His sheer size filling the room, cocooning Theo in the aura of his presence. "Thank you, Lady Theo, I have enjoyed our discussion"—he glanced down at her, his gaze following the line of her neck to where her blouse covered her bosom, making her feel as if she'd already stripped her gown away and stood before, awaiting his approval—"immensely."

She released her breath with an audible whoosh, unaware that she hadn't drawn air since he stood. "It wasn't as if you gave me the opportunity to turn down your visit."

She smiled to cover her discomfort.

Alistair's hand shot to his heart. "You wound my pride, my lady."

"Certainly no more than being bested by a female on the archery field." It was Theo's turn to laugh.

"Oh." He bowed low before her. "Do not be so convinced my defeat wasn't a planned loss."

She sucked in a breath. Could he have allowed her to win, thrown the competition in her favor? That was insulting.

"You did not!" Theo narrowed her eyes. "I demand a rematch, Mr. Price."

He chuckled, straightening from his bow. "Name the time and place."

"Now," she rushed. "I will collect my bow, and we will meet at Regent's Park."

"That would be most agreeable if you hadn't a previous engagement at the museum, and I did not have a hellion of a sibling to track down." He moved toward the door as it opened to reveal Jude, Theo's sister-in-law, ready to accompany her to the museum.

The unsuspecting woman let out a yelp of surprise when she came face-to-face with Mr. Price. "Theo, I was unaware you had a visitor. I was coming to collect you. Cart is expecting us shortly."

"More's the pity," Alistair mumbled under his breath.

Her sister by marriage kept her eyes trained on Alistair, not hearing his last words, yet scrutinizing his every move, awaiting a proper introduction.

"Lady Cartwright, may I present Mr. Alistair Price, Miss Adeline's eldest brother." During the years of their acquaintance, Theo had come to know the reaction men had to Jude. Her fiery red hair crowned her head like a halo, and her slender, swanlike neck only added to her poise and grace.

"A pleasure to meet you, my lady." Alistair turned his riveting smile on Jude.

"And you, Mr. Price," Jude said, clearly unaffected by the man's charm.

"He came in search of Adeline," Theo rushed to explain the man's presence in the dowager's receiving room…the door closed. "But I informed him that she is not here. And now, he is leaving. Is that not correct, Mr. Price?"

Jude's gaze flitted to the tea service and half eaten sandwiches. "Is that so?"

"It is," he said in agreement as he took in Theo's pleading look. "It was a pleasure to see you again, Lady Theodora. Thank you for your assistance." He winked before turning to Jude. "And it is lovely to make your acquaintance, as well. I look forward to meeting Lord Cartwright. With our siblings being close friends, we are likely to see one another often during the coming season. I would love to invite your family to dine with us."

Jude remained silent, turning to Theo with an awkward smile. "Yes, I dare say Theo is very much looking forward to the coming season, and Adeline has been bursting at the seams with talk of new gowns and invitations already arriving."

Her sister-in-law expertly avoided acceptance of any invitation to dine with the Melton family.

Theo was in no way looking forward to the coming season, specifically the endless soirees and midday luncheons with matrons and debutantes she didn't know. In fact, one more dress fitting, and she was likely to take to her sick bed until the holidays.

"Very well," Mr. Price said. "I will leave you ladies to your afternoon engagements."

The butler appeared at the door as Alistair left, leading him to the foyer, leaving Theo to answer Jude's questioning stare.

"Are you going to force me to ask?" The fiery-haired woman crossed her arms, signaling that they would not be leaving for the museum until her unspoken questions were answered to her liking. "Because I can do that."

"Truly, he only came in search of Adeline."

"And did you lie?"

"I told a very minor fib—"

"You said you hadn't seen her this morn. That is not a minor fib, it is outright deception if you have, in fact, seen her." Jude huffed, uncrossing her arms and placing them on her hips—a far more menacing pose. "Which I assume you have, judging from your wide-eyed stare."

"I may have seen her for a few moments," Theo admitted, forgetting whom she'd told the truth to and whose questions begged for white lies. The web she'd woven was tightening around her like a far-too-snug scarf. "I departed Regent's Park in the Cartwright carriage as Adeline left in Georgie's family coach."

"The footman passed me upstairs, your bow and quiver in hand," Jude said. "How has your practice been going?"

"Adequate, thank you for inquiring." She hadn't spoken with her brother or Jude about her instruction of her friends; yet, as always, her sister-in-law knew far more than she let on. "It has been nice spending time with Adeline, Josie, and Georgie before the season starts. I have missed them since departing for London. I fear we will be ever so busy. And if Monsieur Cassini's family is so inclined, I may not be attending nearly as many gatherings as Momma has planned."

Jude glanced at her muddied gown and boots. "We shall never know if you do not prepare for us to leave. They will be at the museum today for a tour of the current exhibits. Cart plans to introduce you and your studies to them before your lecture, in hopes they will deeply consider your offer and take in your knowledge of their latest topographical project."

"Of course," Theo replied. "I will only be a few moments."

"The carriage is being brought round now. I will meet you in the foyer after I call for Daisy to remove the tea service. Your mother would not be pleased to arrive home to a messy room. Now, be on your way— let us not be late for what could be the most important introduction of your life." Judith gave her a quick hug and pushed her from the room.

Theo hurried to her bedchamber, a fresh gown lay on her bed with matching slippers and gloves.

Slipping into the dress, Theo couldn't help but muse over her situation. She was living two separate lives of late—possibly three. She was one person when her friends surrounded her, another when her mother was present, and still one more when she ventured to the museum with Cart. Today, she'd discovered her penchant for witty conversation as she'd mercilessly teased Alistair, holding over his head the information she held. Certainly, a person could not last over long attempting to be three separate people. At some point, the different facets of her life would collide. Archery, mapmaking, lectures on land elevations, dress fittings, and musical recitals, they were all parts of her life, but Theo did not feel that any of them fully expressed who she was. She hoped the day would come when the many people around her—her family and friends—could be a part of all her different passions.

Theo longed to tell Josie of her position with the museum, giving lectures on many subjects. A part of her suspected her dear friend would enjoy attending, or possibly giving a lecture of her own on modern medical practices.

In kind, Theo anticipated showing Cart how she'd taken their force and trajectory equation and put it to use with her archery. He would be proud, especially knowing she'd made the discovery six years before and managed to instruct others on how to apply her method. In the future, she'd teach her niece and nephew the same skill—when they grew old enough to hold a bow properly.

She tied her hair back in a severe knot to hide her long waves. It was something she'd learned from Miss Dires long ago—a woman's mind was diminished in others' views if their beauty outshined their presence. Satisfied her hair would not come loose and no tendrils would escape her knot, Theo grabbed her journal with the notes she planned to discuss at the museum. Her mornings had been spent at Regent's Park, and her afternoons dedicated to accompanying her mother to various appointments—not including her time spent in Whitechapel or entertaining Gladstone. Her spare time, which was scarce, had been spent expounding on her topic of levies and their durability during heavy bouts of rain.

She'd have to make the most of what she'd detailed the night before after her mother had found her bed, leaving Theo a few hours of solitude in Cart's library.

Quiet. It was something Theo had grown accustomed to during her time away from home. Days spent surrounded by books from all over the world, study sessions with other girls, discussing the merits of modern scientific methods as opposed to those from years past, even the hours she spent outdoors, taking walks to the village and practicing with her bow; Theo had come to enjoy that, as well.

She longed for the simpler time spent away from the hustle and bustle of London—maybe after her season, she could convince Cart and Momma to allow her to return and teach the new students. Could she find fulfillment in such a post?

Jude was donning her cloak when Theo entered the foyer. "Are you ready?"

"I am." Theo held up her journal for Jude to see, her confidence not as it normally was.

"Cart is very anxious—and proud—to hear your lecture. I dare say he is overjoyed to have you speak before his peers." Jude nodded in thanks when the butler opened the door for them to depart. "I spent an hour after dinner last night convincing him that the children were far too young—and full of energy—to sit through your lecture."

Theo laughed at the vision of Olivia and Samuel fidgeting and fussing as she spoke. "Yes, this discourse may be a bit advanced for their liking."

#

Cart beamed with pride as Theo concluded her lecture and closed her journal as loud applause filled the room. Not as thunderous and unruly as the cheers from Whitechapel, though far more fulfilling. There was to be a question and answer session after the talk, but it had been postponed to give her the opportunity to meet the Cassini family before they departed the museum for their accommodations.

During her speech, Monsieur Damon Cassini nodded as she expounded on the need and usefulness of maps that denoted elevation levels in areas that may be susceptible to flooding during heavy storms. His sister, Comtesse de Salnome, had taken an interest in Theo's hand-drawn ledger with the symbols outlined to make map deciphering easier for readers.

Theo had nearly lost track of her words when she noticed the pair whispering to one another, each with an expression most serious, their appreciation clear by their intense attention when she moved from one side of the dais to the other as she spoke. It was hard to remember a time when she'd been frightened—almost to the point of inaction—at performing before an audience. In only the past several days, she'd shown her archery skills before a crowd of hundreds, and now, she'd spoken intelligently in front of a room brimming with London's keenest minds.

But her time at the podium was at an end for the day, and Theo looked to the clock at the back of the large room. She only had an hour's time before she was expected at Georgie's townhouse to accompany her friends to Greenwich Park, the location of the Grand Archers' Competition of London. The area was formally used for hunting, and one of the largest open areas in London—the ideal place for a gathering that might spill over into the thousands.

Theo had promised her friends she'd accompany them during the start of the tourney, to calm Georgie's nerves and remind Adeline to exhale before releasing her arrow. If Adeline were able to outsmart her brother for a few days longer…

"Wonderful, insightful, and thought-provoking, Lady Theodora," the comtesse said with glee as she rushed to the front of the room, her brother, as well as

Cart and Jude, close behind. "It is truly an honor to hear you speak so passionately about a topic most do not find interest in."

Monsieur Cassini nodded, far more reserved in his outward appreciation of her lecture. "We are looking forward to discussing your suggestions for changes to our topographical maps. I agree a set of maps detailing only flood plains would greatly benefit our two nations."

Normal introductions and greetings were commonly pushed to the wayside when minds of great intellect congregated—as if names and titles mattered far less than the notions and thought processes of the individuals.

Theo should feel more at ease around her educated peers. Unfortunately, the moment she stepped off the dais, her feelings of discomfort returned, and she felt out of place.

Cart smiled broadly at his sister's success, but remained quiet, allowing her to speak for herself and assume the spotlight. It could also be the hold Jude had on his arm that kept him silent. He was still adjusting to Theo's return—not as the precocious child who'd demanded to travel alone by coach to her new school, but as an educated, free-thinking woman who he was proud to call his kin.

"I am happy to hear you found my lecture insightful." Theo's face heated at the attention bestowed upon her. "And I am grateful that you have chosen to meet with me during your short stay in London."

"My sister could barely contain her excitement during our crossing," Cassini confided. The comtesse elbowed her sibling. "I mean, she finds much inspiration in discussing topics of import with others, especially women in possession of sound minds."

Theo's nervousness increased. The siblings considered her of sound mind, despite her young age. She only hoped she said nothing to embarrass herself.

Cassini and his sister were akin to Cart and her—both men were proud and open about their respective sister's accomplishments. They didn't seek to place them in a drawing room surrounded by other fawning women to preserve the illusion of a delicate nature.

"Until our meeting, Lady Theodora," Cassini grasped her hand and brought it to his lips, gaining a severe glare from Cart and a soft giggle from Jude. "My sister and I look forward to our coming appointment—and working with you in the near future."

"And I, with you, *monsieur*." Theo gave her hand a quick tug and turned to the comtesse. "Thank you for your kind words, Comtesse de Salnome."

"Do call me Samuela, Lady Theodora." The woman, while ten years Theo's senior, was the epitome of French classic beauty with her midnight-black hair, crystal-blue eyes, and willowy frame. Widowed at age seventeen—if Theo remembered correctly—her inheritance gave her and her brother the funds to continue with their ancestor's passion for mapmaking. "As my dear brother said, until our meeting. Come, Damon. We have many exhibits to see, and not nearly enough hours to accommodate all I seek to explore."

Theo smiled demurely at the man, a male replica of his sister in every way, including his lanky frame, which was seen as appealing in a woman, though did not have the same effect when attributed to a grown man.

His dark hair and complexion should incite a sense of handsomeness—but Theo did not find Cassini the least bit charming or captivating to the eye, nor did she seek to gain a deep acquaintance with him. No, she much preferred a certain sun-kissed shade of blond, as if spun from gold, and eyes not of an icy cobalt, but aquamarine, almost clear at times, and at others, pools of deep, turbulent, ocean blue. A broader build was also something she hadn't realized she favored—or that a man's shoulder set would be a factor in his appeal. But Cassini's frame was that of a man untested in any physical capacity. It was likely he'd never held a saber or bow.

Physical ability had always come second—or third—to a person's mental capacity in Theo's mind. Yet, it seemed that had changed for her at some point.

With one last look, the pair turned to speak with another museum patron before leaving the room in search of interesting exhibits.

"Splendidly done, my dear Theo," Cart whispered, patting Jude's hand where it rested on his arm as he rocked back and forth on his heels. Theo had not seen her brother this animated in years, as he was normally the solemn type. "I am certain you will become a regular lecturer here, and possibly be asked to speak in other locations around London. There is a gathering at Eton in a month's time. I think we should journey there to attend, what say you?"

Theo didn't have a moment to consider his invitation before Jude spoke, solidly dispelling the idea. "It will be Theo's first season. There will be no time for her to journey outside of London until"—she paused—"possibly the holiday break for Parliament, but until that time, you agreed to allow your mother to introduce her properly to society."

It had been another condition her brother had agreed to in return for Theo being allowed to attend Miss Emmeline's and receive a proper education, far more suitable than hiring tutors to attend her in town.

"Completely slipped my mind," Cart said shaking his head, and Theo thought it probably true. He had a tendency to focus only on what interested him most while forgetting everything else—like eating and sleeping. "I am certain I can speak with Mother, possibly offer her a more favorable deal, to allow Theo to join me at Eton."

Theo turned to Jude, holding her breath and awaiting her answer—it was far too much to hope for that she'd agree and potentially face the wrath of Anastasia Montgomery, Dowager Countess Cartwright.

"Absolutely not, Simon," Jude said, using her husband's given name, a sure sign her declaration was concrete and that she would not be trifled with or made to entertain further discussion on the subject. Theo deflated, the air gusting from her lungs. "Your mother has worked very hard preparing for Theo to enter society. You promised her one season—only one—and you will give her that. After, it is up to Theodora where her future lies. If she deems societal life is not to her liking, then your mother has conceded to that outcome."

"Well, certainly next year," Cart granted. "Will you both be joining me on the tour with the comtesse and her brother?"

Theo glanced at the clock, noting another fifteen minutes had passed. "I am sorry to say I cannot, Cart. I am to meet with my friends for a turn in the park." She purposely neglected to mention what park or that she would in fact be there to support Adeline and Georgie in the competition; however, she would be *walking* about *in* a park. Her brother nodded, not seeming to notice or consider her plans for the afternoon.

"And you, my lovely wife?" He placed a kiss to her cheek. "May I interest you in a *private* tour of the museum? I have heard in good confidence that a forgery has been found among the exhibits—maybe you can apply your skill and find it."

Jude's light laughter filled the room, gaining the attention of several other patrons before she nodded. "I certainly enjoy a challenge, especially one that will not end with me under the magistrate's lock and key."

Jude and Cart's love had been born of a mutual interest in antiquities and had been put to the test several times, yet they continued to prevail. Theo could hardly believe it had been over six years since Jude and her four siblings had entered her life. Even Cart's son had been named for Jude's twin, Samantha.

"The only place you will ever be locked within is our chambers," Cart jested, a concept he was still exploring. "Come, my love."

"I will take the carriage to meet Georgie, Josie, and Adeline," Theo called as the couple moved toward the double doors leading into the main museum.

"That sounds marvelous, Theo," Cart said over his shoulder, leaning in to place a kiss on his wife's neck. "We shall join you and Mother for a meal this evening."

The audience had slowly filed from the room as she'd spoken with Cart and Jude—leaving Theo alone. An outsider. Invisible and forgotten. It was a feeling she'd lived with all her life, but had found easy to suppress in her youth for it allowed her the freedom to lose herself in a story or study a map without anyone pestering her.

Why did it suddenly trouble her so to be overlooked and left behind? Something had changed, though Theo hadn't any notion what it was.

Everyone had someone: Adeline had Georgie, Cart had Jude, her mother had Mrs. Gladstone and her other charitable friends...even Samuel and Olivia had each other. She supposed she had Josie, but Theo hadn't even been completely honest with her.

Perhaps she and Comtesse de Salnome could become friends, sharing their deeper secrets and longings.

The clock chimed loudly, its deep gong filling the room and pulling Theo from her pitiful musings. The carriage ride back to Mayfair would take far longer at this hour, but Georgie's townhouse was the safest place for them to meet. Her family did not seem to take much interest in her whereabouts.

Theo hurried to her waiting carriage and instructed her coachman back to Mayfair.

After the incident in Whitechapel, Theo demanded that they never venture to any tourneys alone, nor leave one another unattended. Thankfully, Greenwich Park was in a far safer area of London—being one of the royal grasslands. They would remain out of harm's way, and her coachman would not think overly much about depositing the women at such a heavily congested park.

The women waited outside as she pulled into Georgie's drive—their bows slung over their shoulders and cloaks over their arms. They would all wear their hoods raised, knowing if one of them were recognized, it would be simple to connect the women to one another. Greenwich—and the Grand Archers' Competition of London—was heavily attended by many members of society who were trickling into town for the coming season, tripling the girls' chances of being recognized if they were not properly concealed.

"It is about time you arrived," Adeline snorted, plopping onto the seat across from Theo while Georgie and Josie handed their bows to the coachman. "If we do not hurry, we will not be allowed to compete."

"We will arrive at the end of the cataloging period, in time to pay your and Georgie's fees, but not so early as to gain undue notice before the tourney begins." They'd settled on their plan that very morning; unfortunately, it hadn't been Adeline's suggestion; therefore, she hadn't found favor in the decision. Instead, she'd proposed they arrive very early to pay their fee and spend time walking amongst the other archers to assess their skills. "How will we ever be seen if we arrive so close to the start?"

"We do not want to be seen, Adeline," Georgie rebutted. "We must blend in. Our goal is to win the entire purse prize, not be the center of attention."

Adeline huffed, her petulant mood certainly caused by the rift between her and Alistair.

Which reminded Theo of his visit to her that morning. "Your brother came looking for you again, Adeline. He arrived moments after I returned home from Regent's Park. Was he cross with you when he returned home?"

Their carriage pulled out of the drive, the women swaying with the movement as they made their way toward Greenwich.

"I find I do not care how cross Alistair is with me. It does not matter if I sit in my room for days on end or flee out my window, he will find something about me that vexes him."

"How did you manage to leave the house for the tourney?" Josie asked.

"I walked out the front door."

Theo glanced out the window nervously. "Were you followed?"

"Heavens no," Adeline said with exasperation. "Alistair and Abel left for Tattersall's shortly after he was done berating me for climbing out my window. 'You could have been hurt' and 'Think about your future,'" she mocked her brother's warnings. "He made me promise—with a threat of sending me back to the country to Mother—never to climb out my window again."

"I truly thought he'd be far more furious and redouble his efforts to keep you locked away until the season commenced next week," Georgie said with a laugh.

Adeline smirked. "Oh, he did. He nailed my windows shut and posted the twins outside my door. Unfortunately for him, the pair have the attention span of a squirrel and were easily distracted. Long enough for me to slip from my room and out the front door," she proclaimed with satisfaction.

Josie's eyes rounded. "You will be in an awful amount of trouble when you return."

"I am always in an awful amount of trouble." Adeline chuckled.

"Do you not fear being sent away?" Theo felt a sliver of remorse for the discipline her friend would face. "I know how much you are looking forward to wearing all your pretty new gowns."

"Oh, Alistair will not follow through on his threat. He's spent far too much money for me to fail in society," she confided. "I've heard him talking to Abel about it. I must be wed—and during my first season—for there is not enough coin to fund a second one for me. Besides, he no more seeks a return to the dull country existence than I do."

"You know I can help," Georgie offered, always the one to slip Adeline spare coin when she ran low on her allowance. "You can stay with my family and me next season."

"You think I will not have suitors?" Adeline asked, tossing her blonde curls over her shoulder to gain a better look at her friend. "I suspect I will have eligible men offering for my hand before the season truly gets underway."

Georgie and Josie shared an exasperated look at Adeline's incessantly overconfident demeanor. Her arrogant behavior hadn't won her any true friends, beyond her roommates, at Miss Emmeline's, and it would likely garner her less female companions in society. Though if it would deter men from courting her was yet to be seen.

"I did not mean any insult, Adeline, I am certain you will marry and marry well, indeed."

Theo listened as Georgie apologized, though the woman's offer was meant as a gift—a way for Georgie to help her dear friend.

The carriage swayed as the coachman took a sharp turn, causing the women to lean into one another.

Theo pulled the curtain back and peeked out the window to assess their progress. "Ladies, it is time to don our cloaks—Greenwich is fast approaching, and the traffic will slow shortly," Theo announced, pulling her own cloak from below her seat. She'd requested that the stable master stash her gear and long cloak in the carriage when she'd arrived home that morning. "Remember, keep your hood securely raised, and your face averted if someone stares too closely. We keep to ourselves and depart when the tourney halts for the day." She looked to each of her friends, gaining their agreement. "Georgie and Adeline—may the wind be in your favor, and your arrows find their mark."

"Friendship, loyalty, and honor above all," the trio chanted.

Theo nodded her approval as she tied the drape back, allowing the afternoon sun to shine in.

Chapter Fifteen

Alistair slumped against the padded seat in his carriage, the weight of his obligations receding, at least for a few brief hours. The time away from his townhouse—and his siblings—had done as he'd hoped by easing the constant tension.

"Thank you for accompanying me, Abel." He took in his younger brother, now a man, sitting across from him. One and twenty years of age, but still the boy Alistair remembered. Also, the closest thing to a friend he had growing up so far from town.

"Any time, Price," Abel said with a smile using their surname as Alistair had yet to inherit his father's title. "It is about time you and I take a turn about town. All this talk and preparation for Adeline's season is getting old rather quickly."

Alistair sighed. "Yes, and to think we will have to repeat it four more times."

Abel chuckled. "*You* need repeat it on four more occasions. I cannot imagine Adelaide, Arabella, Amelia, or little Ainsley being as much worry to you as Adeline."

"One can hope—and say innumerous prayers to that end." Relief had flooded Alistair the moment he and Abel departed for Tattersall's, and had continued as they'd surveyed the stock up for auction. "But as luck would have it, they will be the death of me."

"Do you think Adeline will be home when we return?" Abel shifted in his seat, stretching his legs in the cramped quarters. "We've been gone several hours—there is no telling what scheme she concocted to gain exit."

"Her scheme did not include shimmying down the side of the townhouse, I can tell you that." Part of him longed not to care. He was losing the willpower to continue fighting her determination to ruin herself. The rest of his siblings counted on the success of Adeline's launch into society as it meant that their chances of favorable matches would increase tenfold. Everyone realized this except, apparently, Adeline.

She seemed not to notice all he'd given up in his life to make sure her future was bright. Not that his commitment to his family had derailed his own choices in life—he would give up anything and everything if his siblings needed him to.

Alistair could be spending his time in London focused on his own path, securing a wife for himself, starting a family, working to build a partnership that would help him in the future when he inherited his father's estate. However, he was locked in a battle of wits with Adeline. It was maddening, infuriating, and altogether unnecessary. He would hate to look back on his many years focused on his family to discover it had all been for nothing; his sacrifices going unrewarded.

He'd asked one thing of her: behave until the season officially began.

It would please him greatly if she acted with a measure of decorum and grace until she was properly betrothed; however, even Alistair knew that was far too much to ask of his sister.

"After the tongue-lashing I gave her, she should be fearful of leaving her room even at mealtime." Once Adeline was introduced properly, he had no doubt that she would make a huge splash and become the debutante of the season—that was if she could keep her name unconnected to scandal for a few more days. "Besides, I have the twins watching her. They cannot do any worse than you."

"Thankfully, I'm not seeking a position as a governess or nursemaid," Abel retorted.

Alistair let the comment be, knowing his brother knew the time was fast approaching for him to make a decision on his own future—he was the first spare, after all. The Melton Viscountship was nowhere near grand or wealthy enough to support four sons and their families. Abel, along with Adrian and Alfred, would need to select a career, a way to earn an income to support themselves—a trade, possibly.

The subject of a commission in George IV's navy had been discussed, with Alistair promising to find the funds, but Abel had shied away from the offer. It was hard enough knowing he could not provide for them all for the rest of their lives, but even worse to try and force his brother down a path not of his choosing.

As Alistair had been forced to do.

There was little reason to contemplate or blame his parents' role in their current situation. Yes, they should have been more aware what funds were needed to support a family with nine children, let alone dowries large enough to secure five females a proper husband. The daughters of a lowly, impoverished viscount were not exactly sought after or the favored choice among eligible men. Take himself for example, if he were to marry, his choices would be limited to women with large enough dowries to replenish the Melton coffers—it was a dreadful excuse to be chosen as his wife, yet there were no other options open to him; which was why Alistair refused to consider marriage as a means of solving his financial problems. Thankfully, his sisters would never know such a fate, as their dowries were barely substantial enough to be called *actual* dowries.

No woman deserved to be taken as wife for her wealth. It would be a doomed relationship with little chance of happiness, let alone mutual love.

In all honesty, Alistair hoped his sister chose a love match over a marriage of convenience or for money's sake, it would make her dowry—while paltry, to say the least—irrelevant when drafting the marriage settlement. Though it would be more to Adeline's liking to select a man who doted on her, thinking she could do no wrong because, frankly, she did a lot of things wrong.

"What has you frowning so?" Abel kicked Alistair lightly in the shin to gain his attention. "You look as if you discovered the existence of several more female Price relations you'll be responsible for."

"Heaven help us all if that were to happen," Alistair said with a chuckle. "I would disappear at sea—leaving you, my beloved Abel, to pick up the pieces and finish the puzzle that is our family problem."

"I would swim all the way to Spain to find you, Price," Abel said. "And drag you back. You know I am not the man to lead this family—nor rescue us from a financial ruin of father's making. Besides, you know account ledgers and arithmetic, in general, do not interest me."

"Ah," Alistair sighed, knowing what was to come next and deciding to beat Abel to the topic. "You are still interested in going on an archeological dig in the West Indies?"

Abel's jovial nature dimmed, hearing the frustration in Alistair voice. "As I have detailed for you, it will be far less costly than purchasing a commission for me."

"But no safer." And certainly not preferable—at least not for him. If his brother were lucky enough to survive the journey, he might well succumb to an epidemic and expire without Alistair being any wiser.

"Come, Price," Abel said, leaning forward. "I would not be journeying to war. I would be gaining a wage and earning living expenses—and possibly, one day, garner mention in a serious historical journal if I am lucky enough to find something."

"Will you be lucky enough not to catch a serious illness or succumb to famine if you are stranded in some godforsaken country?" Alistair argued. "I am more than willing to take the loss of money, but a loss of life if something were to happen to you…absolutely not."

Abel sat back, crossing his arms in defiance.

"What of your sisters?" Alistair posed his final question. "What will come of them if you perish? We may never know, never see you again, would you make them suffer such heartbreak?"

"That is not fair." Abel narrowed his eyes, a sign he'd settled on another proposition for Alistair. "What if I were able to secure a position at the museum? I would remain in England—go no farther—but would still be able to work and gain a living in a manner I would enjoy."

"Is there a position available that compensates you for your time?"

"Not that I am aware of at present, but possibly soon. Or I can inquire." Abel's voice gained confidence as he spoke. "There are certainly hundreds of men—and some women—working at the museum at any given time. Maybe I can continue my intern position—without pay—until something more viable becomes available."

Alistair thought of Theo's brother, Lord Cartwright—acting curator of the British Museum, but he halted himself before mentioning the fact. He'd already used Theo to keep track of Adeline, he would not use her again. And it was unlikely they pair would run across one another without someone making the introduction. "I will concede to a position in England, but nowhere else." He knew he had no right to limit Abel's activities; he had reached his majority. He could simply tell Alistair he was leaving, and he would be helpless to stop his brother and friend.

Mercifully, Abel loved their family as much as Alistair.

"Would you entertain a trip to White's this evening—take our meal there, maybe find a card game?" Alistair asked, hoping to distract Abel and banish his sullen mood. "That is if we ever arrive home with all this traffic."

Alistair leaned forward to look at the window when Abel remained silent and brooding.

"There must be something afoot today, for I swear every carriage is out." The season had yet to officially begin, and he'd noticed an increase in peers arriving in London already. He dreaded the hectic traveling of the city streets. There was a break in the carriages ahead, and Alistair called to his driver to speed up as the traffic moving in the other direction continued its sluggish pace.

Female laughter caught his ear over the shouts of vendors along the street and men on horseback yelled at passing carriages to move out of the way.

Alistair's head was not normally turned by the sound, as it was something he heard day in and day out at his own home, but something about the tone was familiar.

He craned his neck, leaning slightly out the carriage window, careful not to collide with a vehicle moving in the opposite direction.

The laughter—from more than one woman—still drifted through the air, but one in particular still held his attention. "Do you hear that, Abel?"

His brother looked at the window, as well. "Yes, I think it is—"

His words cut off as they both spotted the source of the familiar sound as a carriage with a window uncovered rolled past them—a head of long, pale blonde hair could be seen right before the woman raised the hood of her cloak, as did the other three women in the enclosed conveyance.

"It is Adeline!" Abel shouted.

"That blasted female," Alistair retorted. "Driver! Follow that carriage."

"I guess your tongue-lashing was not as persuasive as you thought," his brother said with a chuckle, his jovial nature returning.

Alistair kept his eyes trained on the fleeing carriage as he caught sight of Theo, sitting across from Adeline. Mercifully, the women's carriage continued in a southerly direction that led away from the East End and Whitechapel.

"Where are they going?" Abel shouted over the din of the wheels on the hard-packed street as the conveyance picked up speed in pursuit.

"I haven't the slightest notion, but it seems they are following the many carriages traveling in that direction," Alistair said, though he feared he did know exactly where the group of women was going. "We will follow and collect Adeline. Her friends are free to do as they wish."

Alistair hadn't been completely honest with his brother about where he'd discovered Adeline a few days prior. Abel only knew that their younger sister had been caught gallivanting about town without a proper chaperone or Alistair's permission.

The carriage his sister rode in slipped into an opening, the conveyances ahead thinning, leaving Alistair and Abel stuck between a cart loaded with fruits and vegetables and a phaeton driven by a man wearing the most obnoxious coat of deep plum—a feather of all things in his hat.

"You, sir!" Abel called to the man driving the cart. "Where is everyone headed?"

The man glanced at Alistair's carriage, eyes narrowing to see within the dim interior to who had called for his attention. "It be da first day of the Grand Archers' Competition of London." He lost his Cockney accent as he pronounced each word. "Every'ne be going ta Greenwich Park."

Alistair sat back in the carriage, allowing the velvet seats to comfort his irritated soul; confident he now knew where the women were headed and what their plans were.

"Price," Abel called, leaning farther out the window. "Their carriage is moving out of sight. Do something, or we will never find them."

The worry in his brother's voice matched the dread filling Alistair. "Sit back," he said. "They are on their way to the tourney."

"Whatever for?"

"To compete, naturally." At Abel's puzzled stare, Alistair continued. "Our dear sister has been sneaking about London, practicing with a bow and arrow—she's actually quite good." Not as skilled at Theo, but Alistair needn't share that tidbit.

"Adeline? Outdoors? I do not believe it." Abel shook his head.

"Believe it," Alistair commented.

"Why did she not include me?" he asked, wounded. "She confides in you—not thinking that I would gladly have accompanied her. She would not be in the trouble she is now, and I may have taught her a few new tricks."

"She did not 'confide in me,' as you say. And Adeline would likely teach you a thing or two." Alistair waved off his brother's glare. "She has been practicing for years, or so Lady Theodora Montgomery informed me."

Abel's brow drew low in confusion as the carriage took a sharp turn, casting both men to the side as it straightened out and gained speed.

"Adeline's friend."

"And you have spoken to her?" Abel's brow rose.

"Yes, I was forced to call on her this morning when Adeline went missing." It was all Alistair was willing to share on the subject. He'd thought he and the woman had come to some sort of agreement to keep Adeline out of trouble, but, apparently, he'd misjudged their conversation. "She was of little help but to inform me that Adeline would likely be home safely before I returned."

Abel wasn't convinced or satisfied by his answer, but something else caught his notice. "Lady Theodora Montgomery?"

"Yes, she attended Miss Emmeline's with Adeline. Why?"

"As in Lady Theodora Montgomery, the only sister of Lord Cartwright, Simon Montgomery—known to his friends and associates as Cart?" Abel didn't take a breath between words. "Lord Cartwright, who currently holds the title of acting curator at the British Museum?"

"The one and only…" Alistair confirmed, watching the wheels spin and the dots connect in his brother's mind.

"You must introduce me." A spark entered Abel's eye at the thought. "I have been about the museum since our arrival in London and haven't secured so much as a glimpse of the man."

"I am not acquainted with Lord Cartwright as yet." He despised dashing his brother's hopes, but there was no cause to allow him to think Alistair could help him in his quest to secure a position.

"But you know his sister, correct?" Abel persisted.

"I have met her on occasion since Adeline's return home, yes." Pressed his lips to hers, and dreamed of her every night since.

Abel clapped his hands as if the situation were resolved and his future bright. "Splendid."

"I do not understand what you speak of."

"You will introduce me to Lady Theo," Abel said slowly as if his brother had gone daft.

"For?"

"Why, I will court her—meet her brother—charm them with my intellect, and I will have a position at the museum before the season ends."

Alistair's nostrils flared as a spike of jealousy coursed through him, setting his skin on fire. "You most certainly will not court Theo—Lady Theodora. You have little interest in marriage."

"But if playing the doting suitor will gain me what I want, what is the harm?" Abel asked.

"And you are resigned to marrying the chit?" His final word stuck in his throat, knowing Theo was much more than another chit making her first introduction to society.

"Certainly, if that is what it takes—unless she is hideous to look at…" He paused, his eyes growing round. "Tell me she is not revolting—long in the face and portly around the middle!"

If they'd been speaking of any other woman than Lady Theo, Alistair might have found the jest in his brother's words, but they most certainly were not speaking of any other woman.

Abel was making light of Lady Theo—and Alistair had half a mind to reach across the carriage and knock the smile from his brother's face.

Instead, he counted to five to tamp down his irritation at the subject of using Theo for her connection to the museum.

"She is most assuredly not revolting to look at," Alistair said once he'd deemed his anger had receded. "I do not know her well, but she is intelligent, witty, and…" He hadn't any idea how to capture all that was Lady Theo in simple words. The notion of sharing with Abel the softness of her lips was highly improper. "She is Adeline's dear friend."

And, therefore, off-limits to Alistair.

And Abel.

For so many reasons other than her bond with Adeline.

"Interesting." Abel looked out the window. "We are almost to Greenwich Park. Can you believe I have never attended an archery tourney? Haven't so much as picked up a bow since we were children."

The area was crowded with pedestrians entering the park, street vendors hocking their wares, and carriages depositing spectators. He spotted several men moving through the crowd, their bows and quivers slung over their shoulders. The competition would be far larger than the one he'd narrowly lost in Whitechapel—which meant a greater risk of Lady Theo and the others being recognized.

When had Lady Theo and her reputation become more important to Alistair than Adeline's chances of suffering a tragic season at the cold, merciless hands of the gossip rags?

"Oh, how have I not realized that Adeline is the fun sibling, and not you, Price?" Abel asked, leaning so far out the window Alistair feared he'd topple from the moving carriage. "A meal and card game at White's cannot compare to an archery tourney at Greenwich Park."

Alistair covered his face with his hands in surrender, the faint smell of livestock filling his nostrils from their time at Tattersall's. His entire family was beyond hope, him included.

Is this what the decade would entail? Chasing his wayward siblings through the London streets, each determined to ruin themselves and their futures?

"There it is!" Abel shouted, looking over his shoulder at Alistair.

"What, dear brother? Ruination? Scandal? The Melton family disgrace?" He was certain these should not be visible to the eye, but alas, Alistair was far from believing they were not, indeed, tangible things. "Because I see all of those crashing down upon us."

"No," Abel fell back into his seat with a satisfied grin. "The carriage! I found the carriage carrying Adeline. It is stopped ahead, outside the park."

"Wonderful." Alistair longed to pack up his entire lot of siblings and move back to their father's country estate—marriage, futures, society be damned. It all took far more effort than he'd bargained for.

Chapter Sixteen

"I did not think there would be so many people," Josie squeaked, pushing closer to Theo, increasing the strength of her grip on her arm. Theo could almost feel the woman's nails through her cloak. "Mayhap I should wait in the carriage."

"That is not safe," Theo chastised. "We stay together, as planned."

"There are not so many people," Adeline proclaimed. "Maybe a hundred more than Whitechapel, but with the practice, we've been doing each morning, I have little doubt we will be victorious." She glanced to Georgie with a smirk. "Or at least I shall be."

Adeline's confidence could be seen in the set of her shoulders and the defiant tilt of her chin. However, images and feelings from their last tourney assaulted Theo at every turn. She looked at the passing men from under her hood, searching for the man who'd attempted to harm her—she was ready for him this time. He would not overpower her, nor get his grimy hands on her friends. The likelihood that the miscreant had found the means to travel from Whitechapel to Greenwich Park was slim.

Nevertheless, Theo was alert and watching for anything untoward that could befall her friends—and herself.

Adeline and Georgie stood in front of her and Josie, waiting their turn to give their names and entrance fees for the Grand Archers' Competition of London. The line was longer than Theo had anticipated, and she wondered how so many archers were to cast their arrow before the sun began to set on the first day of the competition. If she weren't home by dark, Cart and Jude would be alarmed and ask questions.

A man made to leave after handing over his fee, his bow and quiver slung over his shoulder as he strode back down the line of waiting archers, inspecting each as he passed.

"Oh, he does look fearsome," Josie commented as the man grew closer.

"And ever so handsome," Georgie cooed.

"He would certainly have us think so." Adeline adjusted her stance, hitching her bow up on her shoulder as she leveled a glare on the man from beneath her cloak.

Unfortunately, the man slowed as he came closer to the hooded foursome—taking pause a few feet away to take a closer look. Had he been in attendance at the Whitechapel tourney? The man was not familiar, though that did not account for much as she'd been distracted by Alistair the entire time.

Regret flared within her at the thought of Adeline's elder brother—and her agreement to keep his younger sister out of trouble, knowing the entire time she was to travel to Greenwich for another tourney that same afternoon. Adeline was going to come—and compete—no matter what Theo did or said, so the least she could do was attend and make sure Adeline remained safe and anonymous.

And Theo was committed to doing that.

The man continued to stare, turning his head at an odd angle, trying to gain sight of their faces below their hoods. His quiver slipped from his shoulder.

Theo knew for certain that unless one of their hoods slipped, their faces were completely covered—their cloaks ending at the ground, shielding even their boots from sight.

With a sigh of relief from Josie, who'd stiffened beside her at the man's intense scrutiny, the archer moved down the row, giving the next archer his intimidating stare as he hoisted his quiver back to his shoulder.

"That was close," Georgie said over her shoulder.

"Move up," a gruff voice called from behind them.

Something bumped Theo's shoulder, and her hood fell back a few inches as her hands flew from her pockets to return it to its place.

They shuffled forward in line, and Theo returned her hand to her pocket and the velvet pouch nestled within that held enough coin for Adeline's and Georgie's entrance fees.

"Do ye think one of 'em be the Lady Archer who won at Whitechapel?" a female voice hissed behind them.

Theo looked to Josie, but the woman remained oblivious to the conversation behind them.

"It canna be," a man retorted. "It surely only be some'ne seek'n ta copy 'er."

Standing on her tiptoes, Theo noticed the line in front of them was shortening, and it would be Adeline's and Georgie's time very soon, she only hoped the pair could keep their boasting to a minimum long enough to keep attention from them.

Obviously, everyone in London was still abuzz with tales of the Lady Archer. News circulated in *The Post* the very next day about the mysterious Lady Archer winning the tourney in Whitechapel and disappearing as quickly as she had appeared—with the writer making it known he would discover her identity, and even pondering the notion the cloak had shrouded a petite male. Theo had laughed at that—hysterically—but also hoped the report took hold and distracted the London gossips long enough for them to win at Greenwich Park and disappear once more. Surely, they would continue to practice—and maybe even compete—but more as was proper for young ladies of the *ton*. Archery was meant to be a pastime enjoyed by women at garden parties and country house parties, not for monetary benefit and at the expense of men who'd trained their entire lives for competition—as Mr. Price had so willingly told her.

Theo knew well and good her actions—and that of her friends—would be met with scorn and disgrace if the *ton* ever found out. They were all in jeopardy of being exposed, their reputations tarnished beyond repair. But they hadn't found any other financial means to help Miss Emmeline. Georgie, while the daughter of a wealthy duke, had been limited to a small allowance since the new duchess was currently with child. Cart and

Jude were still working to repair the ruined financial situation their uncle had left them all in years before after making off with everything of value from the Cartwright Earldom. They'd known from the start that Adeline, her aging father already struggling to maintain a family with nine children, would dedicate her skill at archery in lieu of money to help Miss Emmeline. And Josie's family was worse off than Theo and Cart had been in their lowest hour—and even if her family had the funds, the woman would expire from terror asking her guardian for even the smallest allowance.

They hadn't any other option if they wanted to support a school that had given them so much—as well as each other. It was their hope Miss Emmeline's would remain and be a place they'd send their own daughters to, to learn and grow, but that would be impossible if the buildings themselves crumbled and deteriorated.

An archer bumped into Adeline, pushing her bow from her shoulder. As she leaned over, her hood caught on her quiver, pulling the material back and revealing her crown of pale, golden hair.

Theo reached forward and easily tugged the hood back into place.

They were risking much by being here—flirting with danger—but none of them were prepared to take danger's hand and allow it to lead them to certain ruination. Certainly, it would never come to that.

"Maybe we should not be here," Georgie whined. Her confidence only fled her when it came to competition—and singing. "My father would be angered so if he found out."

"And your evil mother, the duchess, would delight in anything that would send you away again," Adeline said, knowing it would bring back Georgie's resolve. "Where is the girl who proudly sang her heart out on her first day at Miss Emmeline's school, knowing her voice broke at every turn, never hitting a single note correctly?"

Theo wanted to laugh, but Adeline was being mean-spirited—to rile Georgie's aggression toward her new stepmother.

They'd all done their best when Headmistress had pushed them to ply their talents before their new classmates. All except Adeline; though Josie, Georgie, and Theo hadn't been present to see their friend scoff at being made to perform like a common circus animal.

"My singing voice is heavenly," Georgie challenged, her stern tone calling to Adeline to deny it.

"Now it is," Adeline conceded. "But there was a day when your voice mimicked the dying cries of an infected alley cat."

"Adeline," Josie hissed. "That was rude and uncalled for."

Theo gave Josie's arm a reassuring squeeze, letting her know she agreed with her comment and was proud she'd spoke up in Georgie's defense.

"Let us quiet down." Theo kept her voice low. "We do not want to draw any more attention than we already have."

"I cannot go anywhere without undue attention lavished upon me," Adeline giggled. "It is the burden I am cursed to bear all my days. It is difficult for any person—man or woman—to keep from staring."

"You're cursed, all right," Theo mumbled under her breath, rewarded when Josie stifled a laugh.

Georgie threw an exasperated glance in Josie's direction in response to Adeline's haughty tendencies. Again, Theo returned to her place on the outside of the group. She felt the same vexation at Adeline's arrogant comments, yet neither woman looked to her.

"Step up, archers," a man called, his looming form and obvious musculature spoke of his athletic nature. "Pay your fee and move on to the practice area."

Georgie and Adeline stepped to the table, a simple rough plank of wood supported by two large tree stumps, and gave their names as Lady Archer One and Lady Archer Two. The man turned an intense stare on the pair, trying to see their features below their hoods. As planned, Georgie lowered her gaze to the table, decreasing the risk of the man seeing her face; however, Adeline tilted her chin up slightly, allowing the afternoon sun to reflect off one golden lock that had escaped its confines beneath her cloak.

He seemed satisfied with the small glimpse he'd gotten and the names provided. "Fees please," he said, holding his palm out.

Theo reached between the pair and dropped the velvet bag into the man's hand, as it held only enough for their entrance fees and not a pence more. She ducked her own head as the man stared, and she jerked her hand back, crossing her arms.

"Only two entries?" He opened the pouch and poured the coins into his other hand, counting them twice before throwing them into a large pail next to the table. When Adeline nodded, he continued, "You are archers number one hundred and ninety-nine and two hundred. We are anticipating three hundred archers to compete over the next three days. The practice area is that way." He pointed to a large, open, grassy area to his left—the area already filled to bursting with archers and targets. "Move along and await your numbers to be called."

"Thank you," they mumbled in unison and moved toward the practice area.

"Remember," Theo warned. "We stay together. Our practice this morning was enough—there is no need to show your skills or draw attention before you take the field."

Arriving at the practice area, they fanned out into a straight line—taking in the many archers present. Some were dressed finely, as if they'd only stopped by the tourney on their way to afternoon tea with their wife or mother. While others were dressed in tattered trousers and wrinkled shirts of cotton prepared to work after departing the tourney grounds. Not only did the competitors vary greatly, but so did their gear. Many used older bows, much like the Whitechapel tourney, but some held gear crafted from wood that even Theo hadn't seen in books—fitting an archer better than a pair of well-made Hessians.

"Maybe it is not best I take our second place," Georgie gasped as the man closest to them released his arrow and found his mark at the direct center of the furthest target. "I think I have seriously misjudged my abilities."

"Do not be silly," Josie said, leaving Theo and moving to Georgie's side. "Your skill has steadily improved since we've been practicing. You can best any archer here."

"With the exception of me, naturally," Adeline said with a smirk, her eyes flitting between her friends.

"Undoubtedly, you all agree my skill is far superior to Georgie's? Theo, we've worked hard to calm my nerves—and Josie, you've seen my aim stay true even in heavy winds. Do you remember that holiday your family came to Canterbury and we showed our archery talents to them?"

Theo, as well as the other two women, remained silent, refusing to add to Adeline's self-serving boasting which commonly turned into a scolding ridicule for her friends.

"We must focus, Adeline," Theo finally said. It was the way of things: Josie and Georgie ready to do as Adeline commanded, and Theo stepping forward to correct the injustice of their friend's words and actions. You'd think the woman was completely lacking in compassion and empathy towards others. She'd certainly not lacked training in those baser emotions during her youth, as Theo had met Alistair. He was the height of propriety and took his responsibilities as guardian for Adeline very seriously. "Now, let us assess the competition. See if we can learn anything."

Theo led by example, turning her scrutiny to the many men—and a few women—who took their positions and released their arrows.

A group of young men dressed much like merchants debated another competitor's stance, one man arguing the merits of a solid shoulder posture in lieu of a frame less restrictive. Theo noticed the anxious tone to the man's voice and the dark blue circles under his eyes—his own posture a bit stooped—as if he hadn't slept the previous night. Did the man not realize without proper rest one's body couldn't achieve the correct balance?

She almost spoke to the fact, but an abrupt shout drew her attention to another group of men as a volley of angry cursing erupted. Theo turned in time to see one man push another, causing him to stumble to the ground, his forgotten bow coming to rest at Theo's feet.

Josie quickly moved to the far side of Adeline, not one for shouting or roughhousing of any sort. A loud laugh was enough to send the woman scurrying for safety.

Another man charged toward the group. His target was unclear, but he managed to catch another man off guard as he barreled into his midsection.

Before they could move clear of the scuffle, the burly man who'd taken their entrance fees jumped into the group of men, now wrestling on the ground, all fists and legs, punctuated with an *oomph* and grunt as feet and fists connected with faces and backs.

The women froze with terror. Theo's pulse raced, as she stood rooted to her spot, watching the men tousle.

"I have never seen anything like it," Georgie whispered as the crowd gathered, pushing Theo and the other women closer to the fray.

"Adrian and Alfred wrestle all the time." Adeline moved to her tiptoes to see over a man who'd disengaged himself from the brawl and stood to watch. "The man there…the one in that awfully bright coat…" Adeline pointed to the man and the trio shifted to gain a better look. "He will likely have a bloodstained shirt before this is over. He does not know how to properly guard his face from the punches."

They all turned to stare at Adeline, horror filling their faces. "How can you possibly know any of that?" Georgie shouted above the noise of the crowd.

"Simple, Abel would act as a sparing tutor, of sorts." Adeline smiled with glee as another punch connected with a particularly hard jawline. "That is until Alistair came and ended everything. He is such a bore, I tell you."

The tangle of bodies, undaunted by the jeering crowd and shouts from tourney officials, moved across the ground—directly toward Theo. She grabbed Georgie's arm and tried to take a step back, only to collide with the unmoving wall of the people behind them. Theo glanced down to her friends, stark terror etching Josie's face as she bit her lower lip, a small droplet of crimson appearing.

"Adeline," Theo called, her voice high with fright. "We must find a way out of here before we are overtaken."

Adeline stiffened. Georgie pulled on her arm as they gawked at the scene before them.

The only thing flooding her thoughts was how she'd explain Adeline's battered and bruised frame if she were unable to get them away from the fighting men.

Theo should have left word with Jude—or sent a missive to Alistair—about their whereabouts. They were at Greenwich Park, and no one besides the four of them knew. Adeline had obviously snuck out of her house, while no one cared about Georgie's location. Josie would likely be the first to be missed—though one less mouth to feed in her family would be appreciated.

Theo cursed her tendency to come and go as she pleased with little word to her brother or their mother.

Would Olivia and Samuel notice if she missed their nightly bedtime story?

Surely someone would notice her absence—or would it not become apparent until she failed to arrive for her meeting with Cassini and his sister? Even then, would the Frenchman write it off as the fickle workings of a female?

"Theo!" Josie called, scrambling to avoid a man who'd stumbled to his feet as another tried successfully to pull him back into the fray.

She stared at the commotion now separating her from Adeline, Josie, and Georgie.

The crowd shoved behind her, sending her careening toward the fight—her hood falling from her head. She braced herself for the fall—the possibility of being trampled below the many spectators a stark reality.

Theo closed her eyes. No matter what she did—or how loudly she screamed—it would not change her trajectory, which was aimed directly at the men still scuffling on the ground, fists continuing to find their targets.

Chapter Seventeen

Alistair stood on a large crate to gain a better vantage point and searched the ever-increasing crowd of spectators, archers, companions, and tourney officials. Mixed in with the lords and ladies were miscreants who'd somehow collected enough coin to enter Greenwich Park to behold the spectacular show promised to come. An unclean scent had already settled on the green expanse as far too many people crowded into the area.

The park was much as Alistair remembered it from his childhood, green and well maintained; though he suspected after the Grand Archers' Competition had ended, so would the pristine nature of the park be ruined by thousands of feet, garbage and spoiled food strewn about the many acres of lawn, any remaining wildlife fleeing for safer ground.

Very unaccommodating that he had no way to clear the area, enabling him to swiftly spot the four hooded women he searched for.

"Price," Abel called from below him. "The practice field is beyond that grove of trees, hidden from the spectators. Adeline must be there."

His brother took off toward the secluded area, and Alistair jumped down from the crate to follow. It had been more difficult to gain entrance to the tourney—their progress slowed by the long line of carriages depositing the many lords and ladies in attendance, but also, they'd been denied access through the archer's gate and made to dash around the park and pay an entrance fee with the general crowd.

The dense throng grew even denser as they made their way to the practice field—many spectators flocking to the rope that kept them in the general area, trying to catch a peek of the competing archers.

"This is jolly fun," Abel called breathlessly as they pushed and elbowed their way through the throng of people. "I am certainly going to take up with Adeline from now on."

"Not a wise choice," Alistair said. "She will not be leaving her bedchambers for some time after I catch her." Although, with both Adeline and Abel locked in their townhouse, it would do away with his need to keep watch on at least two of his siblings. "She will be lucky if I don't send her back to the country after this exploit."

Abel laughed. "You are far too serious, brother."

Alistair had no choice. His siblings were relatively unconcerned with their future prospects—which left him to worry about them all. "Stay close, Abel. I will not have you disappearing."

To prove Alistair's hold on his sanity—and his grip on his wayward relations—was slipping further from his grasp, Abel ducked under a man's arms and slid through the middle of a gathering group of lords. He hopped over the rope meant to keep spectators off the practice field. Not only was he fearful of Adeline being discovered unchaperoned at Greenwich Park, but now the chance of Abel being struck by an arrow seemed a definite possibility.

He had little choice but to follow. No one stopped him from passing as he kept watch on Abel, moving through the crowd toward a gathering group on the fringes of the practice area. Maybe he should consider installing shackles in each of his siblings' bedchambers, chaining them to the wall before he left the townhouse? News of his barbaric behavior would cause no less gossip.

"Abel!" His shouts went unanswered as his younger brother arrived at the grouping of archers. "Blasted, bloody—" Alistair arrived at Abel's side, cutting his tirade short as he noticed the crowd had begun to break up, revealing a group of men entangled on the ground, fists flying and legs kicking as if they were a group of toddlers fighting over a toy in the nursery.

Alistair scanned the scattering crowd for Adeline and the other women, spotting a trio of hooded figures fleeing in the opposite direction. But one was missing.

"Abel," Alistair called, pointing to the group. "Go to them, I will find the fourth."

Abel hurried to catch the trio of women. The tangle of male bodies regained their footing but continued to lunge at one another.

It was utter chaos.

Alistair spotted the fourth woman—Lady Theo—her hood pushed from her head, revealing her face as the brawling men collided with her.

He was too far away. Alistair started toward Theo. He wouldn't be able to stop her from hitting the ground, but he should be able to reach her before the crowd trampled her.

His heart fell from his chest, and sweat broke out along his hairline.

There was no other option. If it weren't him who reached her, she would be seriously injured, if not permanently marred.

Alistair pushed two gawking men aside and hurried along the fringes of the foray, attempting to reach Theo. His blood boiled at the crowd's malicious chanting, pushing the men to continue their assault on one another. It was barbaric and highly uncivilized.

He couldn't take his eyes off Theo as her arms pinwheeled, attempting to right herself.

He should have known about the tourney, he should have figured they'd risk their very lives to compete, and he should have been prepared for it. Any harm that came to Theo was of his own making. His overbearing tendencies had pushed the women further down this hazardous path.

There was nothing he could do…she was falling fast.

As he pushed ever closer, a hand reached out of the crowd, abruptly stopping Theo from hitting the ground. Relief flooded Alistair as he expected to see Abel step from the parting crowd with Theo's arm held tight.

It was not Abel he saw.

Theo's naturally serene face contorted in shock, which turned to pain, and finally settled with a grimace she attempted to hide.

Alistair watched as her eyes darted across the crowd in search of someone familiar—anyone to rescue her from her rescuer.

Moving around the final man in his path, Alistair came face-to-face with the man who he'd wanted to give appreciation to a moment before, but Theo's utter terror had him holding his tongue.

Gladstone.

The despicable man clamped on to Theo's arm so forcefully she winced, trying unsuccessfully to pull from his grasp.

Alistair's hands balled into fists, prepared to jump into the fray if only to have one swipe at Gladstone, to wipe the sneer from his face—and remove his hands from Theo. The man had no right to grab Lady Theodora in such a manner, no matter the harm she would have come to had she fallen into the fighting men.

He gained her side as Gladstone attempted to pull her from the crowd toward a small clearing, Abel not far behind him with the trio of hooded ladies in tow.

"Lady Theodora Montgomery," Gladstone chastised, his voice raised to such a level that anyone within twenty paces could hear his every word. His stride was long and sure for a man of his portly size—and Alistair did not doubt he had nefarious intentions where Theo was concerned. "I am ever so pleased that I chose to attend the tourney today, for you would have come to serious harm if I hadn't been close at hand. A white knight, shall we say."

Gladstone was more suited to play the part of black knight as he posed far more of a risk to Theo's safety than the ever-threatening crowd, which had finally begun to disband as officials led six men from the park, their gear left forgotten in the scuffle.

He took several deep breaths, unclenched his fists, and plastered a hospitable smile to his lips—though he felt anything but welcome at Gladstone's appearance. "Gladstone, I thank you for coming to my sister's and her friends' rescue until I made my way to them. The line to pay their entrance fee was dreadfully long and tiresome."

Gladstone turned a scathing look to Alistair, doubt mixed with his fury for having been interrupted.

Theo's eyes bore into him, as well.

"Mr. Price," Gladstone commented. "I was unaware of your interest in archery."

"Not my interest," Alistair said with a light laugh, inserting himself between Theo and Gladstone, forcing the man to release her arm. "My dear sister—Miss Adeline Price—finds great passion in archery, as do her friends. When they begged me to accompany them to the tourney in hopes of competing, I was no match for their female persuasion. But what man can turn away from their pleas?"

"Jolly fun this is," Abel bounded to his side before clapping him on the back and moving to watch any excitement left to be had after the scuffle.

Gladstone's face reddened, and he rubbed the back of his neck.

"I am certain Lord Cartwright—and his mother, bless her compassionate, charity-minded soul—would be agreeable if I escorted Lady Theodora home after the fright she's just had."

Alistair noticed that Theo rolled her eyes at the comment as she used Gladstone's distraction to inch away. She was not in agreement to being escorted anywhere by the scoundrel, and he was more than willing to inform the man of that fact.

"That will not be necessary, Mr. Gladstone." Theo's voice was a bit shaky. "I will remain with my friends. Mr. Price will see us home when our day is completed."

Gladstone turned away from Alistair and pivoted back toward Theo, his brow raised in shock as if he hadn't realized the woman would object to his offer. "Well...see..." He stumbled over his words.

A trumpet blared, calling the first twenty archers to the field laid out before the spectators.

"As you can see, I have everything under control, Gladstone." Alistair held out his arm, allowing Theo to set her hand in the crook of his elbow. "Abel and I will escort the women back to their places. Thank you again for your service. Do enjoy the tourney."

Alistair pushed past Gladstone toward Abel and the Ladies Josephine and Georgina—Adeline stood closer, her arms crossed as she stared daggers at her brother—Theo securely clutching his arm.

"Lady Theodora?" Gladstone called in a severe tone. Theo stiffened at his side, though she did not look over her shoulder at the man. "I will call on you on the morrow. I do look forward to another afternoon in your company."

"Shall we, Lady Theo?" Alistair whispered softly. "There is no need to answer."

"I am thankful for his help," she said, the shakiness gone from her voice. "But I cannot think of a worse fate than an afternoon with Gladstone for company."

"Did he insult you, my lady?" Alistair was prepared to turn and challenge the man—not to a game of wits as they'd played for years, but rather a duel with either pistols or swords. Gladstone deserved nothing less for his thinly veiled threat. "If so, I will handle the matter with swiftness."

"No, he only made it known he looks forward to speaking with my family about our future." Lady Theo continued, her stride even, though he felt the tension riding her body, making her steps jerky. "There is nothing to be done at the moment, Mr. Price, I assure you all is well."

"There is much that can be done *at this moment*." Alistair's temper rose once more, realizing the remaining three women had done away with their hoods, revealing themselves to the gathering of archers preparing to take their positions on the field. "Firstly," he hissed. "I was under the impression that we had an arrangement of sorts—you were to keep my wayward sister from embarking on any more foolish ventures."

"Arrangement?" she asked. "That sounds like an explicit way of describing our conversation from this morning."

"Did you not agree that your actions—along with my sister's—could jeopardize both your chances at a suitable marriage?"

"Yes," she retorted. "Although, I distinctly remember informing you on at least two occasions that marriage was not something I actively set out to achieve this season."

"But my sister must wed. And wed well."

"So you have said." Her curt reply angered him further. The group of women combined hadn't a speck of sense between them. "However, I believe you have neglected to discuss the topic with the one woman it matters most to."

"And I presume you have spoken with your brother and he's agreed to your outlandish notion of putting off a match until you've, what did you call it, explored your many options?" He pulled her close and spoke a bit softer to avoid being overheard as they reached Abel and the trio of women, each looking in any direction but at Alistair. "I am saddened to inform you that Adeline does not have this luxury. My family will not have the funds for a second season, and your actions may very well have doomed her to a lifetime of spinsterhood. Or worse yet, the necessity of marrying a man in need of a wife in name only." The threat was harsh and no better than Gladstone's words; however, Alistair needed Theo to understand the grim position his family was in. It embarrassed him to have to speak it aloud. There was no way around it, though.

At her gasp, Alistair knew he'd used the correct approach. No woman would relish being the reason behind her friend needing to wed for any other purpose but love—as horrid as that sounded.

His parents had wed because of love...given life to nine children due to their continued devotion to one another, and left Alistair with the burden of caring for them all while his mother took care of the man she'd promised to love unconditionally until they were both no more.

It was the same commitment Alistair had promised to his siblings.

He halted before the women, Theo at his side. "Do you have any notion how much danger you are all in?" Alistair looked between the trio, attempting to make eye contact, but the only one to return his glare was Adeline—and she was spitting mad, her cheeks flaming red with her fury.

The color drained from one of the girl's faces—Lady Josephine, he suspected, as she'd been absent at Whitechapel—while Lady Georgina's chin notched up a few degrees, consistent with the spoiled nature of a duke's daughter. Alistair had encountered far too many entitled, flippant women during his short time in London…and he found not one to his liking, no matter the dowry attached to them. An eternity with them by his side would be worse than a fate with all nine of his siblings under his roof.

All the while, Adeline stared directly at him, a challenging air to her posture.

"Adeline Price. Do not look at me thusly," he seethed. "I have half a mind to send you back to Mother and Father, allow them to marry you off to the local blacksmith!"

"You would not dare!" Adeline's rage boiled over, the red moving all the way to the tips of her ears. It was something he'd witnessed many times before. "I would run away."

"That may very well improve your siblings' chances of making a favorable match." Alistair widened his stance, prepared to take all of Adeline's anger. "And I would certainly help you pack your belongings."

Theodora

The collective gasp of the other three women told Alistair he may have taken their argument too far.

Chapter Eighteen

Theo stepped away from Alistair, taken aback by his threats aimed at Adeline and her future. No more had she acclimated to the realization that she was going to be injured in the scuffle, then she'd been pulled from the foray by Mr. Gladstone—possibly the last person she'd ever want to come face-to-face with in a situation that could be viewed as scandalous—and then Alistair had appeared. Her very own white knight to rescue her from the evil clutches of Gladstone, only to turn into a man who should be feared far more than Gladstone. At least Oliver offered no true threat beyond his ability to ruin her in the eyes of society, which meant very little to Theo and her brother. But Alistair could very well punish Adeline, impacting her ability to find a suitable husband, and in turn, having to settle for a match devoid of affection.

The possibility did not scare her. Theo was confident Cart and Jude would never allow her to wed a man who did not suit her—both in daily life and love. They'd pursued a match born of mutual interests that had blossomed into true love without either realizing it. They'd never expect anything less for her.

No matter the Dowager Lady Cartwright's plans for her only daughter, Cart was responsible for any decision concerning her future.

She'd misled Alistair when they'd spoken. Theo did indeed plan to wed, at some point, and share her future with a man she loved. It was on her mind, though not something she longed for during her first season.

Theo understood the burden on Mr. Price's shoulders, but threatening to offer his sister to any man willing to take her off his hands was unacceptable—and appalling. It would be much the same as Cart offering *her* hand to Cassini because Theo met his requirements for an educated, demure, and titled wife. Though the match might actually suit them both, she would need to discuss the possibilities and forecasted outcomes of such a match with Cart. Though Theo was fairly certain such a match would be dire for a woman such as Adeline.

"I believe I shall take each of you to your father— or guardian, whatever the case may be—and tell them of your less than appropriate escapades about London." Alistair scrutinized each of them in turn before continuing. "Maybe that will have you all thinking through your actions with a mind on what is important."

"You…you…you…" Adeline attempted to find her words. "You are a loathsome man, Alistair Alexander Price, and I mean to never call you brother again."

"Yes, dear sister." Alistair's words dripped with sweetness while his eyes were stone cold. "I may be loathsome to you, but it is what my duties demand."

"You do not know what you are doing." Adeline stamped her foot, gaining a whistle of surprise from Abel. "You will not—"

"Calm yourself, Adeline." Georgie set her hands on Adeline's raised shoulders.

"That is not your place, Mr. Price," Theo commanded, rising her hood to shield her face once more, nodding to Josie and Georgie to do the same. He could have all the say over Adeline and her activities, but he was helpless to command Theo and the others to do his bidding. Alistair was free to seek out each of their parents, but by then, the tourney would be over and the prize purse safely in their possession. "Ladies, it is almost time for Adeline and Georgie to take their places in line."

Theo nodded when Josie turned rounded eyes on her, and she lifted her hood.

"Do you think those ridiculous cloaks will keep you hidden now?" Alistair asked. "Gladstone knows your identity, Lady Theo, and likely that of my sister, Lady Josephine, and Lady Georgina, as well. Your names and directions will be front page in *The Post* on the morrow. I can only hope that none of you is connected with the female archer who won at Whitechapel."

Theo's anger spiked at his overreaching manner. "I am proud of my accomplishments at archery, Mr. Price."

"I do not doubt that, Lady Theodora." He turned to her, his mouth etched in a straight line. "I, myself, am overly impressed with your skill; however—"

"There is no 'however,' Alistair."

Josie gasped at Theo's use of his given name—and Adeline smirked triumphantly, though she pressed on, unwilling to allow him to think he held control over her and the other two women.

"I understand if you forbid Adeline to compete, no matter her good intentions, but that is where your involvement ends. Josie, Georgie, and I are committed to assisting Miss Emmeline in any way we can. If that means risking our future prospects, so be it."

"Is that right, Lady Theo?" he inquired, turning his scrutiny to her. "Do you speak for Lady Josephine's and Lady Georgina's families? I know you do not speak for Adeline."

She didn't understand his unforgiving tone. No, she hadn't listened to his requests or heeded his warning about competing in public and its consequences, but they had a connection that transcended Adeline, this situation, and society—they'd kissed. Correction, he'd kissed her. She knew for certain now it meant nothing to him.

Theo had mistakenly enjoyed the brief moment...longed for it to happen again.

He obviously did not desire any such reoccurrence for an intimate moment.

It had meant less than nothing when it came to his sister's reputation.

His fearsome look said it would not come to pass again.

And that wounded her deeply, for reasons she had not time or energy to explore as yet.

She feared what Gladstone would voice to Cart—and if her brother would believe the vile man.

Theo was hard-pressed to believe Cart would side with another against her.

"I speak for no one but myself." It wasn't Theo's place to lead her friends into peril—no matter whose decision it was to help Mrs. Emmeline.

Alistair shook his head, a bitter smile of disappointment etched on his face. "That is wonderful, but I do pray you have thought of a backup plan if this foolhardy adventure causes hardship for each of you."

Josie clasped Theo's hand, ever the timid woman, the color draining from her face.

"Adeline." He turned to his sister. "Gather your things. Abel will see you home."

"Wait, no," Josie and Georgie cried in unison.

"She is to compete," Theo said. "Her fee is already paid."

Alistair turned sharply, his penetrating glare sending a shiver through her. "Then I suggest you take her place, as you took Lady Georgina's spot in the last tourney."

"But I cannot—"

"You will allow your friends to take the risk while you stay hidden and away from the view of society?" he accused.

"No, it is not like that..." Theo shook her head in a vain attempt to convince him to see reason.

"I do not mind overmuch what it is or isn't." He glanced over her shoulder as if she weren't standing before him. "Abel, please escort Adeline home and make sure she remains there until I arrive."

"Ah, Alistair." Abel lumbered over to the group. "Come on, why must I leave? The fun is only just beginning."

He was going to insist Adeline forfeit her place in the tourney; they would lose their money unless Theo or Josie took the empty spot.

Josie was frightened by her own shadow. No amount of confidence would help the woman stand before a crowd of hundreds.

"You cannot seek to order me about as if I do not have my own mind." Adeline's hands fell to her hips, her golden hair and defiant, icy stare trained on her brother. "I am a grown woman, out of the school room and prepared to enter my first season. I am not a child, and do not expect to be treated as such."

Alistair's shoulders stiffened, becoming so rigid she feared his body would crack from the tension.

"Adeline…" Theo stepped between the woman and her brother. "Georgie and I will compete, do not worry any further. Go home. I will send word when the day is done."

With one last scathing glare over Theo's shoulder, Adeline's resistance crumbled. They were no match for Mr. Price and his demands—at least where Adeline was concerned.

Theo gave Adeline a reassuring smile. "Do not fret. All hope is not lost."

"But you cannot be here—"

"We shall not dwell on that now." Theo could think of little else but her meeting with Cassini and his sister; her chance to discuss the changes necessary to create a topographical map that would help so many people. "Everything will continue as planned."

Her friends hadn't any idea what kept Theo from competing, only that she had a family obligation she was unable to miss. The thought of letting her friends down—or dashing their hopes of helping their beloved school—wounded Theo. She prayed it did not come to having to choose between two things that meant such a great deal to her.

"Adeline, go!" Alistair commanded, his tone letting Theo know there was no point in trying to persuade him.

"This is highly unfair, brother," Adeline sniffed before pulling from Theo's grasp and following Abel as they moved away from her. Alistair trailed the pair at a distance.

There was naught Theo could do but compete in Adeline's stead and pray her friend was able to slip from her brother's watch or that she was bested in the first or second round, leaving Georgie as their only hope. For a brief moment, she debated throwing the competition with a shot that was not likely to secure her a spot in the final round, but that was not in line with anything Theo could do. The guilt would hurt more than letting her friends down.

Theo took Adeline's bow and quiver from Josie. "Let us find our place in line," she said, determination filling her. She must prove she could best the other archers to win the prize purse, but that would mean sacrificing her dream of meeting with Cassini, thus eliminating any hope of her ideas being incorporated in his next edition of England's master guide of topographical maps. She would need faith that another opportunity to meet with Cassini would present itself in the future.

But she couldn't worry about that now. It was still two days away, and she must make it through several rounds before the possibility of missing her appointment came to light. At the moment, her larger concerns involved the two men who'd indisputably inserted themselves in her life without invitation.

If Mr. Gladstone—or Alistair, for that matter—thought they could dictate her future, they were going to find themselves sorely disappointed.

She was not to be the pliable, demure bride Gladstone sought.

Nor did she relish being a woman who would betray her friend's confidence, no matter Alistair had Adeline's best interests at heart.

Tomorrow, Theo would convince Gladstone she wasn't the woman he thought her to be—her dreams and plans for her life in no way aligned with his criteria for a wife. He would alter his pursuit of courtship to a woman far more consistent with the pious, obedient bride he desired.

As far as Alistair—Mr. Price—was concerned, their association had expired. There was little doubt Theo would see him and Adeline during the season, though there was no need for them to playact there was anything more than a passing acquaintance between them.

And their kiss…it must be forgotten.

As if it had never occurred.

As if her desires hadn't been awoken by their one chaste kiss.

As if, in that brief, startling moment outside her townhouse, her heart hadn't stopped beating.

Chapter Nineteen

"But what of you, Alistair?" Adeline pulled to a stop, stomping her foot. His sister had returned to the petulant young child she'd been when their father had sent her away to school almost eight years prior. "Why must I leave and you can stay?"

"Who said I am to stay?" he asked.

"Someone has to remain to make certain Theo, Georgie, and Josie arrive home safely, and you, being ever the *gentleman* to others besides your own kin, will see to them."

"So, I am the one being sent home?" This time the protest came from Abel. "I haven't disobeyed your commands—at least not today—why must I leave? The fourth round of archers is taking the field. I haven't seen anything but a bunch of overgrown children throwing fists at one another. We have established my skills as a nursemaid leave much to be desired. I am not the person to escort our disobedient sister home."

Alistair stared into the matching blue eyes of his younger siblings. He'd fully intended to escort the pair home and return to watch over Theo and the others, but Abel was more than capable of returning his hellion sister to their townhouse, no matter how much he spoke to the contrary.

Another trumpet blared, and a man called for the next set of archers.

"Oh, it is Theo's and Georgie's turn on the field," Adeline whined, grasping his arm. "Can we not stay for just this one round? I will go home with Abel willingly as soon as Theo and Georgie release their arrows."

"Yes, Price," Abel sided with Adeline.

Alistair was outnumbered—and likely to face a mutiny if he refused.

"We can stand just over there. No one will notice us." Abel stared expectantly.

Alistair glanced at the small break in the crowd with a view of the next set of archers taking their places, then back to his siblings. "We watch one round?" When Abel and Adeline nodded, he continued. "Adeline, you are to keep your hood raised…and Abel, you are to stay close by. You will depart immediately after this round."

"Of course." Their agreement was followed by Adeline's huge smile, knowing she'd won.

He would give her this small victory if it meant she would not despise him forever.

They squeezed between two groups of spectators close to the seating area, mainly occupied by other *ton* members. Alistair searched the seated audience for Gladstone, but failed to spot the man, though he noted several other men of his acquaintance. It was too much to hope Gladstone had departed the tourney altogether after Theo had rebuffed his advances.

"Oh, look," Adeline shouted, clapping her hands. "There they are, on the far end. They will be the final two archers this round."

He was unsure if he wanted Theo to do well or be outdone in the first round. She excelled at the sport, far more than anyone he'd met previously. Her victory at Whitechapel, no matter how much it incensed him, was well deserved...and earned from years of practice. Dedication such as Theo displayed was not a trait Alistair had witnessed in many men, let alone a woman of the *ton*.

He stood behind Adeline's cloaked figure, certain Lady Theo hadn't spotted him. He also kept watch over Lady Josephine where she stood in the archer's area, awaiting the pair.

The line of competitors took their turns, most hitting their target, if not sending their arrow through the center ring. The men would be little competition to Theo—a smile crossed his face at the thought. Very rarely did Alistair find moments when he wasn't being watched or observed, wasn't agonizing over the future of his family, wasn't meeting with his father's man of business—a time when he could stand with ease and allow his mind to wander.

Of late, he'd found his mind wandering at the most inopportune times, however, such as the carriage ride to and from Tattersall's. Abel had noticed but hadn't questioned him. Adeline and Abel's intense stares remained on the archers, and away from Alistair, which gave him time to inspect Theo at the far end. Though she was petite, her courage was mighty. She'd recovered from her near stumble with ease—and with enough wit to put Gladstone in his place.

Why Alistair had ever worried she'd allow herself to be led into a false sense of mutual affection by the scoundrel, Alistair would never know. He had faith—something he routinely lacked in himself—that she'd not allow her family to marry her off to the highest bidder.

It was not his place to be concerned in regards to Adeline's friends. His sister, and his other siblings were more hassle than he could muster the energy to wrestle. If he were to survive the season, he need focus on *his* responsibilities, not those of others.

Before long, the many archers had taken their aim and released their arrows, leaving only the two hooded lady archers on the end: Lady Georgina and Theodora.

Lady Georgina pulled her bowstring back, releasing her breath as she did, and sent her arrow flying. Alistair craned his neck to get a glimpse of her target. As anticipated, she'd sent her arrow through the red circle, though a little below the exact center of the target. That did not stop the crowd from applauding her effort and shouting their good tidings.

He leaned forward, whispering in Adeline's ear. "After Lady Theo releases her arrow, you and Abel are to depart."

"Of course, *dear* brother." She didn't bother glancing over her shoulder at him. "Now, do be quiet while she takes aim."

Perfectly reprimanded, Alistair stood tall to see over Abel's head as Theo prepared and hefted his childhood bow.

Even with her hood raised and the cloak's bulky set, Alistair could see that her form and stance were flawless. Her chin tilted up ever so slightly, causing him

242

to worry her hood would tumble back and reveal her face to the crowd. Immense satisfaction coursed through him at the sight of Theodora expertly holding his bow aloft.

The gawkers huddled around the brawling men earlier had been distracted, and he prayed no one had paid attention when Theo's hood was knocked from her head during the scuffle. That would leave only Gladstone to contend with, and there was little reason for him to reveal Theo's escapades, especially if he sought her hand in marriage.

The crowd gasped in unison. Alistair had been so preoccupied he'd utterly missed her shot.

"She did it!" Adeline shouted, covering her mouth to stifle her girlish, joyous outburst. "Theo is certainly the best archer in our group." Adeline turned a severe glare on her brothers. "If either of you tell her I said so, I will deny it…do you both hear me?"

"The woman is utterly perfect…captivating even," Abel sighed. "We should go congratulate her on a shot well placed."

"*We* shall do nothing of the sort," Alistair said, placing a hand on both their shoulders. "The pair of you will return home and send the carriage back to collect me." The difficult part of the day would greet him when he arrived home—addressing Abel and Adeline's fury over being thrown from the tourney grounds. He needed Adeline to understand the precarious position their family was in and agree to behave, or he'd have little choice but to return her—and their entire family—to the country. "Adeline, I will return after the day's competition is complete. We have much to discuss."

She didn't argue further, her arms falling listlessly to her sides. "Very well, brother. I shall heed your demand and return home, but please make sure Lady Theo arrives home as safely as I."

"That is my intention." That was Alistair's *only* intention. He would not repeat his past follies and attempt to pull her close—and by no means, would he kiss her. Not that she would entertain any such thing after his boorish behavior.

The pair had started toward the park entrance and the waiting Melton carriage before Alistair noted the significance of Adeline's comment.

Adeline had bid him deliver Lady Theo home safely, no mention of Lady Josephine or Georgina.

Certainly, Lady Theo hadn't told Adeline of their kiss.

Before he could gain her attention to ask, his siblings had disappeared into the crowd.

He turned back to see Theo and Lady Georgina, who'd returned to Lady Josephine's side as they huddled together, walking to the practice area to await the next round.

Alistair skirted the crowd in pursuit of the women, bows and quivers over their shoulders. The other archers practiced in hopes of improving their next shot.

Neither Theo nor Lady Georgina made any move to remove their bows and send a few arrows toward the worn targets, and the men preferred to act as if they didn't exist, that two hooded lady archers hadn't just bested them.

He'd laugh if he weren't worried about drawing attention. There was no need to irritate Theo further. If she sought to act as if she weren't in need of someone to watch over her, that was her right, but he would be unable to live with himself if he departed and something untoward happened to her—to any of them.

Adeline attributed his concern to his upbringing as a gentleman, and no doubt she was partly correct. However, it went far deeper than a proper rearing by their parents. His muscles tensed, and his fists itched to lash out when he remembered the sight of Gladstone attempting to drag Theo away. There was no denying the man had saved her from tumbling into the pile of belligerent men, but that had been where his good deeds and intentions ended. Alistair shuddered to think what Gladstone would've done if Alistair hadn't been present. It certainly would not be above Gladstone to drag Theo back to her family home and insist she be more properly escorted and watched. Ever the hypocritical, righteous man.

He was no more pious than Alistair was the indifferent viscount-to-be. His chest tightened with foreboding at Gladstone's promise to call on Lady Theodora the next day. Alistair wanted the man nowhere near Theo, though he told himself he'd have the same reaction to Gladstone being around his sister or one of her other friends. Gladstone's only concern was in keeping Theo's reputation and name unsullied. Arguably, Alistair's intentions, as well, though not because he had any designs on wedding the woman. Clearly, that was Gladstone's ulterior motive. He no doubt saw Theo as his chance to climb the social ladder and enter the *ton*. As brother-in-law to an earl, his membership at White's would be reinstated with no chance of it being revoked again. His creditors would look the other way at his insurmountable debts, planning to address their notes with Theo's brother, Lord Cartwright. And what option would Cartwright have but to settle the debts or risk bringing scandal to his family?

Alistair's interest in Theo only went so far as to make certain Gladstone did not dig his claws into her. The woman deserved so much more, and would find no happiness with a scoundrel for a husband. Any man worth his salt would do the same.

At least, that's what Alistair tried to convince himself as he blended into the crowd and awaited Theo's next turn with her bow.

# # #

As Alistair anticipated, both Theo and Lady Georgina continued to release their arrows with steadfast accuracy any archer would find daunting to sustain. He'd watched the tourney from his position in the crowd as the lady archers continued to dazzle and enthrall the captivated crowd of both peers and commoners. They'd been dubbed the Dashing Lady Archers by the second round, and now, as they completed their fourth time before the targets, the crowd chanted loudly for the pair. With ease, they released their final arrows for the day, each finding the exact center of the target and solidifying their continued participation in the tourney.

The pair embraced quickly before leaving the field and returning to Lady Josephine's side. The trio moved swiftly through the gathering crowd of spectators coming to give their congratulations on a successful tourney day—or comfort the men whose arrows hadn't found their mark.

Alistair kept pace with the women as they moved along the fringes of the park toward their waiting carriage.

He quickened his pace as the women arrived, handing their bows and givers to the waiting servant. Stepping from the crowd as the man opened the carriage door and step down the steps.

"Allow me," Alistair offered, holding his hand out to assist the women into their conveyance. Lady Josie and Lady Georgie's eyes rounded in shock as their mouths gaped, unable to turn away his offer, while Lady Theo only looked on, amused. "I extend my services as chaperone to see you all safely home."

Lady Theo laid her arms across her chest. "Is it due to the fact that you sent Adeline and your brother home in your carriage, sir?"

Alistair made a production of looking up and down the long row of waiting coaches, his nowhere in sight. "I am certain it is here somewhere; however, what sort of gentleman would I be if I did not accompany the trio of you to your doorsteps?" he asked, a brow raised in question.

"I assure you, the trio of us would not think any less of you, Mr. Price."

"Be that as it may, I would think less of myself," he countered. He risked a glance at Lady Josie and Georgie to see they'd recovered enough to close their mouths, but still gazed between Theo and him in shock. "Lady Josephine, may I assist you into the carriage?"

The woman glanced to Theo for her approval.

"Come now, my lady," Alistair prodded, issuing his most dashing smile. "If we do not depart with all haste, we may very well be caught in a horde of carriages moving through the London streets."

Lady Josephine gave in and took his hand, stepping up into the carriage, Lady Georgina following quickly. Lady Theo reluctantly took his offered help and joined her friends. He stepped into the carriage to find all three woman sharing the rear facing seat. They appeared quite crammed, not unlike a tin of sardines.

"I do not bite." Alistair harnessed the chuckle that threatened to escape him. He would allow the trio to travel in discomfort if they so chose. Meanwhile, he settled into the seat across from them, stretching out his legs to accommodate his height as all three women had tucked their legs close.

"Now, who are we to drop off first?" He glanced between the women as the carriage pulled into traffic.

"Me," Lady Georgie and Lady Josie said in unison.

Alistair did laugh at that. "You all would likely jump from the moving carriage rather than enjoy your short jaunt with me as chaperone?"

"They likely do not agree with your heavy-handed manners, Mr. Price," Theo volunteered.

"And you, my lady?" he inquired. "Do you enjoy my heavy-handed tendencies?"

"There is little need to make Josie and Georgie uncomfortable. We have agreed to allow you to see us home safely."

He would not point out not one of them had willingly agreed to anything, but seemed more fearful of what he'd do if they denied him. However, he allowed them to sit in silence as they traveled into London proper and across Piccadilly Street.

"My house in only two down," Lady Georgina replied. "If you will drop me at the street, Josie and I will see ourselves inside."

The carriage slowed, and Alistair called to the driver to remain on the road.

The women scampered quickly out of the carriage and collected their things from the boot before hurrying to the door of the residence.

"That was uncalled for, Alistair." Theo moved to the center of the velvet covered bench. "I think you possibly frightened poor Josie half to death."

"They should be terrified," he countered, pulling his feet in and sitting forward. "If it is determined you were at Greenwich without a proper chaperone and surrounded by men of undeterminable scruples, it will be all of our undoing."

When she only glared at him, Alistair sighed.

"What? Am I not falling in line and doing as you bid with enough swiftness?"

"I am worried, that is all."

"That is kind of you, but you needn't worry." She relaxed a bit, her shoulders not quite as rigid, and her eyes not as glaring. "I am a superb markswoman, as is your sister."

"I meant no affront, Theo." Alistair's mouth grew dry as he scrambled to collect his thoughts. "I've seen your skill, and it is far superior to mine. I can appreciate that, but I was speaking to your independent nature. While I sincerely appreciate a person—man or woman—who can adequately care for themselves, a group of proper ladies in a less than savory part of town is just not acceptable."

"I have been caring for myself for quite some time." Theo smirked. "And I do not see that changing in the foreseeable future. Maybe you should give Adeline a chance to show you she can do the same."

Alistair slipped his hands into his pockets to avoid reaching out to her—pulling her to him. Setting his lips upon hers.

And never letting go.

Her confidence drew him, as he so lacked his own fortitude of late. His admiration of her swelled, though he did not dare speak of it.

"We are almost at my townhouse," she said, pulling him from his musings.

Alistair pulled the curtain back and shouted for the driver to halt.

"Mr. Price?" Theo grabbed for the seat as the carriage came to a sudden stop, just out of sight from her townhouse. "My heavens, what are you doing?"

Alistair opened the carriage door and jumped to the ground. "Cannot have me seen in your drive, my lady. What will your family think?" He winked. "I shall continue home on foot. Farewell, Lady Theo."

With a dashing bow, he slammed the carriage door shut and called for the driver to continue on.

Thankfully, the day was mild, and a brisk wall would do him good. He looked in the direction of his own townhouse before glancing over his shoulder toward her carriage that was pulling into her drive. She'd pulled back the drapery and watched him. With a final wave, he turned and started off.

The short walk home left him little time to ponder his motivations for keeping watch over Lady Theo. She didn't require his assistance; she'd made that clear on several occasions. And after Adeline's departure with Abel, there'd been no reason to remain at the tourney. However, he'd been unable to convince himself to leave, part of him wanting to see how she fared in the following rounds, and another part wanting a few more moments in her presence, even though she was shrouded in a cloak and positioned across the tourney field from him. He could imagine the tilt of her chin, the sparkle in her brown eyes, and the set of her lips— compressed tightly together in concentration.

Alistair had no right to think of her lips, squeezed in concentration *or* pressed against his for a delicate kiss.

Lady Theodora was not his to dream of or lust after. She was not a common trollop, and he had other duties that more than occupied his every moment. But the challenge in her eyes and the smirk on her lips when she issued a witty retort were hard to forget.

Entering his townhouse, Alistair was first assaulted by the sheer quietness within its walls. With nine Melton siblings in residence, their home was never without laughing, shouting, arguing, or running feet. Occasionally, all four at one time. After the echo of the closing front door receded, Alistair stood stock-still but heard nothing.

No laughter. No arguing. No piano from the drawing room. No running feet. No slamming doors. No arithmetic or poem recitation.

Nothing.

"Mr. Price," his butler said, clearing his throat. "This came for you while you were out."

Alistair glanced at the envelope, delicately placed in the center of the silver tray, his mother's familiar elegant penmanship appearing bolder than normal against the crisp white paper.

"Thank you, Squires," Alistair said, taking the letter and slipping it into his pocket. If his mother was writing, it must be good news. "I will be—"

"Your siblings await your attendance in the study."

The study? Only business and scolding were issued in his office—correction, Lord Melton's study.

"Should I be worried?" he asked.

"I would not know, sir." But the man was unable to meet Alistair's stare.

"Very well." Alistair gave an uneasy laugh. "Do send in help if we have not disbanded by mealtime."

The servant's eyes rounded, and Alistair clapped him on the shoulder in good humor. A good humor Alistair was not certain he felt.

But there was no avoiding his family.

Alistair started down the corridor toward his father's study, unprepared for what would greet him.

The door stood wide, revealing all eight of his siblings. His four youngest sisters were positioned on the low sofa closest to the windows overlooking the stables. Each dressed in varying shades of pastel, they appeared like a springtime bazaar. Adrian and Alfred sat on the rug in front of the desk, playing with wooden men, their British soldiers proudly in red. Abel paced before the unlit hearth, not noticing Alistair had entered the room.

Adeline notched her chin up defiantly from her position behind his father's desk, arms crossed. If looks could wound, hers would strike him dead in his tracks.

"What is this about?" He moved farther into the room, dropping into the single chair positioned before the desk Adeline sat behind. "Are we gathered to discuss your mutual displeasure with me?"

Adrian and Alfred shrugged as if unconcerned with anything except the current battle between their wooden men on the floor.

Alistair looked to Arabella, Adelaide, Amelia, and Ainsley on the sofa, but none met his stare, each occupied with their own musings or fidgeting with their skirts.

Strange. Though Adeline found great discord with her eldest sibling, the younger females in his house generally sought out his attentions. Unease filled him at the sight of all his siblings in one room, no one saying a word. No arguing. No elbowing one another. No teasing or jeering.

The mood was bleak, and Alistair's mouth set in a straight line as he tugged at his coat, straightening it from the carriage ride.

Abel had yet to cease his pacing long enough to speak—or so much as acknowledge Alistair's presence.

"Adeline." He adjusted in his seat to face his unruly sister. "I presume you are responsible for this gathering. Please state your purpose so we may all return to our day. I am certain the children still have lessons to study, and Arabella and Adelaide's musical tutor should be arriving any moment."

As if on cue, his siblings stood to depart.

"Wait," Adeline shouted, holding up her hand to stop them all from fleeing the coming battle. "This concerns all of us, not only me."

"Do not be ridiculous, Adeline." Abel threw his arms wide with annoyance. "You are the only one causing us trouble." Alistair wanted to pat Abel on the back for his support, but drew up short when next *he* received a scathing look. "We were having a marvelous time at Tattersall's with a trip to White's this evening, but you had to go and ruin it all. I do not favor being assigned as your companion. And Alistair," Abel said, moving to stand before his eldest brother, "if Adeline is determined to ruin her good name, let her do as she pleases. I shall not waste my time in London locked in this townhouse in an effort to keep an eye on her."

He didn't wait for Alistair to reply before nodding to Alfred and Adrian and departing the room.

His sisters followed suit, closing the door behind them, leaving only him and Adeline.

"Traitors," she mumbled, pushing her chair back to stand.

"You cannot fault them for not wishing to be in the middle of another of our arguments." Alistair reclined in the chair, crossing his ankles. He was ready for another long shouting match that would end with Adeline reluctantly agreeing to behave, and Alistair promising to curb his high-handedness. The truce would be forgotten within a day, and they'd have the same confrontation again within a fortnight.

It was the way of their youth…and the path their adult relationship would continue down.

"Will you ever see me as an adult, able to make my own decisions?" she asked with a sigh. "Trust me enough to know I would not willingly and recklessly shame our family. Is that too much to ask?"

Alistair was stunned into silence, his anger disappearing with each word. It was the most rational argument she'd set before him in all her years. Normally, she yelled, screamed, and cried to get her outlandish point heard, but today, she spoke like a sensible woman—a grown woman, ready for her society debut.

And he was at a total loss for how to react. No part of him wanted to admit he'd overreacted or that she'd matured without him noticing the transformation.

"Theo, Georgie, Josie, and I are trying to help Miss Emmeline and her school, a place we all dearly love and hope our daughters will someday enjoy. But with the limited funds the school receives from parents, Headmistress is unable to perform general upkeep of the property. The roofs need patching, the stables need new fencing, the dormitory needs new beds, and the classrooms would benefit from a fresh coat of paint. Are you willing to donate the funds needed for all of this?"

It was the same story he'd heard from Theo's lips only hours before.

Theo's lips…

He shook the wayward thought from his mind. "You know Mother and Father barely collected enough coin to pay for your schooling," Alistair said. "At the moment, I am uncertain if boarding school will be an option for your sisters. What about Lady Georgina's father? He is a duke, why not ask him for help before risking your reputations?"

Adeline frowned. "His new duchess has withheld anything but the bare necessities from Georgie for her upcoming season. Her Grace, Duchess Balfour, is with child, and they have every hope that the child will be the future heir to the Dukedom."

"What of Lady Josephine?" Alistair knew nothing of the woman—her family or financial position.

Adeline laughed, finding something humorous in his question. "She is worse off than we are, Alistair. Her father passed away, leaving her mother to care for them all, her guardian only giving enough coin for Josie's continued education. She will likely not be presented to society at the start of the season, but married to the quickest bidder."

She stared at him, waiting for him to say something, anything. But Alistair couldn't give her the reply she sought, and for that, he was conflicted. It would put his entire family at risk. But he owed her something...even if it was only to commend the good deed she'd set out to accomplish.

"Do you understand that our plan must succeed?" she prodded.

"I do, but I still cannot allow it to continue." If it were in his power, he'd tell her to do whatever was needed, but he was not even remotely influential with the *ton*. A Viscountship on the verge of poverty did not make the rules, nor risk breaking them.

"Why ever not?" Her over-bright stare silently pleaded with him.

"Bloody hell, because I care too much about your future," he confessed. And he cared too damned much about Theo's. His feigned relaxed posture fled, but he continued, "This family means far too much to me."

Not Lady Theodora. Not Lady Theodora's family or future, but his own family's prospects. He repeated the words over and over in his mind, hoping they'd take root and return him to his senses.

"Father entrusted me with the duty of presenting you to society while caring for Abel and the others," he continued once he had his rebellious thoughts under control. "You cannot fault me for attempting to secure the future you deserve, Adeline."

"Even if it is not a future of my choosing?"

"You have no idea what the future of your choosing resembles." Alistair stood, pacing before the hearth, following Abel's exact path. "I can assure you a future locked away in the country would not be to your liking. I can guarantee a future wedded to a man seeking a marriage into the *ton* or a bride of convenience will not make you happy." He sighed, his tone softening. "And I can promise you a forced marriage to a commoner would be filled with a life of hardships I will not be able to rescue you from."

He needed her to understand—silently begged her to see reason as she wordlessly begged *him* to understand *her* reasoning.

"And what of you and Lady Theo?" Her change in topic took him off guard, exactly as she'd planned he suspected from her intense expression.

"What of Lady Theo? There is no 'me and Lady Theo.'"

"Do you think I have not noticed the way your eyes follow her, or how you stand a bit taller when she is around?" she asked. "She may not notice, but I do. And Alistair?"

"Yes," he replied, preparing himself for her sharp retort to stay away from her dear friend, that an overbearing, insufferable man like he was not the correct fit for a woman as perfect as Theodora. These were all things he was already aware of, and he despised it. He didn't want to hear her state the obvious truth, the thing Alistair had shied away from since he'd met Theo. She was a headstrong, determined, intelligent sister of an earl, while he was the heir to an almost impoverished estate with eight siblings depending on him—and him alone. There was nothing he could offer a woman like Lady Theodora.

"I will not have you setting your aim on my dear friend," Adeline said softly. "The pair of you would not suit well. Keep your attentions where they belong, on making a successful season for me."

"If it is any interest to you, Lady Theodora and Lady Georgina were triumphant and will compete again on the morrow." Alistair hoped his comment distracted her enough from her previous train of thought, though if she begged him to return to the tourney the following day, he would likely not give in to her request.

"I have already received word of that, not that I expected any other outcome." With a smug smile, she stood. It was nothing like any argument they'd had in the past. Her words were spoken with no yelling; to the point, and her threat unveiled. Her brother would need time, and silence, to come to terms with his shifted priorities and the new path his sister had openly said was denied to him. A future he dared not hope would come to fruition, for that would only increase the hurt when it was taken from him.

Alistair was certain of one thing: he owed Lady Theo an apology. For his brutish and intolerable attitude, his high-handed manner, and for thinking he had any right to command her about and involve himself in her daily life. And to make it all the worse, he'd unwittingly thought to turn Theo against her dear friend. He should have found solace in knowing a person cared as deeply about Adeline as he did, enough to keep his sister's confidence when it would have been so easy to alert Alistair of Adeline's whereabouts, allowing him to handle her unruliness.

He hadn't trusted Adeline nor treated her as an equal, so had he perpetuated the behavior with Theo.

She was a grown woman, an intelligent lady who likely had her life more in line than Alistair could ever hope to achieve in the next fifteen years. His entire existence was a burden—not him, exactly, but the family he brought with him. They were inexplicably tied together, a package of sorts. A daunting task to care for them all…something he wouldn't wish on anyone.

Which was why Alistair needed to push any thoughts of Lady Theo from his mind. Certainly, he owed her an apology and confirmation he would not trespass in her life again, but that was all he was able to give her.

"I will leave you to your ponderings." Adeline moved toward the door with nary a sound. "Good day, brother."

Alone, the weight of his responsibilities settled on him—heavier than a thousand stones of sand.

Alistair was tired. No, not just tired, he was exhausted.

"Maybe a bit of rest," he mumbled to the empty room. Though his hand instinctively reached into his pocket, retrieving the letter from his mother. If it held good news, then certainly his relief would aid his rest, allowing him to find a deep slumber he'd been unable to obtain since arriving in London.

He slipped his finger under the wax seal with his family crest, breaking it easily and removing a single folded slip of paper.

Not a long note. Mayhap his mother was only informing him she would journey to London after all, and Alistair could soon relax, knowing the viscountess would arrive before long and rein in her many children.

His hopes were dashed as he unfolded the letter to see many of the words smudged.

She'd cried when writing him.

There was no other explanation for the droplets that had marred his mother's perfect script, making several words undecipherable.

My Dearest Son,

I know the burden I've placed upon you is one of great obligation and sacrifice. For that, I will be forever sorry and in your debt. However, I would never forgive myself if I were not at your father's side during his time of need. My children need me, as well. This I understand, but when a person truly finds love, they will make many sacrifices others may not truly comprehend. This is my time to sacrifice. But I am blessed beyond measure with an honorable son, Alistair. I have no fear or unease, knowing you are caring for my babies. I hope we are all reunited before the season is over. Please do not speak of your father's declining health with the others. The weight may very well be too much for them to carry.

Take heart, my dear, sweet boy.

My love,

Mother

Damn it, but Alistair understood every word she'd written, the concept of an affection so great one would sacrifice everything to hold onto it, keep it close…and alive. He'd thought his mother neglectful and selfish. In a way, she was being exactly that, but not in her eyes. She was unwilling to sacrifice her remaining days with the man she loved.

The viscountess was correct: her children needed her—her guidance, her love, and her support here in London. She'd journeyed through the *ton*, causing quite a stir during her first season, even capturing the eye of a viscount, his father. It should be her duty to help Adeline successfully navigate the intricacies of society.

Alistair was unprepared and lacking in many ways. His siblings were besting him in every way, and he feared his hold on them would not last until his mother could be with them once more.

Would the day come he would make a similar decision for the woman he loved?

He shook his head. He had many years yet to explore that question.

Slipping the letter back in its envelope, Alistair set it on his desk, ready for a few moment's rest. Certainly, he could sacrifice a few hours to slumber.

Chapter Twenty

Theo rushed from her dressing closet and glanced around her bedchambers for the fourth time in the last several minutes. Her desk was strewn with books and maps spread wide from the previous night's work by candlelight. Her boots from the day before were aligned neatly against the wall with her gloves on her side table. Her bed cover lay askew, as Daisy hadn't called on her mistress as yet. The only place she hadn't searched was *under* her bed. Dropping to her hands and knees, she lifted the edge of the bedcovering and stared into the dark space below. Nothing. Not a single dust mite or misplaced hair ribbon.

A loud gong sounded below stairs, followed by the echo of a knock at the front door.

Georgie and Josie must be early to collect her for the tourney. Of all the times for Georgie to be prepared and arrive on time, today was the day Theo wished she'd be late.

Where had Daisy put her cloak?

Theodora

After the incident yesterday, Theo feared her name would be reported in the morning's *Post*, but other than a short article summarizing the Grand Archers' Competition and detailing the number of entering contestants and the forecast for the remaining two days of competition, there'd been no mention of any lady archers.

She pushed to her feet, her hair falling into her face. She huffed, attempting to blow the tendrils from her eyes.

Of all the days for her cloak to go missing.

Theo snatched a ribbon from her dressing table and hastily tied her hair back, unconcerned with her messy locks, knowing it would be hidden under her hood—if she ever located the thing.

"Lady Theodora?" a light voice squeaked. "I did not expect you to be dressed so early. You were up awfully late working."

She turned to see Daisy standing in the doorway. "Oh, heavens. Where is my cloak?"

"It is downstairs," her maid said. "I had it cleaned last night. The hem was filthy, and I feared the material would stain if left to sit. My apologies for not attending to you sooner, my lady."

"I am quite capable of dressing myself, Daisy. Do not fret, I would have rung for you if it were necessary." Theo glanced in her mirror, confirming her hair was tied securely and her linen shirt buttoned to her throat and neatly tucked into the waistband of her riding skirt. The attire was non-constraining and allowed Theo the freedom to pull her bowstring back without fear of tearing her shirt.

"My lady," Daisy cleared her throat. "You have a visitor downstairs."

"Yes, I know," Theo snatched the drawstring bag that held enough coin for a meal while at Greenwich Park and made to leave the room. "Of all the days for Georgie and Josie to be early. Please tell them I will be right down and to await me in the carriage." She gave Daisy a peck on the cheek before slipping past her and out the door.

Her jovial mood for the day ahead was undeniable. It had felt amazing to take the field the day before, to allow her skill with a bow to be appreciated by such a wide array of spectators. Not that Theo desired affirmation from others. Certainly not. She was most commonly the woman noticed last when in Adeline, Josie, and Georgie's company—always overlooked, though she didn't think that a horrible thing, especially the previous day.

After spending several hours noting all the details she would speak with Cassini about when they met, Theo had crawled into bed exhausted; however, she'd been unable to find solace in slumber. She'd lain awake for hours, assessing every shot she'd taken, and thinking through ways to better her stance. It was highly improbable Adeline would successfully slip from her home, and that left Theo to continue in her place. Much rested on her and Georgie's shoulders. If they failed, all the money they'd collected for Miss Emmeline would be gone, with no time to gather more. They'd agreed to compete only until the season officially began.

Their free time would be scarce between morning social calls, afternoon tea, rides in Hyde Park, and their many evening engagements. There would be no hope of morning practices.

She hadn't time to dwell on her appointment with Cassini and his sister the following day. She would find a way to accomplish both, even if Adeline were unable to escape and compete in the final.

Theo bounded down the stairs to meet Georgie and Josie in the carriage. They would arrive at the tourney grounds earlier today and find a more secluded place to wait their turn. It was highly doubtful another fight would ensue between their male competitors, but the trio had decided to take no added risks as there would be no one present to protect them today.

"Let me collect my cloak and gear and we can depart," Theo called, turning on the final landing and taking the remaining stairs in one leap. "They are just over—"

Theo stopped in her tracks, her booted feet skidding across the polished floor.

"Lady Theodora, good day to you." Mr. Gladstone stood, clutching a rather sad display of wilting flowers before him, hiding his paunch from sight.

An older woman, a decade older than Theo's mother, stood at his side. Her hair was pinned back in a severe knot, and a gown of the darkest grey clung to her rail-thin body from toes to chin, a white ruffle decorating the high collar the only frill. The pointed tips of walking boots peeked from below her floor-length hem. The only adornment to the drab gown was a golden broach secured at her neck.

"May I introduce my dear mother, Mrs. Eugenia Gladstone," Gladstone said, his lips parting in a forced smile. "Mother, this is Lady Theodora."

"Dear," the woman said by way of greeting, her mouth remaining in a grim line. "It has been many years since we met." Mrs. Gladstone's eyes traveled from Theo's messily tied locks to her sturdy boots. "You were a precocious child, and I can see boarding school has only added to your uninhibited nature."

Theo had never been called uninhibited before, and she quite liked the term—especially in reference to herself; however, the icy stare Mrs. Gladstone gave her said she'd meant it as anything but a compliment.

She turned to Gladstone before continuing, "Do make note that Miss Emmeline's School of Education and Decorum for Ladies of Outstanding Quality is not the place for future Gladstone females. This one will need a firm hand, Ollie."

Theo stifled a gasp at the woman's cut, aimed directly at her upbringing. And *Ollie*? Did the woman mean it as an endearing pet name? Because the name only brought to mind a floppy-eared, flea-ridden mongrel.

"Mrs. Gladstone. Eugenia," Dowager Lady Cartwright called, entering the foyer. "So lovely of you to call. I must say I was thrilled to receive your request for an audience. The season has yet to start."

It was an odd greeting for two matrons who never left town, the beginning and ending of the season meant nothing to their visiting schedules.

The pair turned to her mother as she sashayed to Theo's side, a welcoming smile on her face, causing a sense of apprehension in Theo. Her mother rarely smiled, and never moved faster than her normal sedated, elegant pace. She infused each step with the poise and grace befitting her social status. A grace Theo had never mastered, much to her mother's purported derision. Her mother's leisurely steps often extended their shopping excursions by hours—dreadfully inconvenient for Theo.

"Lady Cartwright," Mrs. Gladstone said, nodding. "I have not seen you at Chrissely's House in nearly a fortnight. Did you forget your charitable deeds are much needed?"

A blush swam across her mother's face and crept down her neck as if she were ten and receiving a scolding from her school teacher. Her mother had never been so soundly rebuffed, which begged the question of why the dowager sought the companionship of such a severe, disagreeable woman.

Anastasia Montgomery straightened her shoulders, a measure of pride returning—normally never one to cower before another. "Theodora is newly returned from Canterbury, and I have been busily preparing for her coming out. There have been so many engagements with the dressmaker, the stationery shop, the cobbler…and do not get me started on the hat maker. It is all so overwhelming." Lady Cartwright rambled on, something Theo was not accustomed to her formidable mother doing. Maybe Anastasia had changed during her extended absences from London.

Was this the type of submissive behavior that would be expected of her if their mothers settled on a match between her and Gladstone? No one would label Theo as outspoken or opinionated, but to be relegated to a position of no consequence was not a fate she would ever accept. Nor would Cart expect her to agree to a future as the forgotten, subservient wife of Mr. Oliver Gladstone—Ollie.

Her stomach turned at the thought. Nothing like the wings that fluttered when her mind touched on Alistair.

She looked between her mother and Mr. Gladstone and his mother, attempting to keep the dumbfounded expression from overtaking her face. The mother and son stood far too closely. Theo half expected Gladstone to rest his head in his mother's shoulder.

"Do go on, Ollie." Mrs. Gladstone set her hand at the base of her son's back and pushed him forward. "Give Lady Theodora her gift."

He almost tripped over his own feet with the abrupt force behind his mother's shove, but he righted himself and held the wilting flowers out to Theo—buds of blue and orange mixed with leafy, green stems. The combination of colors was no more harmonious than she and Mr. Gladstone would be as a pair. The flowers clashed with one another, fighting for control but none succeeding.

"I handpicked these flowers for you." He held the offending arrangement out for her to take.

She wanted to ask when, exactly, he'd picked the flowers, as they all appeared well past their prime, but no matter her feelings, she'd been raised to be gracious, and so, she took the flowers with an unsteady smile. "Thank you, Mr. Gladstone."

"Let us find a suitable vase for your generous gift, Oliver," the Dowager Lady Cartwright said, taking the bouquet. A footman appeared at her side and whisked the offending buds from the room. "Come, we can retire to my drawing room for our visit."

Theo hadn't the time to spare for a social call, but her mother nodded down the hall. With one last longing look at the front door—and her means of escape—she acquiesced.

The dowager ushered them into her private room, immediately offering Gladstone the chair Mr. Price had occupied several days prior. Alistair's weight was almost enough to cause the Queen Anne to crumble beneath him. Theo shuddered to think what Gladstone's added girth would do to the chair; however, except for a groan of protest—which may have come from Gladstone and not the piece of furniture—the man settled, his grin returning.

The women each took a seat on a long chaise lounge, leaving only a small settee for Theo to perch on, a low table separating the group.

Theo glanced at the clock behind Gladstone, noting the time to depart for the tourney was almost upon her. Georgie and Josie would arrive at any moment, and it was likely her mother would forbid her from leaving until after Gladstone and his mother had satisfied their reason for calling.

Theo assessed the trio as they exchanged eye contact, not saying a word. She had the impression she was the only one in attendance who was unaware of the purpose of their visit. Gladstone would not have spoken of her unchaperoned excursion to the tourney in Greenwich Park. It would cast an unfavorable light on her, which would be all that was needed for his mother to turn her sights elsewhere for a bride for him—not to mention, her mother would have punished her severely if she knew of Theo's escapades about London.

If that were what it took to dissuade Gladstone's pursuit of her, then maybe Theo would benefit from tattling on herself. Banished to her room meant no further contact with *Ollie*.

Mrs. Gladstone cleared her throat, making the silence that had descended on the room all the more prominent and unavoidable.

Instead of speaking, Gladstone rushed to his feet, the front button of his jacket straining at the movement. Theo kept her eye on the rounded knob, prepared to shield her face if the thing burst free from its thread and shot across the room. An injured eye was certain to hinder her aim with a bow.

She couldn't help but think if this were what awaited her during the upcoming season—day after day of endless, mundane social visits with people she had nothing in common with—she may very well throw herself at Cart's feet and beg to depart London.

"Mr. Gladstone?" Theo asked as the man stood before her, his protruding belly only inches from her face, the button straining to be free almost in her eye.

"Do not say a word, Lady Theodora—Theo," he gushed, glancing over his shoulder to their mothers. The women nodded, giving Oliver the confidence he seemed to be lacking all of a sudden. "Will you stand, please?"

Theo pushed to her feet, Gladstone not moving an inch to allow her room, his face now as close as his belly had been a moment before. The image of him gripping her arm and pulling her away from her friends at the tourney sent a cold shiver through her.

Something brushed the side of her skirt, and it took her a moment to realize that Gladstone was searching for her hand, which she kept safely hidden in the folds of her gown behind her back.

"Mr. Gladstone, what is the meaning of this?" She stepped to the side, putting distance between them, but he moved with her. "Do allow me room to breathe, sir."

"Shhhh, Theodora," the dowager hissed. "Mr. Gladstone is trying to speak."

He reached behind her and clasped his clammy fingers about her wrist, drawing her hand between them. He ran his calloused fingers over her palm. "As I was saying," he started again with a sigh, as if she'd purposely interrupted him. "Lady Theodora, we have not been acquainted long, but I find my heart seeks your presence at every moment of every day."

"What?" The hair on the back of her neck stood on end, and her stomach rolled. Theo leaned back, her senses inundated with the smell of his hair oil, making her nauseous.

"Be quiet, Theodora!" her mother insisted.

"Manners, they are certainly lacking in today's young women," Mrs. Gladstone huffed. "A man cannot even offer a marriage proposal without being waylaid."

"Marriage proposal?" Theo squeaked, pulling her hand from his grasp. "No...I...no...does Cart know of this?"

"Anastasia," Mrs. Gladstone said. "Let us leave the happy couple to speak privately while we call for tea to celebrate the coming union of our families, shall we?"

"No." Theo stepped around Gladstone toward her mother. "We do not need—"

"Theodora," her mother scolded. "Mr. Gladstone is not finished speaking. We will return shortly, dear."

Theo watched helplessly as the two women stood, exchanged a knowing look, and departed the room, solidly closing the door in their wake.

The room spun around her, and Theo feared she'd be sick all over her mother's favorite rug. It was all the dowager deserved for tricking her in such a cruel manner.

She was uncertain how long she stared at the closed door, waiting for the room to still around her, but the silence seemed to span into eternity, or mayhap it was her mind blocking everything out, refusing to hear Gladstone's words.

Everything was completely still and silent around her, but her mind was screaming in warning. It pushed her to leave, run as far and as fast as she could...find Jude or Cart, they would make this right.

"Lady Theodora?" he asked. She flinched, pulling her arm away when he set his hand on her. He pulled back, showing Theo the first hint of uncertainty she'd ever witnessed in him—except where his mother was concerned. Theo turned back to him, a blank expression on her face. "As I was saying—"

"Please, stop, Mr. Gladstone." Theo despised the desperation in her voice, hated the way her arm shook when he'd touched her, and knew without a doubt the man saw it as her weakness. "I have much to do today—"

"Continue in the Grand Archers' Competition?" he inquired with a sneer, his hand snapping forward to clasp her arm. "You will not be going. It is exceedingly unfitting for a lady of your station—the future Mrs. Gladstone."

Theo pushed the unease away with a soft chuckle at the lunacy of his comment. Her trembling halted, and she turned an icy stare on Gladstone. "Thankfully, my movements are of no concern to you." She refused to address his insinuation that they would ever be wed.

"Oh, but they are." At her puzzled looked, he continued. "Our mothers have settled on our match. At this very moment, they expect I am in here, reciting the loveliest of proposals, and you, dear Theodora, are accepting my offer graciously. Possibly even thanking me with a kiss."

Theo shook her head, her hair falling free from its ribbon.

"But I am not going to hassle with all those pretty, fanciful notions by proclaiming my never-dying love for you, how I can't see my life without you…how I see you raising our children in the future, and the importance and pride I will feel with you by my side." He paused with a huff. "Oh, no. We both know that your false propriety and unladylike activities eliminated the need for a proper proposal, but you shall accept our betrothal nonetheless."

"I will not, I do not—" She struggled to draw breath. "No…"

His hand fell away from her arm, and he laughed, a deep, malevolent chuckle without any hint of decency. "You have no other option, Lady Theodora."

"That is not true." Theo tilted her chin in defiance. Gladstone was intimidating her into accepting his proposal, but she would not. She could not. "I must speak with my brother."

"Oh, the good Lord Cartwright, is it?" he asked. "Yes, we have not had occasion to meet, but I am certain he will find joy in our union."

"He will find no happiness in a marriage I am not agreeable to." Theo took a step toward the door, ready to find Cart and end this travesty for good. "I will send for him now."

"But you are agreeable to the union, Lady Theodora. In fact, you are so overjoyed and blissfully excited to be my wife, the newest Mrs. Gladstone, that we've decided to dispel with the reading of the banns and gain a special license from the Archbishop to wed immediately. I will handle the details of this, do not fret." The cold finality in his words and stance frightened Theo, as if he knew something she wasn't privy to.

"Why would you ever think I would agree to any match that includes a man such as you?"

"And what type of man do you see me as?" he asked.

"A scoundrel...a coward...a debauched reprobate." Her head swam with a hundred more words to express her dislike of Gladstone. His furious glare sent a chill through her, halting her momentarily. "A man not worthy of any lady's hand," Theo whispered.

"Then allow me to persuade you." Gladstone resumed his seat while Theo stood, her instincts telling her to flee while she could, but it was likely her mother and Mrs. Gladstone stood outside, their ears pressed to the door. "If you do not agree to wed me, I will go to *The Post* with your identity as Lady Archer in both the Whitechapel—"

Theo sucked in a deep breath, averting her stare from his.

"Oh, you were unaware that I knew of it?" His brow rose. "I make it my duty to be informed of everything and everyone whose movements affect me. Let us return to my point. I will go to *The Post* with information about the Lady Archer from Whitechapel and the Grand Archers' Competition. Your name and portrait will be everywhere before the season starts."

His haughty smile said he assumed he'd hit the right angle to push her to accept his offer.

"Your chances of securing a favorable match—or any match at all—would be very slim, you must agree, Lady Theodora."

"Your threat only shows how little you know me, Mr. Gladstone," she replied, sending one last glance at the closed door. Her best course was to sit down and outline all the reasons she'd make a terrible wife for a *charitable* man such as he. "I am unconcerned with making a match this season—or in the next several seasons, for that matter."

She sat primly on the lounge her mother had vacated, awaiting his next move. A man such as Mr. Gladstone would not be so foolish as to think his first argument would completely persuade his target. Ruining her name was not his only tactic, certainly.

"Do you feel Lady Georgina Seaton, Miss Adeline Price, and Lady Josephine—what is her family name?" he asked, tapping his chin with his forefinger. "Oh, it does not matter at the moment. Hopefully, it shan't come to all that. Do you think your dear friends are hoping to secure husbands this season?"

Theo felt lightheaded as the color drained from her face, her fingers instantly freezing.

"Not only will I inform *The Post* of your identity, but I'll also share that of your friends. Possibly even news of your morning outings to Regent's Park." He sat back in his chair, confident he'd said the final thing required to secure her agreement. "But...I can be

275

persuaded to keep your secret. Mayhap give *The Post* a completely different announcement to share with all of England."

He'd threatened the one thing that would ensure her cooperation with his scheme. Remaining silent, she sent daggers his way. If her look of disgust could wound, he'd be dead where he sat.

"Do not look so shocked at my cunning, Lady Theodora. A man *such as myself*," he mimicked her, "is not always given his share of what he deserves. It is quite common for men of my status to find other methods of receiving their due."

"You've been following me…and my friends?" Theo asked.

"Heavens, no." Gladstone set his hand across his chest, affronted at her accusation. "I would never muddy my own hands with such a task."

"You are despicable, and you will not get what you seek from me—or anyone else."

"Mayhap the ruin of your friends, at your hands, is not enough." Gladstone folded his hands, attempting to set them on his lap; unfortunately, his rounded belly left no room, and he was forced to lay them across his protruding midsection. "And your brother, the poor man, has known his share of scandals. How will the article in *The Post* affect his position at the museum?"

…or her hopes of working with the Cassini family?

Theo couldn't ponder any of it. She wouldn't be the one to bring disgrace upon her family, not after Cart and Jude had worked tirelessly to restore the Cartwright title and estate to a fraction of what it had once been. And her friends, her dear friends, they did not deserve this either.

This would be Josie's only chance at a season. Her family had little in the way of funds or standing in society. She'd be lucky to make a match with a second or third son, but sweet, shy Josie would be more than happy to accept any match that would help her family.

Lady Georgina's family was financially secure and the only one of them that would escape the news with little scandal. The daughter of a duke was sought-after, no matter the rust that clung to her silver exterior. But what would become of her if the new duchess delivered her first child? It did not bode well for Georgie and her future. Her only hope was to marry well and escape her family home. She would make a decent match regardless, though if her father sought a happy union for her was yet to be seen.

That only left Adeline, and likely the woman in the most crucial of positions. All Theo had learned from Alistair pointed to financial instability far exceeding what she'd feared with the probability that Adeline would be removed from London if any hint of shame surrounded her name. The woman was by far the most graceful and poised of their group. Her classic, white-blonde hair and clear blue eyes, with a complexion as pure as freshly fallen snow, would draw much notice with gentlemen seeking a prim and proper English rose.

But could Theo live with herself if she caused any of them disgrace? And Cart, along with Jude and the children, would see all their hard work destroyed by her thoughtless behavior. Everything they'd built for their family would be for nothing. Society would shun them once again.

And Alistair, he'd toiled just as hard to give Adeline the season she deserved...and all Theo had done was jeopardize his efforts. He'd warned her that the ladies would be unable to keep their secret from society, he'd begged her to help him keep Adeline from ruining her name. The ironic part was that it wasn't Adeline, but Theo, who would be responsible for Alistair's family disgrace.

Gladstone following her—and her friends—was unsettling enough, but if she agreed to their sham of a betrothal, what would he ask—demand—of her next? She could not be the true reason he was willing to go through so much trouble to wed her. He could blackmail any young woman.

"Why me, Mr. Gladstone?" Theo asked. "I am the daughter of an impoverished lord, the only sister of an academic man who seeks knowledge over power and prestige. I am not settled with a large dowry."

"Money is not everything, Theodora, or did you not learn that lesson?"

"I have never taken much stock in monetary amounts," she conceded. "But I do know many men, especially those seeking to improve their status, are interested when a large dowry is settled on a woman; whether it be pounds, land, or properties—even a percentage of business ventures."

"I have enough coin and many successful business transactions coming to fruition. What I do not have is a title."

The man could not be so daft. "I do not come with a title."

"But you do come with a brother—an earl, no less—who has established quite an impressive influence about town, with many friends in places I have yet to gain entrance to."

Theo remembered Alistair's warning: Gladstone's tendency for gambling, women, and power. She'd ignored his cautions, thinking there was no reason to hear of Oliver's flaws because he was nothing to her. Mr. Price had labored on about the man's false sense of righteousness, his proclamation of his charitable nature. Gladstone had Theo's mother fooled, but he'd never held such power over her.

Not then, and certainly not now.

"You seek to use my brother's connections to raise your status in town?"

"Among other things," he replied, sitting forward slightly.

"Such as?"

"That is none of your concern," he retorted. "As my wife, you will be privy only to what information I deem you worthy of."

"I will not agree to any marriage without knowing in advance what you have planned for my family and friends." Theo sat back, pushing all the tension from her body in hopes he'd see her relaxed posture and take her words for fact—though they couldn't be further from the truth. "If I accept your outlandish proposal, you will have many years of attempting to keep me submissive to your wishes, but that time is not yet. You will answer my question, or I will walk out of this room, the consequences be damned."

Her voice cracked, and she prayed Gladstone didn't call her bluff.

He narrowed his eyes, obviously unused to anyone—especially a woman—demanding an answer he wasn't prepared to give, but her untroubled attitude must have convinced him it would be necessary. "I have certain debts that need handling."

Alistair had been correct.

"My brother is not a wealthy man," Theo countered.

"I understand that, but as my brother-in-law, our association will buy me time to make good on several notes—and keep my memberships in good standing."

It was far more honesty than she'd thought to gain from him. "And after that, you will leave my family and friends alone?"

Gladstone tilted his head to the side, giving no answer one way or the other.

She didn't trust him, but as he'd so pointedly lain out, she had no other option. It was marry Gladstone or be the cause of her family's disgrace and her friends' ruination.

Sacrifice *her* future, or the future of many.

She should feel something—anything—but instead, she felt empty. Devoid of all emotions at the thought of a life married to Gladstone. At least her friends would escape harm.

There was no need to ponder her options, no formula she could apply to the situation to turn the odds in her favor, and little chance of Gladstone not making good on his threats.

"Very well, Mr. Gladstone." Theo stood. "You leave me with no other alternative. I am certain our mothers are waiting with baited breath for your announcement."

"You are a wise woman, Lady Theodora." Gladstone stood with a bit more effort than should be necessary to hoist himself from the chair. "Though, I will tell you, it is not a trait I value in women. But for today, I will allow it."

Chapter Twenty-One

Alistair dismounted, once more outside Lady Theo's residence without an invitation or reason beyond owing her an apology for his brutish behavior. There hadn't been much to contemplate after Adeline had left him in the study. He was wrong. In so many ways, Alistair was wrong. In his treatment of Theo, his overbearing nature with his siblings, and about his unrealistic ideals for all their futures—as well as his influence in each. Most of all, he'd pushed Theo away. She'd had no option but to lie to him, and all in an effort to keep her dear friend's confidence. He could think the secret trivial and not worth mentioning, but Theo was able to look past the surface and realize it wasn't the secret that meant something, but the trust another person needed to share such a private thing.

A servant hurried down the drive from the stables beyond the house and took hold of Alistair's horse. "Beg'n ye pardon for da wait, sir," the stable hand said. "There be much afoot at m'lord's house."

The man led Alistair's mount around the house and toward the stables without another word or the chance for Alistair to ask *what* was afoot. For a brief moment, he worried something untoward had occurred within; however, no black trappings were hung.

He paused a moment longer, allowing the remorse regarding his actions to return. The coming apology would be difficult. He wasn't used to issuing them, and Alistair was not certain Theo would accept his words. Nor was he sure she would even listen to his apology. However, he must make her hear him out fully. It all went far deeper than him offering a statement in defense of his actions. He cared about Theo. He would have little peace until she forgave him.

He imagined the sight of her smirk when she'd bested him at Whitechapel...he was foolish to think it had meant more than it did, but certainly she'd felt the connection between them as much as he.

She was his first stop on his round to make good on his promise to fix the situation he'd created. Next, he'd speak with Abel and Adeline, offer his sincere regret for his behavior and beg them to forgive him...and ask them to work with him toward their future. If the three joined forces toward a common goal, they would be unstoppable. A whole crop of gossiping dowagers wouldn't be able to prevent them from attaining a successful match—if only they could settle on a way to work together. They were blood. Alistair needed their pardon as much as he needed Theodora's.

Alistair was stalling; scared Theo would rebuff him, even though he came in repentance.

He would never know if she could forgive him if he didn't knock on her door. With one final deep breath, Alistair strode down the drive and up the front steps, stopping before the massive double doors before knocking loudly. One, two, three pounds with his closed fist brought a servant hastily to the door.

"Good day, sir," a familiar servant called. "I am afraid Lady Theodora is not receiving visitors at this time."

Alistair peered over the butler's shoulder at the activity beyond as a large bouquet of blue and orange flowers moved through the foyer and disappeared from sight. He spotted Lady Theo inside, hurrying about when the servant departed, the flowers set upon the mantle.

"I will only be a moment, my good man," Alistair confided in a whisper, taking the opportunity to slip past the butler into the foyer. "I see her just over there. I promise I will not keep her long."

Habits were hard to break, and his overbearing nature was proving very difficult to change, but he needed to speak with Theo—to see her—and no servant was going to dissuade his plan.

Stepping into the room, Alistair took in the atrocious sight of the mismatched orange and blue flowers. Certainly, the sender could have coordinated more suitable colors. He shuddered at the offensive bouquet. Startled, Alistair belatedly realized Theo could have another visitor: matrons of the *ton* or Lady Cartwright and the Dowager Lady Cartwright. He was prepared to offer his apologies to Theo but not in the presence of others. That would bring cause for further explanations neither of them was willing to give.

Lady Theo stood inside, staring at the vase of flowers, her back to him—blessedly alone but for the obnoxious blossoms.

It was the first stroke of luck he'd had in some time. Confidence surged through him.

"Please, Mother, I have told you I request some time alone. Please leave me be." Theo didn't turn to face him. Her words were quiet, a deep sadness bordering on defeat casting a shadow over her normally bright demeanor. She sighed, her shoulders sagging as he realized she hoped the intruder exited the room. "I will be unable to attend you this afternoon. I am to meet Cart shortly."

Alistair gazed around the room, but no sign of the dowager was found. It was only the pair of them. The despondency in her tone pulled at his heart—so unfamiliar, so not like the woman he'd met before. Alistair longed to go to her, set his arms about her, and repair whatever was broken.

"Lady Theodora," he whispered. He had no wish to startle her.

"Mr. Price. I thought you were my mother." She swung around, her hands brushing her red, swollen eyes. "Alistair. I do not know where Adeline is."

Did she think that was the only reason he ever sought her out? Of course, she did. It was the truth, or the guise he'd used to mask his true reasoning for longing to be in her company at any rate. He'd hidden the truth so well he hadn't seen past it either.

"Have you been crying?" His voice thundered in the small room. Mayhap today was not the day to hold his commanding nature at bay. Someone had hurt her, and he would damn well find out who, and seek retribution. "Who is responsible for this?"

He had a moment of hesitation when she didn't answer. What if it was her brother, Lord Cartwright? Certainly, Alistair had no right to interfere where her guardian was concerned. There were likely several times when Alistair had made his own siblings shed a tear, and he would not relish the idea of another man—no matter his intentions—stepping in.

Alistair clenched and unclenched his fists to stop himself from going to her. He lifted one foot, about to close the mere three steps between them and take her in his arms—soothe her unhappiness—but stilled himself, despite wanting nothing more than to go to her. He'd promise her the world if only she'd smile, throw a witty retort his way, or tell him of his insufferable attitude.

Instead, she crossed her arms and kept her eyes on the floor at her feet, her shoulders folding in as if she sought to disappear into herself.

"Who are the flowers from?" he asked, sensing her grief began there.

Her brown eyes, like molten caramel, snapped to his and immediately softened. Theo searched his face, apparently judging if she could trust him—and the answer would likely be a resounding no. She'd throw him from her house, unwanted guest that he was. Alistair had given her no reason to confide in him. That was all too apparent now as he stood before her…waiting.

"Mr. Oliver Gladstone," she whispered. "My betrothed."

His knees weakened, and he felt himself sway, off-balance.

"That...I...when?" His ears must be deceiving him. Not long ago, the vile man clutched her arm far too tightly and insisted she depart the tourney with him. A rock the size of a large boulder settled in the pit of Alistair's stomach as he fought to find the words to express exactly what her announcement meant to him.

Now, instead of taking her in his arms, he wanted to shake her, demand her senses return and she call off this damnable union. Or far more preferred, admit that she jested with him. It was exactly as he deserved for his behaviors thus far.

"He asked less than an hour ago." She moved to the chair he'd sat in on his first visit and collapsed. "He was rather persuasive. My mother agrees the match will suit."

"And your brother," he said on an exhale, the only coherent question he could muster. "He is agreeable to this travesty?"

Theo's hands were clasped tightly in her lap, wrinkling the fabric of her dress as her knuckles turned white. Her long hair fell over her shoulders, covering her face from view, but he sensed the tears had started once more. "He knows nothing of it," she replied, her inflection remaining flat with each word.

"Gladstone is an abhorrent, despicable man, Theo. You cannot marry him. He wants nothing but to improve his own social status, and use your family for his own personal gain."

"You think I am unaware of that?" Anger flared in her tone. It was much preferred to the deflated woman of a moment before. She needs must fight this—fight Gladstone's evil intentions. "His proposal was very—for lack of a better word—honestly given. I know what he seeks, and what he expects of a wife."

But, Theo wasn't fighting it at all. He wanted to shout, "what about me?" Where would her betrothal to Gladstone leave him? Alone and longing for a woman he had no right to claim as his own.

"Yes," Alistair fumed. He needed her to understand, even if she did not return his feelings, at least she should be fully aware what awaited her if she wed Gladstone. "He wishes for a malleable bride, a woman who will do his bidding without question. A person he can use, and justify his actions, as a wife is meant for that exact purpose."

"Come now. I have no illusions of love or even affection beyond the physical." She looked up to him, a wobbly smile on her face. "He cannot be so dreadful, for his mother dotes on him ever so much, and my mother is quite smitten, as well. It may take time, but we will adjust to one another. Come to terms with our arrangement, if you will."

"Come to terms? That is not a marriage! You are more a fool than anyone if you think that to be true." She was worth more than what she was accepting from Gladstone. How could she not see that? He could not be the only man who noticed her value, saw her wit and intellect. Gladstone would not appreciate Theo; he'd only seek to suppress her mind and quash her passion. Not physical passion, no, he would graciously use her in that area, but the things that made Theodora…well, Theo.

She stiffened at his harsh tone, but Alistair did not regret what he'd said. It was fact, every damn word.

"He has decided to gain a special license, forgoing a reading of the banns," she continued, dismissing his protest. "It will be a quiet affair with only close family— and possibly a few friends—" Her voice cracked. "It shall be done quickly, as soon as the contract is drawn up and agreed upon."

Her words were empty, devoid of anger, anxiousness, dread, or sadness. All sentiment had left her.

"Not if I have anything to say about it." Alistair paced toward the unlit hearth, shoving his hands in his pockets to avoid going to her—taking hold of her and never letting go. "Where is Lord Cartwright? I will right all of this."

"That cannot be done," she sighed. "I have caused this myself, just as you predicted would happen."

"What does that mean?" He halted, facing her. Begging her to lift her gaze to him, but she kept her eyes on the rug below her chair. "Tell me what is going on." If he could only look into her eyes, he'd see what he needed to do, what Theo longed for him to do to right everything.

"There is nothing to tell. My brother's solicitor will have the marriage settlement drawn up and prepared by week's end." Resigned, she stood. "I am expected elsewhere. I must go, Mr. Price. There is much to do and not enough time to do it in."

He wanted to demand she call him Alistair. Their association had moved past that of social acquaintances long ago.

Fury heated his blood while desperation tugged at his soul. "You are going nowhere until I understand why you would agree to wed that insufferable man."

The irony of the situation was not lost on Alistair. It was the same word commonly used to describe him, but he was not without morals or virtue. Everything he did, everything he said, all of his demands, were only meant to help those he loved. And at some point, that had come to include the woman before him. "Theo, I cannot allow this."

"Thankfully, my life is not in your hands."

Alistair flipped around to face her. "You think your future is so easily decided, that the consequences of this marriage will not affect you?"

Her eyes returned to his, empty and lifeless, though she still had breath in her. "If I do not agree, the consequences for my family and friends will be far more than I am willing to accept. If it is I who suffers while they remain unscathed, then so be it. It is the least I can give them."

"Tell me how I can repair this." He moved to kneel before her. There was no greater urge than that to return the light to her eyes and set her shoulders straight and proud once more. "This cannot be the end of things."

"Alistair." She brought her hands to cup his face, and he closed his eyes, languishing in the feel of her skin against his, though her fingers were cold to the touch. "He threatened to reveal my identity to all of England."

"You do not care about that," he retorted, his eyes snapping open. "You have told me as much yourself."

"Regrettably, that was not the end of his intimidations." Her hands fell away from his face, and she sat, leaning back into the chair. "He knows of your sister's involvement at the tourneys, as well as Lady Georgie and Lady Josie."

Alistair rocked back on his heels, grasping the arms of the chair to still his hands from balling into fists. "I will handle this," he said, pushing to his feet.

"You mustn't," she begged. "He has designs on ruining everyone I care for, including you." She stood, following him toward the door. "I have created this situation, and I will see to it that everyone escapes unscathed. I promise, not a negative thing will come to light concerning Adeline."

He halted, jerking around to face her, his jaw clenching as he bit out his next words. "You think I am worried about my sister? I fear I cannot save her from herself if she insists on embarking on a path to ruin. My offer to help has nothing to do with Adeline."

"I understand the possibilities and adverse light it will shine on you, as well." She set her hand on his arm, her gaze begging him to forgive her. "I never meant for this to harm you."

"Damn it, Theo." He brushed her arm aside, and she recoiled. "I worry about *you*. I care only about *you*. It is thoughts of you that keep me awake at night and send me into my cups during the day to escape the urge to come here. To pull you into my arms...to place my lips upon yours once more. But this time, I would capture you completely and never let go."

Everything crumbled around him: his pledge to his parents to do right by his siblings, his pledge to himself to stay away from Lady Theo, and his pledge to Theo that he would not harm Gladstone.

The reprobate would not get away with his underhanded actions and threats toward Theodora. Alistair would see to that.

Chapter Twenty-Two

Theo took another step back. Alistair was livid, but his words were everything she'd hoped to one day hear from a man. Though not now…not after she'd agreed to wed Mr. Gladstone. And not from Alistair, her dear friend's brother and a man who galled her at every turn with his arrogant actions.

A thrill of alarm coursed through her, at odds with the warmth that had filled her at his words. An uncontrollable whimper escaped her.

There was nothing she could say, nothing she could do but remain frozen as he continued. She couldn't breathe, feared moving an inch or this moment would be gone—the spell broken and Alistair returning to his lofty self. That was the man Theo was most comfortable with, a man she could handle with a personality she understood; however, this Alistair was foreign to her. He was daunting and unpredictable. Her mind begged her to give in to him, listen to his sweet words and accept them for what they were without further question.

Everything about this Alistair was perplexing.

Alistair had kissed her—just that once. He'd never mentioned the incident again, and Theo had thought it just that, an incident best forgotten. An action that meant nothing, with no consequences or promises attached. It had meant far more to her, but he was a man—a handsome one—who'd more than likely kissed many women in his time in London. The simple kiss they'd shared couldn't possibly mean anything to him. Theo reminded herself that it did not have to be the same for her. He was free to pretend the intimacy had never happened while she treasured the moment in that scarce breath of time.

"Are you hearing anything I'm saying?" He moved toward her, overtaking the few steps she'd retreated at his outburst. "Lady Theo, you cannot marry that man."

"Why not?" It was a simple question, though she feared his answer. Did his reasoning have to do with the attraction between them? Or was it Alistair's last gallant attempt to save her from a fate worse than any other she could imagine.

"I have given you many reasons why."

"Yes, but none of them solve the issue at hand. He will ruin not only me but also my family and friends." Cold, icy dread sent a shiver down her spine. It was something she *would not* allow to happen, but she could not admit that it was Alistair she feared for most.

He deserved none of the disgrace his family faced if she didn't marry Gladstone.

If she had to give up on her dreams, at least it was worth it to make certain her three friends attained theirs, and that Cart and Jude would not be taken down once more by scandal, tarnishing their two young children.

But most of all, Alistair would one day—when his obligations to his siblings were fulfilled—find a future that made him happy.

"Then marry me," Alistair countered. "Allow me to set things to rights."

Oh, how she wished she could throw caution to the wind and scream "yes."

"And how would that be any different from marrying Gladstone?" Theo knew it would be a world of difference. Alistair challenged her at every turn, not seeking to conquer her as Gladstone would do. "It might save me from ruin, but it will leave my friends unprotected."

He took hold of her trembling hands, and Theo wanted to cry for all the warmth they gave her—a chill had taken over her body the moment she'd been left alone with Gladstone earlier. "I have affection for you, Lady Theo," he confessed.

"Affection may grow between Gladstone and me," she countered, not believing her own lie.

Alistair laughed, a cold, hollow sound that matched the way Theo felt inside.

"Besides, you have told me you do not plan to marry, that children are not in your future," Theo insisted. "Oliver wants to marry me, and seeks to have an entire horde of children."

"A horde of offspring he has no means to support." Alistair squeezed her hands. "I do not need to impress upon you how difficult it is to properly care for children without significant funds."

"But I shall love them all." Certainly, love was enough. A family of her own...she'd thought it would be many years before the notion would even cross her mind.

"And if love is not enough to keep a dry roof and warm food on the table?" Alistair asked.

"My brother will not allow harm or starvation to come to my family." And Theo needed to believe that loving her children, no matter who their father was, would be enough. It might very well be the only thing she'd be left with.

"Come now, Theo." He pulled her close, circling his arms around her—something she'd imagined happening since their kiss. And it felt right...and good. Theo felt protected in his arms. "The man doesn't know you, not in the slightest."

He pulled her closer at his words, their bodies meeting at every point.

"You know me no better, Mr. Price." It was a lie, but she couldn't have him thinking to sacrifice himself—and his future—to save her while leaving all the others unprotected from Gladstone's ruinous plans. Surely, she would survive, but at the expense of her dear friends. "Nor are you that different from Mr. Gladstone."

Alistair's arms fell away from her, and she stumbled back, unaware how much his hold had been supporting her. Cold dread returned, threatening to overtake her.

Taking a step back, he asked, "How can you think that?"

"Can you deny the statement's truthfulness?" Theo could, but she had no desire to. The simple look in his eyes told her that the accusation wasn't true.

"I've witnessed your compassion, your unconditional love for your friends, and your intelligence." Alistair turned and paced to the door then back again before continuing. "Certainly, with both of us, we can discover a way to keep everyone from ruin. You must trust my word on this."

"But what of your desire not to marry?" she whispered. It was her last point to argue.

Alistair halted, staring at her intently for a moment before sinking into the chair she'd sat in moments before. "I have every intention to marry, Theodora. It is only that it seems impossible to pursue my future until I have seen all my siblings happily wedded and cared for. I cannot use what meager resources my family has toward my own gains until their needs are met."

Another side to the man she thought she knew. His overprotective nature was irrefutable, but his reasoning made sense; though she reminded herself that his treatment of Adeline aligned with the views of most men. "Do you plan to coerce your siblings into accepting a future not of their choosing?"

He scrubbed his face with his hands. "Of course, not."

"But your high-handed actions are not so different than Mr. Gladstone's thus far."

"Because I take my sister's safety very seriously?" he demanded. "Yes, my first duty is to my siblings' well-being. I promised my parents no harm would come to any of them."

"You seek to keep Adeline from competing in the tourney," Theo challenged. "It is her passion and her desire to participate and help Miss Emmeline's School. And you deny her that."

"For her own protection!" Exasperation laced his voice. "Just as I would keep you from competing if it were in my power. Once you wed Gladstone, every freedom you've enjoyed under your brother's care will be stripped from you, taken away with no explanation or promise of security."

"That is my choice to make," she sighed, allowing the fight to leave her. Why could he not see his words aligned so closely with Gladstone's? "Do you think I am unaware of everything I will be giving up? The sacrifices I must make?"

"No, I do not think you are aware of the magnitude of your decision." He sat forward, his boots planted on the ground as if ready to jump to his feet if she tried to depart.

Which Theo must do. Her mother had turned away Georgie and Josie when they'd arrived to collect her. As far as Theo knew, Alistair still kept Adeline locked in their townhouse, and Theo must be at the Grand Archers' Competition to continue if they had any chance of winning the prize purse for Miss Emmeline.

"I must go." Theo attempted to move past him and slip out the door. She could disappear down the corridor and depart through the alley behind her townhouse, waving down a hackney when she made the main road, but Alistair's hand shot out as she passed, halting her. His hold was firm but not painful as Gladstone's had been. "Mr. Price, do unhand me before I sound the alarm."

"Scream, Lady Theo," he prodded. "Hopefully, it will bring someone with an ounce of sense who can help me make you see reason."

Theo clamped her lips shut, refusing to give Alistair what he so clearly wanted: further discussion of the decision she'd already made.

"So, you expect me to depart this room, forget all that's been said, and allow you to burn every hope you had for your future?" He threw his arms wide, releasing his hold on her arm. She had the freedom to move past him and out the door, but she remained, knowing once she left this room, any hope of him understanding why she'd promised to wed Gladstone would be lost. "My siblings are my priority, not you, that is what you are saying. I can walk out, giving you no protection from the nefarious designs Gladstone has for you. Live my life, take care of my siblings…and if we see one another about town—which will very well happen—I will look the other way, pretend we are not acquainted and that I am not utterly, maddeningly, desperately in love with you?"

The air—her every breath—was sucked from her lungs, leaving her begging to inhale deeply and stop the burn in her chest. She had no idea how to process his declaration, if that were what one called it.

He stepped before her, his eyes searching hers. What did he see there? Did he see that she wanted nothing less than to marry Gladstone, that she cared for Alistair as much as he cared for her? That a future by his side—a member of the Melton family—would be the most preferable path for her. Surely, he saw through her denials and claims to the contrary.

Theo could not risk admitting any of it. It would put her family—and his—in jeopardy.

She was doing what needed to be done…for *him*.

Instead, she remained silent, her eyes pleading with him to understand, to let her go, to allow her to make the sacrifices she'd agreed to. She was not the victim in this situation; she was doing all in her power to save everyone. Why could he not believe that? If there were another choice for her, she would have made it.

Her chest seized at the fate she'd created—a marriage not bound by love or respect. Her knees grew weak at the prospect of the hard years ahead of her, but she allowed her determination to flare once more, strengthening her stance. She may suffer, but the ones she loved would thrive. Every part of her screamed it was the right thing to do, the correct outcome for all involved. Except her, of course, but she could handle Gladstone. Women like Josie stood no chance against a man of his vile nature.

Yes, she had to believe she was making the correct decision.

"But instead of accepting me, you will give up your happiness and marry Gladstone." He paused, tightening his hold on her. "My overbearing, domineering, insufferable self will not allow that to come to pass."

She wanted to tell him once again it was not his decision to make, beseech him not to make this any more difficult than it already was. She wanted to push him away and walk from the room, confident in her choice.

Because, with each breath she took, she knew she loved him as much as he loved her.

It was because of this she'd made the decision she had.

Theo set her hands against his chest, meaning to do just that, push him away, but his arms encircled her, pulling her body against his, pressing them together from hips to chest. Her breath hitched when her breasts nestled against his firm, heated torso. The feel of his body against hers dispelled all thoughts of departing the room.

"Look me in the eye, Theo, and tell me you do not want me," he whispered, his breath fanning her cheek. "That your final choice is to take Gladstone as your husband, and not me."

When she hesitated, he pressed his lips to hers, pulling her closer. If that were possible. It seemed their bodies were as firmly connected and inseparable as their love for one another. Surely, that was not possible.

His kiss was not the chaste, delicate kind they'd shared before. There was a desperate air to the movement of his lips, intensity. And Theo found her mouth parting and moving to match his need, her hands grasping his arms to hold him to her, her lips as insistent as his.

It was a parting kiss. The last they would share, but it only awakened something within her. A stirring she hadn't known was there, lying dormant and ignored. She'd sensed the swirling of restless desire during their first kiss, but this, this longing, this passion to consume him, to never let go—to leave her family and friends without her protection—overpowered her in that moment.

However, Theo knew this moment—with this man—would end. Leaving her exactly where she'd been before he took her in his arms and showed her the true depth of her feelings for him.

All that she'd sacrifice to remain in his arms.

But the cost was too great and would come at the expense of every other person she loved.

"Alistair," Theo said breathlessly against his lips, releasing his arms and planting her palms solidly to his chest to push him away. She must make him see reason. Gladstone had the upper hand; there would be no stopping him if he did not get what he wanted. "We cannot do this. I am all but betrothed to Gladstone. The papers are being drawn up, and the license procured. You must go before my servants—or my mother—catches you here. The gossip would only incite Oliver's anger."

Alistair flinched at the use of Gladstone's given name. His arms remain on her, moving to settle at her hips, but he refrained from pulling her close for another kiss.

"I cannot allow you to do this, Theo," he said. "No matter what you think you must do, or your sense of responsibility toward my sister and the others, this is wrong."

Her eyes filled with tears—tears that must remain unshed.

Just as her desire to make Alistair hers would remain unspoken.

Chapter Twenty-Three

The house was painted a grotesque, pastel shade of orange, obviously a tactic to keep visitors from noting the less than stellar upkeep of the Gladstone House. Nestled not far off Bond Street in an area primarily housing shops, offices, and work fronts, the townhouse was lackluster in its appeal. The blue shutters, many leaning, cockeyed, and missing nails to secure them in place, only added to the travesty that was Oliver Gladstone's family residence—and left no doubt either Gladstone or his mother had hand-selected the flowers in Theo's drawing room to match their hideous abode.

The symbolism was not lost on Alistair.

The sound from the busy thoroughfare several buildings down was deafening and caused Alistair's head to ring. It had nothing to do with the scotch he'd imbibed when he'd stopped at White's to inquire about Gladstone's directions. He'd thought the servant jesting at the address so close to Bond—certainly it was Gladstone's father's old mercantile and not their actual home. Alas, it had proven to be a true residence. Though sorely neglected in both care and upkeep.

Alistair walked to the front stoop, no steps or grand double door, only a dirt walkway with loose rock landing before the unassuming entrance.

No silver or brass knocker hung for him to use to sound his arrival.

With one swift knock, an elderly man—surely past his own father's age—pulled the door open only far enough to peek out the crack and take in Alistair from head to toe with one eye. The eye narrowed, its milky surface struggling to focus on Alistair.

"Good day, sir," Alistair said in way of greeting. "I was hoping for a visit with your master, Oliver Gladstone." At the man's puzzled stare, he continued. "This is his residence, is it not?"

"Cornelius calls no one master."

"Good for you." The eye narrowed once more at Alistair's retort. "Allow me to rephrase my request. I seek to speak with Mr. Oliver Gladstone."

"The senior or the portly, disagreeable young buck?" Cornelius's eye widened with his inquiry.

Under any other circumstances, Alistair might very well enjoy this man's company; mayhap offer him employ at his own home. "The portly, disagreeable one."

"He ain't receive'n guests."

"And the senior Gladstone?"

"He ain't at home," the man huffed. "Someone needs ta be work'n to earn every'ne's keep."

"Very well." Alistair could find no fault with the man's words. He understood the hardships of supporting a large family in London proper without benefit of a study flow of coin. "When will the portly Gladstone be available? I will return to speak with him."

The door shut in Alistair's face with a thud, a mere inch from his nose. The man's curt dismissal stung as he returned to his mount, determined to find Gladstone—and make him pay for all the threats he'd levied against Theo. The man hid inside his townhouse, a coward used to badger women, but unprepared for the repercussions Alistair would see he faced for his devious actions.

Alistair led his horse down the drive and around the modest house, toward the stables beyond, tying the beast to a post before inching toward a set of large windows, the draperies pulled back to allow in the midday sun.

He shielded his eyes to look through the panes. A flurry of activity was afoot as he witnessed servants moving to and fro. With no sight of Gladstone, Alistair moved to the next set of windows, set a bit higher off the ground but bordered by a pair of solid double doors.

The window ledge was encrusted with dirt as he grabbed hold and hoisted himself high enough to peer into the room. Sure enough, Gladstone sat behind a large desk, a quill poised as he read through some document or another. Certainly, the marriage contract hadn't been prepared and delivered already. He dropped softly to the ground, hoping to escape the notice of the stable hands working not far away around the back of the house.

With any luck, the double doors would be unlocked, and Alistair could walk right into Gladstone's house. The element of surprise would be enough to throw the man off his high stool.

The knob turned easily in his hand—the second bout of luck he'd had that day.

Alistair entered the room with Gladstone's back to him. The door did not make so much as a squeak, but his determined footsteps brought the man swiveling around in his chair and jumping to his feet when Alistair slammed the door wide against its frame.

The windowpanes rattled, and Gladstone's chair toppled to the floor, taking a stack of ledgers with it.

"Oliver?" a woman called from the hall outside the closed study door. "Is everything as it should be?"

"Tell her everything is fine," Alistair hissed.

"Every…everything is as it should be, Mother," he called, but his eyes narrowed on Alistair. "What are you doing here, Mr. Price?"

Alistair strode farther into the room, inspecting a small table to his right that held a chalice with a biblical passage inscribed on it, knowing his ease would worry Gladstone. "Your butler informed me you're not receiving guests, but I assumed that must be a mistake."

"And why would you assume my butler is wrong?"

"Because," Alistair paused, turning a pointed stare on the man. He wanted to see his reaction—and watch him squirm under his penetrating glare. "When a man finds himself newly betrothed, they are normally open to good tidings and wishes for their happy future."

"Ahhh, well, news certainly travels fast," Gladstone commented before bending to right his chair. "I have yet to finalize the agreement with Lord Cartwright and make a public announcement. I am certain *The Post* will catch word of our pending nuptials and broadcast our good news across all of England."

"Oh, that is interesting to hear," Alistair said, once again pacing slowly about the room, his eyes taking in every shelf, but settling on nothing for longer than a second as he struggled to keep his composure...and not tear the man limb from limb. "I was under the impression you'd forced Lady Theo's hand into a hasty marriage by special license, surely no time to alert *The Post* before the deed is done."

Gladstone smiled, an odd smirk he likely thought resembled the joyous smile of an expectant bridegroom. "Lady Theodora is not one to seek attention or fuss."

"Is that so?" Alistair stopped to admire an old tome, allowing a moment for the tension to drain from his body. Every part of him wanted to rush across the room and take the portly, arrogant bastard by his neck cloth and pin him to the wall until he agreed to call off his intentions to wed Lady Theo. Even hearing her name on his vile lips made Alistair's blood boil.

However, any hasty movement would cause the man to shout for help, ending Alistair's ability to reason with the scoundrel—and if all else failed, offer his own threats. It would only cause gossip to spread, and Gladstone would work quicker to secure the special license.

"Yes, as a matter of fact, it is." He set his arms on his desk, entwining his fingers. "And one does not start off on good footing with his soon-to-be wife by going against her wishes."

The man had gumption, Alistair would give him that. He must know Alistair had been to see Theo and knew he'd blackmailed her into accepting his offer of marriage.

"Let us dispel with the niceties, shall we?"

The man's eyes flashed, and Alistair noted the first hint of fear in Gladstone since he'd entered the room unexpectedly, though he quickly hid his unease. "I know not what you mean, Price."

"Then allow me to explain it to you." Alistair moved to stand before the desk and slapped his palms against the hard surface. The inkpot shook, sending a droplet of black ink flying, landing squarely on Gladstone's white shirt that strained to cover his expanding middle. The stout man glanced down at the growing stain, the spot widening as the ink entered the material. "You will withdraw yourself from Lady Theo's life, end your betrothal before anyone but myself knows of it, and refrain from so much as glancing in Lady Theo's direction in the future. If you see her at Hyde Park, you will turn around. If you see her at the opera, you will depart immediately. If you so much as attend the same ball, you will withdraw promptly."

"Her name is Lady Theodora." Gladstone balked at Alistair's furious expression. "And I will do no such thing. It would be the height of dishonor. Her brother would have every reason to call me out for such an action."

"You speak of dishonor?" Alistair leaned across the desk toward Gladstone. "All the while blackmailing an innocent woman into a marriage she does not want?"

"Did you ask her if she was against the match?" Gladstone asked with a sneer. "She was more than happy to agree to my proposal this morning."

"You gave her no choice, you bloody, sniveling scoundrel!" Alistair pounded his fists on the desk for emphasis, and Gladstone jumped to his feet. "You are a coward, applying threats and coercion to gain what you want."

"Oliver," his mother called again. "What are you doing in there that is causing all that racket?"

"Yes, Oliver," Alistair seethed. "Do tell your mummy all your treacherous dealings."

"I will have you know my mother selected Lady Theodora to be my wife," Gladstone hissed. "You will not gain sympathy from her."

"You think it is sympathy I seek?" The man was in danger of being the recipient of all of Alistair's rage.

Gladstone swallowed, gulping down air, but smartly kept his mouth shut, leaving Alistair's question hanging in the air unanswered.

Alistair chuckled. "Sympathy is a useless emotion. If you do not withdraw your offer for Theo's hand, I will be forced to seek vengeance." He glanced down to the widening ink spot marring the man's crisp shirt. "Instead of an ink stain, that will be a hole from the shot of my pistol."

"Are you challenging *me* to a duel?" Gladstone squeaked.

The tradition had gone out of fashion a decade before—and was a punishable offense now—but Alistair would gladly spend his time in the tower if it meant Theo was free of Gladstone.

"You are requesting a petticoat duel." It was Gladstone's turn to laugh. "Jeopardizing our mortality over a woman? How rash of you, Price."

"I am an honorable man, and will do what is necessary to protect Theo from the likes of you."

"I am no less honorable." Gladstone stood, putting space between him and Alistair. "Is it so horrible to have aspirations in life?"

"When it is to the detriment of another, yes."

"The line between right and wrong is often blurred. When that happens, I hover on the side that favors my future. Lady Theodora has something I do not, connections to a title through Lord Cartwright and a tolerable demeanor. She will give me what I seek, and she will, in turn, receive what she wants."

Theo hadn't mentioned receiving anything in return for agreeing to marry Gladstone. He was hard-pressed to think of one thing this scoundrel could give Theo in return for all she was giving him. "And what might she gain by wedding you, Gladstone?"

"Her reputation—and that of her friends, your sister included—will remain intact and free from scandalous gossip to the contrary."

Alistair raised one brow. "You offer all this in exchange for Theo's future—control over her dowry, and connection to Lord Cartwright?"

"I am certain you understand the fairness of the deal."

"There would be no fear of their identities and activities coming to light if you, Gladstone, were not the one to spread the gossip."

"Ah, yes, I must admit my negotiation skills are born from generations of Gladstone men fighting to receive their due," he said. "But be that as it may, Price, I have information Lady Theodora does not want known—scandalous tidbits, if you will—and I aim to use it to my advantage."

"Society will not dwell long on a foursome of young women who seek pleasure in competing in archery tournaments." Alistair was certain of the fact, as he'd been in society long enough to watch the *ton's* interest in one scandal or another wane within days—or even hours—when the next grand distraction presented itself.

"Lady Theodora does not seem to be under the same impression."

"Is it money you are after?" Alistair stayed himself from reaching forward and knocking the smug smile from the man's face. Improving his societal status could not be all he sought, for there were several impoverished heiresses to a duke for Gladstone to set his sights on. "I will collect whatever her dowry promises. Double it, in fact."

"Double it…" The words trailed off as Gladstone pondered the proposal. "I am afraid the entire Melton estate would not be enough for my liking. My mother did briefly consider the notion of me taking Miss Adeline Price as wife, but with your family's limited associations in London—what is your father, past his eighty-second summer, if he is a day?—and the penniless state of the Viscountship, a union between our families is not advantageous to my future."

Alistair's wrath rose once more, and he didn't bother breathing deeply to tamp down his fury at Gladstone's comments. He allowed the rage to roll through his body, tightening every muscle, and making his hair stand on end. Gladstone was more of a reprobate than even he had assumed.

Gladstone's chest puffed, and he stared down his nose with disdain when Alistair remained silent. "If you would like to test my resolve—and wager your sister's good name—then please, continue with this absurd crusade against my betrothal to Lady Theodora Montgomery. We will see who escapes unscathed and in possession of what they sought in the first place." Gladstone glared at Alistair, leaning into his desk. "Do you think Miss Adeline Price's reputation can survive the gossip to come if Lady Theodora turns away from our betrothal?"

Our? Nothing between Theo and Gladstone would ever be label as *our* as long as Alistair was in command of himself.

"I will call on Lord Cartwright. He will put a stop to this."

"You are certainly able to try that tactic; however, if the betrothal is called off, I will see that *The Post* knows immediately of Lady Theodora and her friends' escapades about London—hooded and unchaperoned. Quite improper and worthy of gossip, if you ask me." Gladstone organized his forgotten papers that scattered his desk, turning an unperturbed smile on Alistair. "Be advised that if Cartwright voices his objection to the match, I will have little other option but to warn all of society to the impropriety of Lady Theodora, Miss Adeline, Lady Georgina, and Lady Josephine."

The man looked down at his ruined shirt, annoyance written across his face.

"Now, if you will excuse me, I must change my shirt before venturing to Greenwich Park." He looked Alistair over from head to toe, disgust taking over his face, his nose wrinkling as if his uninvited guest smelled of rotten food scraps. "You can see yourself out, I am sure."

"I know of your expansive debts. I will make sure they are all called in," Alistair challenged, bringing the man up short. "What will Mummy and Daddy do then? Destitute without the possibility of an advantageous marriage for their thick-witted son."

Alistair would throw himself before a moving carriage before he allowed Gladstone to get near Theo again.

"If that comes to pass," he said, glancing over his shoulder, "then Miss Adeline will never marry—along with your other siblings. Ludicrous. Your parents were addled...having nine children. The man was either in love or insane. I hope the same fate does not latch on to me. I will ruin your entire family, as well as Lady Theodora's, if you do not cease."

Had the man sought to gain some sympathy from Lady Theo by dangling the thought of children before her?

Gladstone hurried from the room, securely closing the door behind him to stop Alistair from pursuing him.

The vile man thought he held the upper hand. He would shortly learn to regret the day he'd gained the displeasure of Mr. Alistair Price, heir apparent to Viscount Melton.

A man in love was a man capable of scaling the highest mountain—and leveling it with one fell swoop. Gladstone was the mountain, and Alistair would bring him down.

Chapter Twenty-Four

Theo sucked in a quick breath as she watched her arrow soar toward the target, her aim as accurate as it had ever been despite the added pressure she was under. The arrow stuck with a resounding thump, and the crowd cheered, along with Josie and Georgie.

Her heart soared at the same time her hands trembled.

"You've done it!" Josie screeched, rushing onto the field, wrapping her arms around Theo in a tight hug. "There is little chance your shot will not qualify you to take a place in the top ten archers."

Theo disentangled herself from Josie's grasp and looked to Georgie, who stood a few paces away.

"Within the smallest circle," Georgie said by way of congratulations, though Theo spied no smile or sense of excitement from her. It was understandable, as she'd been outshot by every other archer in the last round. She was in a bitter mood over her disqualification, something Theo could fully understand. "Let us await the next round in the training area."

It was only proper to suppress her own elation at her victory, so as not to further wound Georgie and her pride.

Theo sighed, keeping her smile at bay as she faced her friends.

Georgie didn't wait for Theo or Josie before turning sharply and stomping off the field as the shouts from the crowd began to lessen. They would have a bit of time before the next round of archers—the final ten—were prepared and ready.

She'd competed far better than even she had anticipated, continuing round after round and placing either first or second in each. The next round would secure the superior three archers to participate in the final round the follow day…at the same time Theo was to meet with Cassini and Cart at the museum, along with Cassini's sister. Adeline needed to slip away and take Theo's place or all their hard work—and the trouble she was in—would be for nothing.

There was no time to think about Gladstone and his devious plan for her and her family. Theo need to concentrate on making the final round and pray Adeline found a way to escape for the day.

Knowing the true danger his sister was facing, the chances were very slim Adeline would be able to slip from the house unnoticed with Alistair watching. Georgie could step into her place, but the archers left in the tourney were superior to anyone she'd every shot against. Even Theo was amazed at the lofty skill of her competitors. Other than her, only Adeline had any hope of besting everyone in the final round.

Thoughts of Alistair had taken up far too much of her mind of late, even more since he'd been so furious with her and still, in the heat of the moment, had pulled her close for a kiss that Theo would likely never forget. She'd allowed him to gather her in his arms, press their bodies together until she was unsure where she ended and he began, or if she'd ever be able to let him go.

It was meant to be a farewell embrace, a final act to end their association. Resolution of Theo coming to terms with her impending betrothal to Gladstone. However, it hadn't been any of those things. She'd imagined their kiss—their embrace—ending and Alistair walking from her home, taking with him her newly discovered longing for him. Instead, he'd left her in a state of need so great she'd nearly told the hackney driver the wrong park to deliver her to. Theo didn't know what passions lie beyond the feel of Alistair's hands and lips on her, but her body seemed to know there was much, much more he could show her.

It was all too distracting and could jeopardize her accuracy on the playing field; something she could not afford.

At the moment, the most important thing was putting Alistair—and her newly recognized desire for him—aside. Her dread over her upcoming nuptials to Gladstone was easier to push from her thoughts. She'd made the correct decision, and with any hope, Josie, Georgie, Adeline, and Theo's family would never learn of the disgrace that'd loomed over all their heads.

Theo had no misconceptions about her life after she wedded Gladstone. Her mornings practicing with her dear friends would be taken from her—and likely her bow, too. Any hopes she'd had of working with Cart and Cassini on new ideas for topographical maps would be denied, and there was no guarantee she'd be granted permission to even see her friends and family except at social gatherings and with luck, the holidays.

Her meeting with Cassini might well be her last if Gladstone and she were betrothed. She'd be required to let go of her hopes for the future, but that could not come before she'd passed on to Cassini all she'd studied and the discoveries she'd made while at Miss Emmeline's school. Theo was not an expert in maps, but her passion for them could lend advancements for every future endeavor. There was much more she hoped to learn from Cassini, if the opportunity was afforded her, but if not, she would be satisfied with passing on her limited knowledge thus far.

Her endless days would be filled with Gladstone's charitable endeavors, and with any hope, he'd disappear during the night to seek out the gaming hells Alistair had mentioned he favored.

Alistair had been correct, Mr. Oliver Gladstone was indeed a vile, corrupt man who only sought to marry her for his own personal gain. Any expectation of affection between them developing had been dispelled the moment Alistair had kissed her for the second time. No, even after the first kiss they'd shared, she'd known no other man would be right for her.

Her traitorous body trembled at the mere thought of Alistair taking hold of her once more. Things would be different if he did, she'd beg him not to let her go, allow him to force her to see reason and call off her betrothal to Gladstone, propose once more to make everything right. Theo had dreamed of walking into her first ballroom, arm in arm with her friends, watching as they danced late into the evening as Theo spoke with dashing men of the *ton*. She'd never been one to find a thrill in fancy gowns and extravagant outings. No, thought-provoking conversations and heated discussions about current events were what she most looked forward to. Would she someday be able to experience the simple pleasure of society or would Gladstone deny her even that?

Odd that she'd miss something she'd never thought she'd enjoy to begin with.

Though her betrothed had made it very clear intelligence and wit were not something he favored in his soon-to-be wife.

"Are you feeling ill?" Josie set her fingers on Theo's arm to gain her attention. "You are as white as the walls in my family's stable."

Theo gave her friends a weak smile. "I am only nervous, that is all." She wanted to reassure the women, but it would only give the pair pause as it was extremely rare for Theo to be worried over something that she had complete control over. For a brief moment, she debated telling them about everything—her betrothal to Gladstone, her meeting with Cassini at the museum, and most tempting, her intimate moments with Alistair—but it would merely incite more questions from them, pushing her to give answers she was unprepared to share. Answers she didn't know herself.

The truth was, she wasn't ready to dissect all these things in her own mind, let alone discuss them aloud.

"Adeline will find a way to be here on the morrow," Georgie said. Theo was glad the woman thought her distracted by Adeline and her situation. "She sent me a note this morning. She plans to be agreeable today, lead her brother to think she is remorseful for her actions. Then she will slip from the house tomorrow and meet us here."

Theo chuckled weakly at her friend's precocious plan, but doubted Alistair would be misled into thinking Adeline was in any way sincerely apologetic about her behavior. Georgie and Josie hadn't any notion why it was important Theo be elsewhere during the final day of the tourney. She was uncertain if it was due to their lack of interest in her or if they sought not to press her for details when Theo hadn't willingly shared them.

Either way, they hadn't asked nor had Theo spoken her of plans.

She wanted to share with her friends the immense burden on her shoulders. Would they come together and help her find a way out of the betrothal? Likely, each would offer their reputation to save her from marrying Gladstone. But there was little sense in all four of them suffering.

A trumpet blared, followed by a man shouting for the remaining archers to return to the field for the final round of the day.

After making certain her hood was in place, Theo took her quiver and bow from Josie, slinging both over her shoulder.

She gave her friends another reassuring smile. "That is great to hear, Georgie."

"We will await you here," Josie said, placing a quick kiss on Theo's cheek. "Best of luck, Lady Archer!"

Theo took her place in line as the first to enter the field—and the last to shoot her arrow.

The day had grown overly warm with the sun now blazing hot while it slowly descended toward the horizon. Her heavy, hooded cloak did not help or allow any breeze to touch her heated skin.

Theo was instructed to start the procession onto the field. With her bow and quiver slung over her shoulder, she pushed her sleeves up to allow the afternoon air to cool her—and dispel her unease as her knees trembled.

She'd scanned the crowd continually since arriving at Greenwich Park, but there'd been no sign of Gladstone—or Alistair. Even now, as she strode across the field, her eyes strayed to the spectators, moving down the long rows of people and finally skimming the hordes not lucky enough to afford a seat in the spectators' area, those relegated to stand at the side of the tourney grounds.

Not a single familiar face stared back at her.

Though every eye was trained on her.

The scrutiny of the crowd sent another wave of agitation through her, along with the thrill she'd become accustomed to since the tourney in Whitechapel.

How would she ever give it up?

The unique excitement that coursed through her each time she stepped onto an archery field and pulled her bowstring back was unlike any feeling she'd ever experienced.

Competing, it was an experience she'd never meant to have, and therefore, a thrill she should have never known. Much like the kiss she and Alistair had shared. He'd stroked a passion—awakened a need—within her that was never meant to be.

Her footsteps faulted when she realized the thrill of standing before the tourney crowd was in no way different from the hum of exhilaration and longing that had coursed through her the two times Alistair had placed his lips against hers.

But he was gone from her life, as archery would be when she left the tournament that day.

Theo took her place at the very end of the line of archers and watched as one after the next pulled back their bow and released. To soothe her frazzled nerves, she analyzed and noted each archer's stance, posture, and position as they took their turn. One man stood too rigid, another pushed his chest out, changing his aim and causing his arrow to hit the target well above the center mark, and still another man thought it jovial to close one eye and raise one leg as he released the arrow. The crowd cheered with merriment at his stunt, but the exploit sent his arrow far to the left, missing the target altogether. The man, dressed in a tailored suit made specifically for the competition, made a show of throwing his bow to the ground and storming off the field. This sent the audience into another round of clapping as they shouted jeers.

The next two archers, both men garbed in peasant's clothing of heavy, coarse wool, took their time with releasing their arrows. Theo suspected they had much invested in the tourney, and returning home without the prize purse would hurt them more than it would her and her friends.

Each man did themselves proud with their arrows. Finally, it was Theo's turn.

The crowd inhaled as she exhaled and relaxed her carriage, arranging her feet as she'd practiced since her first day at Miss Emmeline's School of Education and Decorum for Ladies of Outstanding Quality, solidifying her reason for placing herself in jeopardy. Her time at

Miss Emmeline's was the best she'd experienced since before her father's passing and the deterioration of her family. Before her mother had changed from a doting, loving parent to the bitter, emotionally broken woman who now existed only to attend her societal charity gatherings and complain about her son's ineptness.

Besides Cart's—and now his wife, Jude—attention, Theo had lived a solitary life of academic pursuit, left alone far too often with only her books as company. That had changed with her arrival at school. It couldn't be denied she'd always been a bit of an outsider with Josie, Georgie, and Adeline; however, she never doubted their feelings for her. They were friends, willing to do what was necessary for one another.

Though they never spoke of it, Theo had witnessed Georgie giving Adeline coins when they ventured into town. Josie was the mother hen of the group, the compassionate soul who, in all honesty, held their group together and kept at bay any strife between Adeline and the others.

Besides her skill at archery, Theo was unsure what she brought to their friendship. Maybe it was now that she saw her true worth. She was meant to be here—in this moment—to secure each of her friends a future of their choosing, free from Gladstone's manipulations. It was a small price to pay for the many years of friendship and love the women had given her.

"Lady Archer, release your arrow!"

As requested, Theo double-checked her aim and freed her arrow.

She had no urge to close her eyes or look away from her target. There was no other alternative...she had to hit the target dead center, or all of her sacrifices would be for nothing. She would be betrothed to Gladstone and have no prize purse to show for it. Certainly, her reputation and that of her friends would stay above the realm of suspicion, but Theo would spend the rest of her days dreaming of another man's kiss; her heart broken and her resilience crushed.

A loud cheer filled the open park, enough to confirm that Theo had not only hit her target but also struck the direct center, making six perfect shots in three days.

Theo didn't bother holding back a triumphant grin. The hood shielding her face would hide her elation at her victory.

The shouts of congratulations gradually began to follow a pattern as the audience came together, reciting a chant...

"Lady Theodora, Lady Theodora, Lady Theodora!"

"They know my name?" It wasn't more than a mumble, though the words took with them any possibility of her identity remaining unknown.

She glanced wildly toward Josie and Georgie, who stood behind the row of archers, awaiting Theo's return. Both women shrugged in response to Theo's questioning look.

The crowd chanted her name, screaming their compliments. The frenzy increased as all eyes stayed on her. How could they know her name? Her mind scrambled to make sense of it all at the same time her shoulders slumped in despair. Each archer had been assigned a number when they entered the tournament. The girls had made sure to give only fabricated first names, and she hadn't even entered, Adeline had.

Besides Josie, Adeline, and Georgie, there were only two people who knew of her participation in the tourney; she hadn't even dared tell Cart or Jude.

Theo was helpless to stop her bow from falling to her side, the bottom of her stomach falling out as the chanting intensified further and someone pushed the crowd on.

The other archers deserted her, clapping as they left the field.

They knew…the entire crowd.

There was no more point in hiding.

Theo pushed back her hood, revealing her dark hair tied back with a simple ribbon.

Glancing away from the spectators, she implored Josie and Georgie to flee before their identities were revealed, as well. They needn't all suffer the consequences. Her friends only stood taller, neither turning to depart.

"Lady Theodora! Lady Theodora! Three cheers for Lady Theodora," the people continued to chant.

She scanned the crowd again, trying to find the man responsible for her disgrace. It had to be Gladstone. Who else would seek to bring such shame upon her?

Apparently, he hadn't been satisfied with forcing her hand in marriage, he also planned to ruin her and dishonor her family and friends, too.

Unfortunately, Gladstone hadn't calculated his major error. With Theo's name—and now her face—revealed to all, there was little reason for her to continue with their sham of a betrothal.

Chapter Twenty-Five

Alistair watched the stark terror take hold of Theo as she pushed her hood back to reveal her face, allowing her a better view of the crowd. For a brief moment, the sight of her splendor stalled him, stopped him dead in his tracks as he allowed himself time to take in all her beauty. What others didn't know was that her magnificence was not only on the outside but infused every part of her being, inside and out.

When her terror turned to fright, Alistair started again, pushing his way through the milling crush to the field as her eyes skimmed the crowd.

It was as if a deep expanse of impassable sea separated them, its depths churning to keep him from her side, much as Gladstone had tried to do.

But Alistair was stronger than any sea.

There had been another choice for Theo the entire time, though not the decision he'd hoped to make in the situation, especially since he'd been unable to consult with her before deciding his course of action. He needed to believe she would forgive him. In time, she would comprehend why he'd done what he did.

It was not beyond him to force her hand, even if it only meant she would be free of Gladstone.

He strode closer to Theo, the invisible draw making it impossible for him to take any other path but directly to her side. Fighting it was beyond him—possibly, it had always been beyond his control. He only longed to hear her say she felt the same.

Gladstone had executed his plan with perfect precision, down to the final detail of threatening not only Theo and her friends but also her family and his. It had been enough to send Alistair running back to Theo's home, only to find both Lord Cartwright and Lady Theo out.

He hadn't any notion she'd go against him and deny his proposal...and truly, Gladstone had given Alistair no way around his next move.

What neither Gladstone nor Lady Theo had wagered on was Alistair ruining Theo himself.

He finally reached the edge of the archery field, and her eyes landed on him. His heart beat almost clear from his chest knowing she was so near, yet not in his arms.

Relief quickly faded to confusion. Alistair suspected she'd be upset with him, possibly furious. Reason would take hold before too much time passed, though.

Lady Theo's behavior was only scandalous to the eyes of the *ton* if someone deemed it so.

Alistair was determined to make sure not a single member of the *beau monde* viewed her participation in

The Grand Archers' Competition of London as shocking or disreputable in any fashion.

He started across the field to her, clapping to continue the crowd's enthusiastic appreciation of her skill, making each person note something special, something *grand* was happening, and they were witness to it.

Her furrowed brow rose in shock, and her eyes narrowed.

His chest seized, making breath impossible. He had a moment of regret over his involvement in taking away her choice at her future; though he'd done the right thing. It was the only decision for him to make if Theo was to avoid Gladstone's suit.

There was no stopping him as he marched toward her across the open field with the crowd still cheering at his back. No one would dare keep him from her side.

The other archers turned, departing the field only to turn and watch him. Alistair was satisfied not a single soul was missing a moment of his grand production. It had to be big, a show no one in attendance would soon forget. This day needed to be the talk of every London drawing room when the season officially started, only to be overshadowed by the betrothal announcement of Mr. Alistair Price, future heir to Viscount Melton, and Lady Theodora Montgomery.

With a few more strides, he stood before her, taking in the captivating woman she was, his eyes begging her to understand...and agree to wed him.

"Lady Theo." He didn't know what came over him, but he dropped to one knee and took her shaking hands in his. "You are the most enthralling woman I've ever had occasion to encounter." His words didn't capture an ounce of the feelings coursing through him: pride at her bravado, adoration at the way she'd captivated the crowd, sympathy for the position he'd had a hand in placing her in, and most of all…hope. Hope Theo would listen to all he had to say and that she'd confess she felt the same. Alistair cleared his throat and started again, speaking loudly enough for the watching crowd to hear. "Lady Theodora Montgomery, Theo, your skill at archery, your compassion for others, your willingness to put yourself and your future at risk for those you love, and especially your willingness to do all in your power to protect my family…these are only a few of the reasons I adore you."

He searched her intense stare, praying for her to say or do something besides gaze at him.

The spectators' cheers had ceased, going quiet as they strained to hear every word he spoke. They sensed the magnitude of the moment, just as he'd hoped they would.

While *The Post* would have the story of the season, *he* was determined to have Theo. All of her. She was selfless and pure of heart. Not meek and malleable as he'd first thought when they met. She had a quiet resilience about her. The notion of her giving up her future and marrying a man who would crush her spirit made Alistair weep inside, but she'd raised her chin a notch and did what needed to be done to protect her family and friends.

That determination was why he'd had to step in and save her—from herself.

"I envy your ability to take the most daunting of paths without fear for your future," Alistair continued, "when I am weak and so often take the easiest path.

327

That does not have to be the way of things any longer. You are free."

Alistair begged for time to speed up and for the silence to end. He may not be the man she chose. Could he let her go if that was what she wanted? Doubt, dread, and desperation threatened, causing tightness in his chest, but he pushed back at the negative cloud settling on him, making from for the light that was Theo. She shone so brightly, she was certain to lighten any dark day to come.

"You can seek any future that makes you happy," he said when she remained silent. "You can travel to France and study or travel across England competing in archery tourneys or stay here, with me, and attend your first London season with me by your side—along with Adeline, Lady Josephine, and Lady Georgina. You are properly, thoroughly ruined."

Theo pulled her hands free from his and shot a quick glance to the spectators—and archers—who pushed closer still, their attention focused on Alistair.

"I think this conversation is better had in private, Mr. Price."

Alistair's heart—and hopes—sank when she turned and bolted to Lady Georgina's and Lady Josephine's side, the trio pushing through the gawking archers toward the tourney exit.

Standing, he watched as Lady Josephine took hold of Theo's bow and quiver, their heads tilting close.

He and Theo had much to discuss, but certainly not as much as she did with her friends.

The discontent of the crowd forced its way into his mind, dispelling his thoughts as the people watching loudly speculated about the outcome of the tourney; the way she'd cut him off and fled dismissing Alistair from their minds.

The chance she would chose a path that did not include him was always in the back of his mind, but this...

Alistair hadn't imagined he'd have to live through her leaving him so soon, without time for either of them to discuss the matter at length. Certainly love and affection were not something easily expressed in words, nor could mere words bring to life love where it did not exist.

Did he have the strength to follow her, only to have every hope for his future dashed?

Chapter Twenty-Six

Theo, Josie, and Georgina made their way back to the practice area, and Theo shrugged from her heavy cloak, allowing the afternoon breeze to hit her overheated skin. Any added weight upon her, and Theo would collapse as her head spun uncontrollably. She could not catch her breath.

What had possessed Alistair to do such a thing? In such a public way?

Every person she passed either stared at her or offered their congratulations on a shot that secured her place in the final round.

She would not deny that she loved archery, but her meeting at the museum with Cassini and his sister was far more important, not for her, but for the many people that would be saved if her ideas were incorporated in the family's next set of topographical maps. Adeline was slated to take her place on the morrow, but that was impossible now. The audience would never be fooled if Theo's chestnut brown hair suddenly turned to a blonde so fair it appeared like spun gold in the sun.

Alistair had made it impossible for her and her friends to secure the prize purse without Theo giving something up.

Oliver had threatened her into agreeing to a betrothal she did not want, and Alistair was doing the same. Did he not see his actions were little better than the man he despised?

"Theo," Georgie said, grasping her arm and pulling her to a stop. "What was Adeline's brother doing out there?"

She should have confided in her friends long ago. Told them everything—about Alistair, Gladstone, and her work at the museum. Would they turn away from her when they learned of her deceptions?

"Your face has been revealed, Theo," Josie said, wheezing as she commonly did when her nerves got the best of her. "And your name was spoken loudly."

"That was Alistair's plan all along, I presume."

"Do not look now, but he is coming this way." Georgie released her arm and took a step closer to Josie. Suddenly, Theo felt more exposed than she had on the tourney field moments ago. "And he wears the oddest expression."

Theo whipped around, knowing she could not avoid him any longer. He needed to know the consequences she and her friends would face at his disastrous actions. He'd not only put her in jeopardy but her friends, as well.

Surely he saw that.

"Lady Theo," Alistair said before turning to Josie and Georgie. "Ladies, I offer my sincerest apologies for my outward display of affection on the tourney field."

Josie brought her hands to her chest and sighed. "That is awfully romantic, Mr. Price."

"And quite dashing, I would say," Georgie said, fluttering her lashes.

Theo's mouth gaped open, and her arms fell to her sides as she looked between her two friends. Josie and Georgie thought his actions valiant, and his emotions true.

"It is my hope that Lady Theo will accept my offer of marriage."

"He has asked for your hand?" Josie turned to her, brows raised in disbelief.

"When?" Georgie screeched, clapping her hands. "I mean, Theo, you never told us."

"I was not at liberty to accept Alistair's proposal." Theo knew the situation was going from bad to worse as both women stared at her, mouths opening and closing but neither knowing what to say. "I had already given my promise to another."

"To another?" Josie said breathlessly, turning a puzzled glance in Georgie's direction. "Who?"

"And what, pray tell, does Adeline think of all this?" Georgie stepped closer to Theo, lowering her voice as if she feared their friend would jump from the shadows and berate them all for keeping a secret from her. "Is she agreeable?"

"I fear this is all rather new, and unexpected," Alistair said. "But now, Theo is free of her other suitor."

Theo's heart raced when she realized Gladstone held nothing over her any longer, any power he'd seized was gone, made irrelevant the moment Alistair had incited the crowd to chant her name.

Even now, the gathering of people shouted for her to return to the field.

She was thoroughly and scandalously ruined…and unequivocally free.

And never in her life had she been happier, except when Alistair had pressed his lips to hers.

"Alistair." She glanced to Josie and Georgie, pleading silently for them to give her a bit of privacy. They nodded in understanding and clasped arms, making their way to a vendor hocking flags to wave during the competition. Certain they would not be overheard, Theo continued. "You have ruined me."

"Yes, I have." His smile encompassed his entire face, as if he were proud of what he'd done. "And now you are free to tell Gladstone to take his offer and sod off."

He didn't comprehend the level of harm he'd done.

"Yes, I can…and a part of me thanks you for that…" Her back stiffened in indignation. "But now there is little chance of keeping scandal from my family and yours."

"Not a person who witnessed us on that field today will think there is anything scandalous about you, or your actions," he replied. "Especially when the *ton* learns we were promised to one another long before your identity was revealed. I was here, watching from the stands as you applied your skill with a bow. You had my blessing—and a proper escort—during your outings at the tourney, as well as my sister, Lady Josephine, and Lady Georgina. Not a single member of the *ton* will find scandal where none exists."

"And what of your family?" she asked. She couldn't ponder the notion—or the excitement that filled her—of them entering society together as a betrothed pair. Yes, she'd been willing to give up her future for the people she loved, but she would never expect him to do the same.

"What of them?" he countered.

"It was not long ago you were resigned to securing their futures before your own." The burden on his shoulders was heavy. Eight siblings to see properly introduced to society with hopes that each made a favorable match. It was a daunting task for even the most skilled London matron to undertake. "What of them and their futures?"

"They will be better off with a brother who has found happiness and a love they can admire," he said. "I need not postpone my own life to make sure they all succeed in theirs. We can all have what we want. And, Lady Theo, make no mistake, I want you."

A shiver of anticipation coursed through her at this declaration. She wanted him, too; desired him more than the air she needed to breathe. He'd filled her every waking thought since their first meeting, and invaded her dreams almost as regularly.

"I know my methods have been rather unorthodox, to say the least." He looked to the ground, almost ashamed. "But I can assure you, I mean well. However, I am resigned to the possibility that your affections do not match my own—"

"Rest assured, Alistair, they do."

His gaze snapped to hers, a new sense of confidence filling him as he continued. "Then you will marry me?"

"Mr. Price, Alistair," she began, holding her smile within. She had much more to say before allowing the man to think she was agreeable to their match, no matter that every part of her was tingling at the mere thought of Alistair's hands and lips on her again. "You are the most high-handed, insufferable, domineering—"

"Do not forget overbearing, dictatorial, and arrogant," he said with a wink.

"Those are certainly on my list, as well," she confided. "However..."

A spark lit his eyes.

"You are a man undaunted by overwhelming situations. You have a mind that solves even the most complex dilemmas, and besides my own brother, I've never met anyone more dedicated to their family's well-being."

"Even though I am an insufferable blackguard?" he asked.

"Especially because you are an insufferable blackguard...but an insufferable blackguard who was determined not to allow me to make the worse mistake of my life."

"I have never been so honored to be called an insufferable blackguard." He pulled her close, settling his body against her. "Would you do me the honor of making me your insufferable scoundrel for all eternity?"

"I think that can be arranged, Alistair."

"There is nothing I adore more than my name on your lips."

"There is nothing I adore more than your lips on my lips," Theo countered, shocked at her suggestive comment.

Alistair paused, his arms holding her tighter to him. Theo knew it would take much convincing to get him to let her go, and that was fine by her. "Are you saying you adore me, Lady Theo?"

Theo smirked. "I am saying I adore your lips against mine. The rest of you I am not completely certain about."

"Then allow me to do a bit of convincing." Theo gasped as his hands kneaded her backside, gently coming to rest on her rounded posterior. "Do you not fancy my hands, Lady Theodora?" he leaned in and whispered in her ear.

"I do, sir." She was utterly helpless to stop him, needing him to continue, anticipation flaring at the thought of his next move.

He did not make her wait long as his tongue darted out, and his lips settled at her earlobe. "And my tongue, my lady?"

"It is certainly rapturous, Mr. Price," she sighed. "Though I must say it is nothing without your lips, which we have already discussed I adore immensely."

"Oh, the things I could do with my tongue—"

"Alistair!" Theo protested, strangely aware of their current surroundings as the noise from the tourney grounds invaded their moment of privacy. "Can we talk of something else—"

The feel of his hips, moving against hers stopped her words, and she focused on the obvious sign of his desire for her.

"You were saying, Lady Theodora?" he asked, allowing his groin one more swirl against hers.

"I…well…I…" She paused. "You scoundrel. You have utterly distracted me from my thoughts."

"I will distract you from more than just your thoughts if you persist in denying me what I want."

Theo didn't seek to deny him anything. In fact, she was prepared to give him everything as long as his hands and hips continued their course, and his lips remained close to hers.

The sounds of the gathering crowd began to push through her haze, and Theo pulled back out of his arms. Though her attendance on the tourney field was no longer considered scandalous, her intimacies with Alistair before all these people was still highly improper.

At his wounded look, she grabbed his hand and began to drag him toward her waiting friends.

"One last question," Theo said, pulling him to a stop several feet from where Josie and Georgie awaited them.

"I will answer anything."

"Did you truly come to the tourney today knowing your plan was to ruin a lady?"

"Of course, not," he said as if appalled she'd think of him in that regard. "I came to the tourney to claim the woman I love—by any means necessary."

Chapter Twenty-Seven

"Are you certain you want to tell her *now*?" Theo's voice shook with apprehension as the carriage pulled to a stop before his townhouse. Her fingers clutched his hand, squeezing so tightly, her nails dug into his palm. "There is always tomorrow, or even after the holidays."

Lady Josephine and Lady Georgina had sat stick-straight on the bench seat across from Alistair and Theo as they departed Greenwich Park in one coach. Both women had held their tongues the entire journey, no matter what outlandish topics Alistair put before them to try and bring out their voices.

"There is no time like the present, Lady Theo." He didn't bother hiding his exultant grin. He was happy, ecstatic even. "Besides, I think it is in all of our best interests—and I do mean *your* best interests—to tell Adeline sooner rather than later. For if she thinks the trio of you were conspiring to keep something from her, she's likely to take out her vengeance on you all."

"And what of you, sir?" Lady Josephine squeaked. "Do you not fear for your welfare?"

"Her wrath is permanently focused on me." He laughed when the meek woman averted her stare, focusing once more on the velvet cushion beneath her. "And, I do not seek to be her friend. I am her brother, her guardian, and her protector while in London. She can rail on me all she wants, but that will never change where my heart lies."

The women across from him gave a collective sigh.

"So we are all clear," he paused to gain both women's notice before continuing, "my heart lies with Lady Theodora Montgomery."

Georgie and Josie *ahhh*'d in delight.

"Mr. Pri—Alistair!" Theo swatted at his arm, clearly beyond acting as if they were mere acquaintances. "Do not send them into a frenzy with your honey-coated words before we have had the opportunity to speak with your sister."

"We will see if my—what did you call them?—marmalade-dipped words can save us all from my sister's vexation." Alistair departed the carriage when the footman swung the door wide and set about down the steps. He held out his hand for the women to alight. "I, for one, am quaking in my Hessians with fear. Let us get this done and see what our fate is to be."

"I do not think it necessary for Josie and I to accompany you," Lady Georgina whined. "I only learned of your treachery today. Why should we align ourselves with your cause?"

"Yes, we should continue home, if your coachman would be so kind as to deposit us at our doorsteps." Lady Josephine kept her eyes lowered but a fraction of force had entered her tone.

"Absolutely not." The pair inhaled sharply at this rebuff. "Theo needs you both by her side in this matter. After all, she was prepared to do much more for her dear friends, the least you can do is stand with her in this decision."

"We certainly do agree with Theo, and are overjoyed you found one another, but..." Lady Georgina dared a glance at Theo. "I am sorry, Theo. Of course, we will be by your side today and every day. Friendship, loyalty, and honor above all."

Alistair was uncertain he had heard the woman correctly, but the smile that lit Theo's face as her eyes came to rest on her friends was all he needed. His heart surged once more.

His sister was a force to be reckoned with—a plow of sorts, who pushed until she attained what she wanted. Unfortunately, Adeline was unaware Alistair was capable of the same. At least, when he desired something enough.

And he desired Theo.

He would take Lady Theodora to wife, no matter his sister's opinion on the matter.

It was only up to him to convince his sister to agree, for she could make his life a living hell if she so chose.

But at least he'd have Theo by his side through it all.

"Lady Theodora, my sweet," Alistair called into the carriage when none of the three women ventured out. "I neglected to ask how you feel about gaining eight wildly out of control, opinionated, and frighteningly honest siblings..."

"Why do I feel as if we are walking off a plank with no land in sight?" Lady Josephine whispered.

"Because, we are all her prey…" Lady Georgina chided in a hushed tone. "Thankfully, Mr. Price and Theo are far more appetizing at the moment."

Theo took his hand and stepped from the carriage, her wide smile revealing her perfectly straight teeth. The light in her eyes was enough to brighten a thousand days but held the promise of dark, stormy nights of passion. "You are an appetizing morsel, indeed, Lady Theodora."

"Mr. Pric—" She attempted to scold, but her laughter cut off her words as she took him in from head to toe.

Alistair imagined the man she saw before her—he was beyond hiding his intense adoration of her. If it showed in his eyes, then so be it. He had nothing to hide from her, not any longer. "Lady Theo, though I jest, it does not mean my feelings for you—and our future—are not deep." He held tightly to her hand as he stared down at her, gauging her mood and determining his next course of action. He could kiss her right here, before his townhouse with anyone watching, even Adeline. He could whisk her into his arms and carry her into his home, straight to the study, and summon his lively bunch of siblings to impart the good news.

Though he was far more tempted to reenter the carriage and command the driver to depart, drive, and…keep driving. Take them straight to the Archbishop and demand a special license.

He wouldn't do that, though. There was no chance their marriage and future would start in such a manner. The banns would be properly read when the time was right. They would meet one another's families. He would not rush their union, but savor the time between this day and the day when he could call Theo is wife in truth—the future Viscountess Melton.

It was everything she deserved. A morning ceremony. Flowers, though not blue or orange. Family. Friends. With nothing but well-wishes and good tidings for all.

It was everything, and yet nothing he ever suspected he wanted—or needed—when, in fact, deep within, he'd longed for this exactly.

"Shall we?" he asked, breaking the spell between them. When she nodded, Alistair called over his shoulder into the carriage. "Ladies, if you have not departed the carriage and taken your place by Theo's side before I open my front door, I will inform Adeline you have both been privy to the affection between Theo and I since the Whitechapel tourney."

Alistair didn't bother with another look over his shoulder as he pulled Theo close and started toward his family home, the woman of his dreams fitting snuggly to his side.

Behind him, he heard the springs of the carriage groan as Lady Josephine and Lady Georgina each hopped from the coach and hurried behind them.

He leaned close to Theo and whispered, "I suppose adding two more females to my list of dependents is not all that horrible."

Theo giggled, her hair bobbing about her shoulders. "Alistair, I am certain they need our mature guidance as they search for their own matches."

"*Love* matches," he declared. "Nothing less will do for any woman under my care!"

"Suddenly you are an expert on love?" They came to a stop at his front door as his butler swung it open wide. "Just the other day, you were prepared to marry your sister off to the first man who showed any interest."

He leaned down and placed a kiss to her cheek. "That was before you showed me how mundane and undesirable a life without love can be. When you took me, you were to marry Gladstone and consent to a life without love or passion. I realized the only means to find my own love and passion was with you."

"Alistair!" Adeline shouted, thundering down the stairs. "You bloody knave! You had the twins sit below my window, and Adrian and Alfred at my door? Abel even followed me to the loo. This is outrageous…"

"Ready or not," Theo whispered, straightening her shoulders as if ready for combat.

"I have been ready since the moment I laid eyes on you, Lady Theodora."

Epilogue

"Aw, *mon petite femme archer*," Monsieur Cassini sighed, rushing to take Theo's hands in his and placing a kiss to each of her cheeks. "So lovely to see you once more."

"Monsieur Cassini," Theo said with a laugh, glancing to Alistair at her side to gauge his opinion of the man's naturally flirtatious manner. "Thank you so much for agreeing to stay a few extra days."

"It is only Damon, Theodora," he cooed. "And once we received word that our Lady Theodora was unable to attend our meeting because *mon petite femme archer* had plied her skill with a bow and earned a place in the final round at the Grand Archers' Competition at Greenwich Park, well, Comtesse de Salnome and I were ravenous to attend."

"You were in the crowd?" Theo gulped, looking between the siblings, the *monsieur* genuinely intrigued by her hidden talents with a bow while his sister was far more entertained taking in Alistair and his broad-shouldered, fair-haired form, so at odds with their olive

344

complexion and dark, ebony hair. "I did not see...I was unaware..."

The comtesse released a light laugh at Theo's muttering. "My dear Lady Theodora, we would not have missed the final day of the tourney, especially once we learned you were the lady beneath the hooded cloak. I hesitate to say you are the talk of the town." She sighed as if envious.

"And to claim the place as victor among so many elite sportsmen?" Cassini gushed. "*Mon petite femme archer* it is a grand pleasure to call you friend."

"Certainly, Lady Theodora," the Comtesse continued, her lip pushing out in a pout. "My brother was so overwhelmed by your generous donation to the school in Canterbury he has professed to match your bequest."

"That is not necessary, Monsieur Cassini." Theo looked between to the siblings, the comtesse's smile tight and at odds with Cassini's open, genuine grin.

"It was in *The Post* this morning that others too will contribute to your cause. You have certainly garnered much attention." Cassini nodded, affirming his sister's words.

But Theo had not desired to be the talk of anything, let alone all of London. "It is a pity we cannot stay in London and experience the season with you."

She shot a pouty look to Cassini, but the man only shook his head in regret. "You know we must return home; we have much work to do."

"But not before you meet with my sister," Cart said, entering the room with Jude on his arm. "Her ideas are highly enlightening and advanced for such a..."

"Young woman?" Jude asked. "Certainly, that is not what you meant, dear husband."

Cart blustered, patting his wife's arm to soothe her. "Of course, that was not what I was hinting at. I meant her ideas are advanced for a person with no topographical map training to speak of, nor has she personally visited many of the regions she's determined need elevation alterations. Hers is a truly spectacular—and ingenious—mind."

Theo felt her cheeks heat as a blush spread up her neck at her brother's praise. "Simon, it is not so truly revolutionary, I promise you." Theo sought to push aside his high regard. "Monsieur Cassini may have likely already determined the changes needed without my input."

Alistair stood silently at her side, as he had on the final day of the tourney, and after, when Gladstone arrived at her family townhouse, fuming with rage at Alistair's clever plot to make a marriage to Gladstone unnecessary.

"I highly doubt that, my lady," the comtesse said with a laugh. "Lord Cartwright has shared with us a bit about your ideas, and I can assure you, we are extremely interested and eager to speak with you."

Cassini nodded at his sister's declaration, but kept his eyes on Alistair's arm, which Theo held.

Alistair's fingers flexed, tightening briefly as if he too noticed the way Cassini was watching.

"Will you excuse me, my lady?" Cassini cleared his voice before continuing. "There is something I must attend to. You are still able to meet tomorrow, no?"

"Of course." Theo watched the retreating man, his sister close to his side as they hurried from the room. "That was rather abrupt."

"Oh, he only needs a moment to nurse his injured heart." Cart frowned, shaking his head slightly. "Though I believe it is impossible for a heart to obtain an invisible wound, the comtesse speaks to the contrary."

"What in heavens are you talking about, Simon?" Theo asked.

"Alistair," Cart said. "I believe you can explain far better than I.

Theo looked between the men, and then to Jude, seeing her smirk. The knowing look that passed between them was similar to the looks that continually passed between Georgie and Josie when Adeline was being particularly troublesome.

Since Alistair had met with Cart and formally asked to court Theo, they'd become fast friends, even having all of the Melton siblings to supper. It was a grand affair, only rivaled by the dowager's shock when Jude and her four siblings joined their family. It had been utter chaos, and Theo had loved every minute of it; especially the dowager countess's discomfort.

"What your brother is trying to explain is that Cassini had a tender for you, even asked Cart to court you properly." Alistair patted her arm as he spoke.

"And why is this the first I've heard of it?" Theo fumed.

"If you'd like, I can speak with Cassini and see if he is still interested…" Cart's words trailed off, challenging her to agree.

"Of course, I am not agreeable to his pursuit; however, I should have been informed of his interest."

"I should hope you are not interested in Cassini," Alistair huffed. "First, it was Abel, and now this oily Frenchmen?"

"Abel?" Theo and Jude asked in unison.

"Oh, he had his sights on you long before he spied you with a bow; although, I believe his interest was more with Lord Cartwright than you, Theo…the sorry fool." Alistair leaned close and whispered, "I would never have allowed him close if I thought his curiosity genuine. You were mine long before you knew it."

A shiver traveled through Theo at the mere suggestion of her being all his.

"Now, now," Jude hissed as Alistair placed a kiss to Theo's neck before drawing up short at her scolding tone. "You both are more than capable of waiting until after you are wed for that."

"May I open my eyes now?" Cart asked, his eyelids squeezed shut.

"It is safe, dear husband." Jude laughed.

"My apologies, Lady Cartwright," Alistair offered. "Maybe we should be off. Theo and I have agreed to a turn in Hyde Park with Adeline, Lady Josie, and Lady Georgie. If that is agreeable, my lord?"

Alistair's comfortable air, calling her friends by their beloved nicknames, infused her with a great sense of rightness.

"A word with my sister before you depart?" Simon held out his arm and Theo moved to his side, leaving Alistair and Jude in their wake as they walked a few steps away.

"What is it, Simon?" Theo's mind had settled on the idea of a few moments alone in the carriage with Alistair before they were joined by her friends.

"A man came by the townhouse yesterday. He requested an audience with me…"

Theo stomach sank. "Who was it?"

But she knew who'd called on him, before he said the name. "A Mr. Oliver Gladstone. He attempted to convince me that you and he were to be wed. The man had a special license signed by the Archbishop of Canterbury."

"What did you say?" Theo would not give away any more information than was necessary.

"I told him to depart my home immediately, and to take the matter up with your betrothed." Theo could not have adored her brother any more than in that moment. "Now, let us not speak of this matter again."

They returned to Jude and Alistair, and Theo immediately moved to his side.

Simon's nod of approval only filled her heart with more certainty. "Do hurry along before Cassini returns with a new scheme to steal you from Mr. Price's arm."

"I fear that would not bode well for the man," Alistair chuckled, pulling Theo to his side. There was not another place she'd rather be.

"I am happy to see Miss Adeline has forgiven the pair of you." Her sister-in-law was not one to pry, but all had been witness to the uncomfortable situation when the Melton family had become acquainted with Theo and her family. Adeline hadn't said a single word, only pushed her food around her plate until she claimed a headache and begged Alistair to depart. "I do hope the situation improves before the wedding."

Remorse tugged at Theo, and she gave Jude her warmest smile. "Adeline is coming around. It just took a bit of convincing to make her understand we had no intention of hurting her."

Alistair squeezed her arm in reassurance. "It turns out Adeline was only worried about having to share her new gowns with my future bride. However, I informed her that no wife of mine would be saddled with hand-me-down gowns, but would rather be afforded a healthy allowance to commission her own wardrobe."

"And how did she take *that* news?" Jude inquired, a spark of merriment in her eyes.

"Oh, she did not take the news at all," Theo cut in. "She stomped from the room and slammed the door shut before the words had left Alistair's mouth."

The group let loose a great round of laughter, the joyous sound bouncing off the walls of the museum and echoing down the long corridors. Several glares from patrons enjoying their time at the museum were cast their way.

"I suspect she was more annoyed that she was the last to know and hadn't been consulted before I offered Theodora my heart." He glanced at her sideways, and Theo couldn't help the pool of warmth that spread through her at his words. "Though she would be loath to admit this fact."

"She would just as soon perish than concede she had naught to do with our love match." Always the leader, always the one to have the final say, and always the one to be most informed…Theo was elated to be the one who showed people that even though she didn't constantly feel involved and appreciated, she did know what she wanted in life—and that was Alistair by her side.

"I think we should depart before Lord Cartwright has no other option but to throw us out," Alistair jested. "Come, Lady Archer, you have friends in need of a lesson in attracting the perfect match."

"Heavens," Theo sighed, her heart aflutter once more. "What advice could I offer to that subject?"

"Your arrow lodged in my heart, surely that was your aim all along, Lady Theodora." Alistair leaned down, unperturbed by Cart's and Jude's presence, and settled a kiss to her lips—a kiss much like the first they'd shared. What she hadn't realized then was that it was a kiss full of promise: promise for a future, a family, and a love to endure until their last breaths.

Books By Christina McKnight:

Lady Archer's Creed Series

Theodora (Book One)

Georgina (Book Two) – Coming 2017

Adeline (Book Three) – Coming 2017

Josephine (Book Four) – Coming 2017

Craven House Series

The Thief Steals Her Earl

The Mistress Enchants Her Marquis – Coming February 2017

The Madame Catches Her Duke – Coming 2017

The Gambler Wagers Her Baron – Coming 2017

A Lady Forsaken Series

Shunned No More, A Lady Forsaken (Book One)

Forgotten No More, A Lady Forsaken (Book Two)

Scorned Ever More, A Lady Forsaken (Book Three)

Christmas Ever More, A Lady Forsaken (Book Four)

Hidden No More, A Lady Forsaken (Book Five)

Available at all retailers!

<u>Standalone Title</u>

The Siege of Lady Aloria, A de Wolfe Pack Novella

A Kiss At Christmastide: Regency Romance Novella

About the Author:

Christina McKnight is a book lover turned writer. From a young age, her mother encouraged her to tell her own stories. She's been writing ever since.

Christina enjoys a quiet life in Northern California with her family, her wine, and lots of coffee. Oh, and her books . . . don't forget her books! Most days, she can be found writing, reading, or traveling the great state of California.

Email: Christina@ChristinaMcKnight.com
Follow her on Twitter: @CMcKnightWriter
Keep up to date on her releases:
www.christinamcknight.com
Like Christina's FB Author page:
ChristinaMcKnightWriter

Author's Notes

Thank you for reading *Theodora, Lady Archer's Creed (Book One)*.

If you enjoyed *Theodora*, be sure to write a brief review at
Amazon, Barnes and Noble, or Goodreads.

I'd love to hear from you!

You can contact me at:
Christina@christinamcknight.com

Or write me at:
P O Box 1017
Patterson, CA 95363

www.ChristinaMcKnight.com
Check out my website for giveaways, book reviews, and information on my upcoming projects,
or connect with me through social media at:

Twitter: @CMcKnightWriter
Facebook: www.facebook.com/christinamcknightwriter
Goodreads: www.goodreads.com/ChristinaMcKnight

Sign up for my newsletter here: http://eepurl.com/VP1rP

There are several people I'd like to thank for staying with me through the emotional journey of writing this book.

To Marc, my amazing boyfriend—thank you for always being *you*!

To Lauren Stewart, my critique partner and best friend, you pushed me to explore new avenues of thought that I never dreamed possible. If we were in a true relationship, it would be one based on co-dependency, but in a good way. My writing would not be what it is without your comments, criticism, suggestions, and guidance.

I'd also like to thank the wonderful women who've supported me in both my writing career and life, including (but not limited to): Amanda Mariel, Debbie Haston, Angie Stanton, Theresa Baer, Roxanne Stellmacher, Laura Cummings, Dawn Borbon, Suzi Parker, Jennifer Vella, Brandi Johnson, and Latisha Kahn. I know I'm forgetting people…You have all been very patient and wonderfully supportive of my eccentric ways.

A very special thank you to my editor, Chelle Olson with Literally Addicted to Detail, your skill and professionalism surpass all that I expected. Chelle Olson can be contracted by email at literallyaddictedtodetail@yahoo.com.

Also, a special thank you to historical and developmental editor, Scott Moreland.

And to my proofreader, Anja, thank you for embarking on yet another journey with me.

Cover and wraparound cover design and website design credit to Sweet 'N Spicy Designs.

Theodora

Finally, thank you for supporting indie authors.